ALSO BY CATE QUINN

The Thief Taker
Fire Catcher
Dark Stars
The Changeling Murders
The Bastille Spy
The Scarlet Code
Black Widows
Blood Sisters
The Clinic

PRAISE FOR CATE QUINN

"A high-society wedding set against the lavish backdrop of a private island, *The Bridesmaid* is a delicious new take on the destination-wedding-gone-wrong. It's brimming with juicy secrets, betrayal, a bridezilla for the ages, and my favorite element, an undercover forensics attorney posing as a bridesmaid, and I couldn't turn the pages fast enough. Readers will be dazzled!"

—May Cobb, bestselling author of *The Hunting Wives* and *All the Little Houses*

"*The Clinic* drew me in from its tense first page and left me thinking long after I finished it. It's a twisty mystery with feeling that kept me turning the pages until well into the night."

—Sara Ochs, author of *The Resort*

"With relentless writing and twists around every corner, Cate Quinn weaves a gripping mystery through the world of luxury rehab that will have you saying 'one more chapter' until you hit the final page. So be warned: Once you step foot in *The Clinic*, the doors lock behind you."

—Tony Wirt, author of *Just Stay Away*

"Cate Quinn's propulsive thriller *The Clinic* reads like an edge-of-your-seat page-turner with clever twists and turns and redirections, all while taking place at an unconventional rehab clinic in the wilds of the Pacific Northwest coast. But at its core, this is a haunting story of addiction, long-lasting trauma, and the power of transformative change—I absolutely loved it."

—Ashley Tate, author of *Twenty-Seven Minutes*

THE BRIDESMAID

CATE QUINN

Copyright © 2025 by Cate Quinn
Cover and internal design © 2025 by Sourcebooks
Cover design by Erin Fitzsimmons/Sourcebooks
Cover images © Vibe Images/Shutterstock, Seth Mourra/
Stocksy, Ilina93/Shutterstock, Steve Collender/Shutterstock

Sourcebooks and the colophon are registered trademarks of Sourcebooks.

All rights reserved. No part of this book may be reproduced in any form or by any electronic or mechanical means including information storage and retrieval systems—except in the case of brief quotations embodied in critical articles or reviews—without permission in writing from its publisher, Sourcebooks.

No part of this book may be used or reproduced in any manner for the purpose of training artificial intelligence technologies or systems.

The characters and events portrayed in this book are fictitious or are used fictitiously. Any similarity to real persons, living or dead, is purely coincidental and not intended by the author.

All brand names and product names used in this book are trademarks, registered trademarks, or trade names of their respective holders. Sourcebooks is not associated with any product or vendor in this book.

Published by Sourcebooks Landmark, an imprint of Sourcebooks
1935 Brookdale RD, Naperville, IL 60563-2773
(630) 961-3900
sourcebooks.com

Originally published as *The Bridesmaid* in 2025 in Great Britain by Orion Fiction, an imprint of The Orion Publishing Group.

Cataloging-in-Publication Data is on file with the Library of Congress.

Printed and bound in the United States of America.
KP 10 9 8 7 6 5 4 3 2 1

To my incredible family.

Prologue

Adrianna Kensington smoothed her couture wedding gown, adjusted a shining lock of chestnut hair, and balled her fists.

"This will work," she breathed. "I will be married, and this will work."

The grand staircase blossomed in airy clouds of white roses. The floristry team, like black-clad bees, hummed at the edges, inserting the twenty thousand blooms, adjusting the invisible wire frame beneath.

Uniformed fitters in plastic shoe covers were temporarily recarpeting the entire downstairs floor of the hotel, rolling a snowy-white deep-pile over the regal red colors of the steps. They stapled the edges with rapid determination.

"Oh God!" The head florist, usually unflappable, made a brief, panic-stricken perfect *O* of rich red lipstick. "The bride! The bride is here! Everybody off the steps. Now!"

Already they could hear it. The gunshot ricochet of a diamanté heel on the marble floor.

The head florist cast about. Where was the planner? No one wanted to deal with Adrianna Kensington without the wedding planner at hand. The dark-haired heiress was poison in a fifty-thousand-dollar bridal dress.

A rustle of raw silk told everyone they were too late. Adrianna had arrived. Every last crew member paused, and all eyes turned to the slim figure in the doorway of the grand stairs. Her bridal gown ran in folds along her narrow body, pooling in thick, wide skirts like fresh-poured cream. Her usual team of assistants and staff was nowhere to be seen. Sweat prickled on the florist's palms. This wasn't good.

"Miss Kensington," stammered the florist, catching a gulp of Adrianna's signature, custom-made perfume. "We were told to be ready for you by ten."

Adrianna's sapphire-blue eyes took in the clouds of roses. The unfinished carpet.

"Where is my maid of honor?" she asked in a tone they had all learned to dread.

"I think...she was in the ballroom earlier," managed the florist. "But we're not ready yet in there, and the floor can't be walked on in heels right now, so..."

Adrianna's lithe honey-hued arms picked up the heavy skirts. She strode up the staircase, encrusted heels peppering the freshly laid pile. The weight of silk skirts rustled like a felled tree across a forest floor.

The entrance to the ballroom was marked by a half-complete floral archway. A scaffold had been erected to access the crystal chandelier, handmade in Venice. Adrianna had agreed with the wedding planner that the golden light of real beeswax candles was essential.

Tables for two hundred guests were arranged and partially dressed. Gilt-framed mirrors lined the walls, reflecting the bride's face—a hundred dewy pink lips, sculpted eyebrows, and artfully contoured cheekbones.

Adrianna rarely enjoyed seeing her features in mirrors, but today, she absorbed herself appraisingly, taking in the three hours she had just spent in the hair and makeup artist's chair. Her glossy brunette hair curled artfully around her shoulders.

"Dream it, believe it," muttered Adrianna, eyeing her reflection. "Dream it, believe it." Her palms, she noticed, unclenching them with distaste, were sweaty. She took a long, steadying breath and nodded. Along the mirrored walls, two hundred sleek-jawed, blue-eyed women nodded along with her.

Why was nothing ready? Where was her maid of honor?

Adrianna twisted to leave, the rustling volume of her dress turning with her. It was then she noticed that one of the mirrors reflected a different color from her white and black scheme.

A flash of red.

Frowning, Adrianna took a step deeper into the room. Hanging at the back, high on the stage, were three wedding dresses. She recognized them from the five she was to wear on the second day of festivities. Planned meticulously with no less than two famous designers.

The crystals of her shoe caught in the unfinished underlay on the floor, and she staggered. Even as she regained her balance, she knew what she was seeing.

For a few moments at least, she was certain it was some kind of prank. In terribly bad taste and bizarre. Reality set in like waves washing onto a strange shore. Adrianna's throat tightened in a silent scream.

Blood. Hanging limbs. A familiar, lifeless face.

One of the three hanging wedding gowns had been used to dress a corpse.

Adrianna glanced about the room, heart drumming at her rib cage. A choking sound broke from somewhere deep inside her. The battered body of her former bridesmaid turned slowly, suspended above the stage, the Swarovski crystals of her floating hemline smeared deep red.

Adrianna could never explain after the fact why her first action was to raise the latest-model cell phone clamped perpetually in her hand and telephone her father.

"Daddy?" she breathed. "Daddy. He's back."

CHAPTER ONE

HOLLY

There's an oil and kerosene smell to the back alleys of New York's Queens in the early hours. It matches the searing yellow slash of POLICE LINE DO NOT CROSS and the steady white solar pulse of evidence photography.

A blare of police radios clouds the air as I approach, the orchestra of my working life.

As I slip quietly below the crime scene tape, an officer I've never seen before heads in my direction.

"Excuse me. Miss? You can't be in here."

I flash him my ID. "I work for Liberation Law," I explain politely. "You have our client under arrest. I'm Holly Stone."

He blinks once. Twice. Matching my appearance to my words. My hair is deep blue and my lipstick violet. The lacy cuffs of my black skull-print dress, its ribbon ties drawn around my curving frame, and a whole clutch of skull and pentagram silver jewelry.

"You're...a *lawyer*?" he manages. His eyes sweep my lip piercing and the unnatural hue of my shoulder-length hair, before landing back on my ID.

"I'm a freelance forensic investigator," I explain. "And I'm *really* not a morning person," I add ruefully, delving in my studded backpack and unearthing a breakfast Twinkie along with my crime scene coveralls.

The officer's uncertain expression hasn't wavered, but he lifts the tape and begins explaining the scene as I put on my protective gear while demolishing the last of the Twinkie in two short bites.

"Whew," I say, yanking the coveralls up and over my waist. "They don't make these for curvy girls, I'll tell you that much. OK. Tell me what's going on with the scene."

"The victim looks to have been stabbed," he says. "Your client was seen fleeing the scene by a reliable witness."

"No witness is reliable," I tell him. "I'm here to look at the data."

The officer leads me to the remains. The victim is a young man in a hooded top, jeans, and sneakers. His legs are splayed on the damp ground, blood soaking a wide pool underneath him. He hasn't yet been loaded into the body bag laid out at his side.

I squat down. It's a strange thing about death. The lifelessness of a corpse always cements in my mind the vibrancy of life. All those cells and vessels lying quiet hold a beauty that never fails to motivate me.

"Whatever happened," I promise him quietly, "there's evidence here somewhere."

I tune out the background noise and let my attention rest on the key areas. Knife wound to the chest. Something about his sneakers. There's a degree of blood soaking that doesn't correspond to what I can see of his socks. A rusting iron fire escape just above us. An arc of blood on the wall behind the body. I stand and walk closer to this last detail until I'm inches away, looking close at the blood droplets. My finger traces the air. Left to right. Right to left.

"Holly?" A familiar voice breaks the spell. I twist to see Lieutenant Howard Green, his mischievous smile belying the age of his lined features. He used to take me on ride-alongs back when I was a kid. "What are you doing here? Doesn't that hotshot law firm keep you busy enough?" He grins.

My smile wavers, and I rub the back of my neck. "I kind of quit."

"You quit working for *Attorney Simone Walters*?" His face couldn't channel more disbelief if he tried. "The two of you were inseparable."

"TV changes people." I can't meet his eye. "Simone started choosing cases for publicity instead of justice."

He frowns, unconvinced. "You sure you didn't just want an excuse to miss the awards dinner last week?"

"You know how I am with fancy dinners. All that cutlery."

He sighs. "So buy a dress. Learn how to use a fork already. Holly, you won two out of three categories in forensic breakthroughs, and you weren't there to pick up your own trophy."

I shrug. "I had work to do. You can never examine evidence too thoroughly."

"Spoken like a true forensic. And for the record, Holly, you might be locked in a basement, examining twenty thousand bloodstains in pursuit of truth, but not everyone in the private system is a purist." He levels an accusing stare.

To my immense relief, we're interrupted by the same nervous-looking young officer who was reluctant to let me on the scene. "Miss Stone?" he says. "There's a delivery guy on the other side of the crime tape."

"For me?" A million questions rise up. In my line of work, I often get urgent documents, but delivered straight to the scene is a first.

"Says he's got a package he can only give to you directly," confirms the officer.

I turn to see a man in a liveried uniform looking in my direction. Tapping my lip piercing distractedly, I head toward him.

"Any thoughts on the victim before you flee the scene?" shouts Howard, cupping his hands and calling after me.

"Blood arc is oval," I shoot back. "High-pressure exit. Consistent with a left ventricle wound, right-handed killer. My client is left-handed. And the shoes were put on the victim after he died. Your perp probably stole the victim's sneakers and left barefoot. Get to Sneakerheads on the Upper East Side today. You might catch them selling them."

"You're wasted in a private law firm," Howard calls back. "When are you going to join the good guys, Holly?"

"When you let me keep my piercings in and choose my own hours."

The delivery guy wears a box-fresh tan shirt emblazoned with the crown logo of his company and looks very out of place in the dark alley. The morning sun is coming up, lighting him from behind like an angel of destiny.

I recognize the branding on his shirt. His company delivers ultra-secure, ultravaluable items, with a price tag to match. My law firm uses them occasionally for state documents. But never to employees.

I swallow uncertainly. He's holding a black cardboard box—the same size as one of the heavy legal books that form a jerry-rigged nightstand in my walk-up apartment.

Legal documents? They come in envelopes.

"Holly Stone?" he asks.

"That's me." My eyes drop to the box. "How did you know I'd be here?"

He looks uncomfortable. "I went to your apartment first. Your roommate told me you'd been called out to a crime scene."

"But how…"

"My client was extremely clear. These must only be delivered to you personally. Would you mind looking into the display?" he asks. "Face recognition."

I wait motionless until he nods, then lowers the device. "Never seen such high-tech security before," I say conversationally. "Couldn't risk this falling into the wrong hands, huh?" I add.

His eyes follow my black-painted fingernails as I take the box. "Let me get you a tip," I tell him.

He raises his hands, appalled. "No. No. That's all taken care of."

I frown. I've never known a delivery guy to refuse a tip before. "Are you sure? Because…"

He shakes his head so vehemently I wonder if I've offended him. "The tip is included in the delivery," he says, backing away. "And perhaps mention to your apartment block manager that there are some…drug people…junkies…outside on the street. You probably don't want them hanging around your building."

"That's Burt and Emerson," I assure him. "They've been there forever. Never cause any trouble unless their methadone scripts get refused."

He retreats with an uncertain expression. I lever off the top of the box, taking extra care, since the contents could be valuable. Growing up in a shabby tenement, my quiet anxiety of damaging something expensive has never quite gone away.

But as the contents are revealed, I see to my surprise it isn't documents.

There's another box inside emblazoned with two names in foiled curling golden letters.

Adrianna & Mark.

I stare at them for a moment.

Adrianna Kensington, famous nightclub heiress and her millionaire fiancé, Mark Li.

Must be a mistake. There's no way in the world those people would be mailing me anything. As I peel back the lid, unease ripples through me.

It's a wedding invitation.

The strangest wedding invitation I've ever seen.

CHAPTER TWO

ADRIANNA

The sun is rising in Uptown Manhattan, and I am surrounded by cake. Tiered, towering, perfectly frosted cakes. The boutique pâtisserie has cleared out their entire display before opening at 9 a.m. and filled it with potential versions of our wedding masterpiece. Our *first* masterpiece, I should say. We're having three. One for each day of the festivities.

I've dressed down for the occasion, my usual high-shouldered blazer swapped out for an unstructured black jacket over a loose silk cami with a swinging pearl necklace and a casual little peplum skirt in a light blush. I've traded my heels for a pair of black velvet wedges. Overall, the effect is casual—Hollywood starlet headed out for lunch. Now I'm here, I wonder if I should have made more of an effort.

I let my gaze sweep the sugary constructions. Candy colors and glittering gold rococo flourishes. I'm disappointed.

"The brief was dark Versailles," I say, taking in the various decorations. The sugar craft roses and golden swirls. "This is more like…Disney or something." I point to a frosted gold twist.

The pâtissière—a glossy-haired brunette in an apron—looks devastated. She plucks out her phone and scrolls.

"We designed those elements based on the cornice in the Hall of Mirrors in Versailles Palace," she says hopefully, showing me a picture. "It's actually an exact replica. We had the molds made especially."

I wrinkle my nose. "Yeah. I guess, but..." I take in more cakes. "I wanted kind of the *vibe* of Versailles rather than just a copy of the interior. It's a Kensington wedding," I add. "Think dark glamour. Sophistication. Decadence. We own nightclubs."

I'm fully aware I might seem picky to some, but like my father says, if you want to be a special kind of person, you need special kinds of standards. And like my father, I have perfect faith in my visions. Even though he might not appreciate that about me just now.

The pâtissière nods in that way I'm used to people doing. Mark—my fiancé—isn't used to this yet. People agreeing with things that regular people might feel are unreasonable. He would likely be gushing with praise. Speaking of which. I check my watch: 6:30 a.m. Where *is* Mark? He is never late. Memories of yesterday bubble up. The body. Cops.

We agreed to try and put it behind us, but...

I pull out my cell. Unable to help myself, I quickly check the news.

Nothing nothing nothing. Dad's injunction has worked. No one is allowed to report on what happened.

When the police piled into the ballroom of the Plaza, you could tell they were completely overwhelmed. None of them were prepared to see what had happened to my bridesmaid.

They asked a lot of questions about who arrived at the Plaza and when.

"You're telling me you're not getting married at the Plaza today?"

asked a young policeman who was obviously completely out of his depth.

"I'm not getting married today *or* at the Plaza," I said exasperatedly. "This is a demo," I explained to him patiently for the second time. "The planner has set it up so my fiancé and I can get an idea of how the wedding breakfast will look."

His colleague kept looking around at the mirrors and tables. "You had the New York Plaza Hotel recarpeted in white," she said finally, "for a *demo* of your wedding?"

"Are you going to find who did this?" I demanded.

They exchanged glances.

The young police officer cleared his throat. "Here's the thing, ma'am," he said, emphasizing the *ma'am* pointedly. "Your bridesmaid. She died in a very strange way. And you don't seem all that upset, if you don't mind my saying."

"I've been raised to keep my feelings in check," I told him icily. "Not to mention I don't know her all that well."

"Excuse me, Miss Kensington." His female colleague spoke up. "But you're trying to tell me you didn't know the lady who was going to be a bridesmaid at your wedding?"

"What in the hell is all this?"

The silence of my nonreply was broken by a familiar voice. I looked up with waves of relief to see my father's short and stocky frame bowling across the white-carpeted floor. He was wearing the Brioni suit, which my half sister and I think makes him look like a Russian oligarch, thinning brown hair combed back and light-brown eyes bulging in fury.

"Hey! You!" My father closed in on the policeman, finger-pointing. "You don't talk to my daughter. You talk to me."

The young policeman visibly bristled, standing a little taller.

Likely he'd already seen my father on a "Most Wealthy" list and formed an opinion of him. Men do one of two things when confronted with the legendary Leopold Kensington: fight or fawn. The policeman looked like he was going for *fight*. It wouldn't last long.

"Excuse me, sir," he began in a bored kind of drawl, adopting an alpha-male, shoulders-back stance.

"You don't 'excuse me, sir,' *nothing*," interjected my father. "I grew up on the Lower East Side, watching you clowns take payouts from mobsters who put bricks through our windows. I got absolutely no time for New York cops. Or any kind of cops for that matter."

The officer was stunned into momentary silence. My father often has this effect. When I was a little girl, he used to let me sit in on the board meetings for his nightclub empire. I've literally seen him make grown men cry. Dad changed his name from Kolowski to Kensington when he married my mom, alienating his Polish father in the process. A lot of people are shocked at how much second-generation-immigrant grit he retains beneath the glamorous retitling.

"Mr. Kensington," the female officer tried. "We're examining a very brutal…very *strange* murder."

"Tell me something I don't know, Columbo. I've seen the goddamn pictures. What I want to know is what you're doing to stop the press getting ahold of this, less than a week before my daughter's wedding."

The police lady's mouth opened and shut. "You have… pictures…of the crime scene?" She was looking around, trying to fit this with the reality of having only just arrived on the scene herself.

"Sure I do. My daughter Adrianna has a problem, she calls me. I told her, send pictures. And from what I saw, we have a serious problem keeping this out of the media."

"I'm afraid it's your daughter who has a problem." The policeman had regrouped but wasn't restored to his former bravado. "From the remains, the way they were…arranged in a bridal dress. It looks as though someone means your daughter harm. A stalker or…"

"Call the newspapers!" yelled Dad, making everyone except me jump. "Howdy Doody here has solved the case. We all *know* Adrianna has a deranged stalker, genius. You knuckleheads in the NYPD have been failing to catch him for three years."

My phone beeps, interrupting my thoughts. A message lands. From Mark:

Got held up. Choose without me. See you for dinner.

My initial gut response is hot fury. How *dare* he stand me up by text when we're choosing our wedding cake? Then I remember. Mark is busy finding someone to investigate the crime scene who isn't NYPD. Like my dad says, you want the best, you pay for it.

I scroll through my image files, selecting a few choice snaps I had taken of me by a very specialist photographer last week. I zero in on two where the silk underwear reveals more than it should. I text an accompanying message:

Did you get an independent opinion on the crime scene?

Then attach two of the more risqué pictures and press Send. He texts back in seconds. Two smiling faces.

Yes.

I hate his use of emojis, but I have our whole married life to cure him of it. The important thing right now is the wedding is going ahead.

CHAPTER THREE

HOLLY

The New York traffic sounds are starting up in the nearby streets as I stare at the invitation.

Rather than a flat paper or card, the wedding invitation is a small rectangular black box, the size of a slim novel.

The front is a thick flap edged in deep foil filigree, like a greeting card on steroids. As I lift it, a tinkling classical music score begins. Beneath is a clear acetate panel, and underneath, top left, is a tiny golden carriage. The kind Cinderella might have. It looks slightly eerie set against the deep black card. As I watch, the carriage starts to slowly roll across the top of the invitation, revealing a trail of words under the clear acetate as it goes.

Leopold Kensington, it writes. The carriage backs up. Begins a new line.

Invites Holly Stone to the wedding of his daughter Adrianna Kensington to Mark Li.

Mark is the CEO of a highly successful tech company, so I'm guessing this is showboating for him. But it still doesn't explain the mystery of why I'm getting an invitation.

Unless... It occurs to me this could be from my former boss, Simone. She's a close friend of Leopold's. Maybe she thinks an invitation to the world's most famous wedding will smooth things over between us.

I shake my head. "Seriously, Simone?" I mutter. "I quit over your obsession with Adrianna Kensington's stalker case. Do you honestly think an invitation to her wedding will fix things?"

An image of Simone's unhappy face flashes in my mind. Despite her tiny frame, pixie haircut, and large round eyes, she is a straight-talking, no-nonsense type. Just like me. Last time we spoke, I accused her of putting TV ratings ahead of justice. The memory prickles me with discomfort.

I watch, mesmerized, as the carriage fills out the rest of the invitation.

Day 1. Teterboro Airport, 11 a.m. Drinks Reception, Elysium Island. White Tie.

Day 2. Elysium Island, 11 a.m. Ceremony. Wedding Breakfast. Black Tie.

Day 3. Elysium Island, 3 p.m.–2 a.m. Celebrations. Party Attire.

My mind drifts to the meager rack of clothes in my room. What in the world is "white tie"?

A final line scrolls out.

Holly Stone, meet Mark Li at the New York Plaza URGENTLY!

OK…so maybe Simone didn't send me this invite? Before I can take this in, my cell sounds its goth-rock ringer. I glance at the display.

Could be: Mark Li

I press to answer.
"Holly Stone?" The voice is male, loud with confidence.
"Yes?"
"This is Mark Li."
He leaves a pause. I don't fill it.
"Did you get the invitation?"
"The one couriered to a live crime scene?" I lift the cutout from its cushion bed for a second time, turning it in my hand. "It got my attention."
There's a pause. "Good. I had twelve staff work around the clock for a week, getting that carriage to roll. Adrianna was insistent the card be a certain thickness, and the weight ratios were a nightmare."
Adrianna. As in the *Adrianna Kensington.* It's really weird to hear him say her name so casually. Everyone has heard of the Kensingtons. Adrianna works hard to stay private, with limited success. With a father like Leopold Kensington, her private life is public property.
"What can I do for you, Mr. Li? Why are you asking me to meet you at the Plaza?"
"I need your help. You work as a forensic for Simone Walters?"
"Not anymore," I explain. "We had…a disagreement."
There's a long pause.
"Mr. Li?" I try. "If Simone is using you as a go-between, you can tell her to talk to me herself."

"I wasn't aware that you and Ms. Walters had had a disagreement," he says smoothly. "I contacted you because I researched you thoroughly and determined your qualifications to be excellent. Your self-taught abilities in the field won you a scholarship at New York University. You're the only student ever to graduate forensics without a high school diploma. Your two years working with Simone Walters was another point in your favor. But," he concludes, "I will now strike this merit from the list. What I *do* know is you are driven by unusual and complicated cases."

"Mr. Li," I say, trying to maintain an even tone, "I'm flattered you researched me. But you should know that I quit Simone's law firm because I want to solve criminal injustice, not garner TV ratings. Simone wanted exclusive access to Adrianna's stalker case. I didn't. I'm just not interested in picking over a dead case for publicity purposes, so I don't think I'm the right person for you."

"One of our bridesmaids has been murdered."

The words send a jolt right through me. Adrianna's upcoming wedding to her tech billionaire boyfriend has been featured in every glossy magazine, and the family employs the best security in the world. The idea of one of their bridesmaids being murdered is as bizarre as it is unlikely.

"I'm...so sorry to hear that," I manage. "I'd advise you to trust the police..."

"We have good reason not to," says Mark.

"Because the Kensington nightclub empire is notoriously shady, and Leopold Kensington is three parts businessman to one part mobster?" I suggest.

"I'm sending you pictures. They'll self-delete in a few minutes."

I can't match his flat voice and emotionless delivery to a man whose bridesmaid was recently murdered.

There's something not quite right about Mark Li.

"Mr. Li—" My phone pings as files arrive. I snatch a look and recoil in shock. The images are close-ups of a gruesomely murdered woman. Her face is obscured, but I can see heavy injury detail to the head and temples. Her body has been displayed in a way that is grotesque, even to a person who routinely visits crime scenes. The forensic expert in me can't help but be intrigued.

"The police haven't been able to remove the body," adds Mark. "They're sending in a specialist team this morning, so we only have a few hours."

"The body is still *there?*" My mind is whirring, wondering at what could possibly be preventing the police from removing it. I glance again at the pictures, but nothing gives it away.

"I can tell you more," says Mark. "But it needs to be in person. Meet me at the New York Plaza, seven a.m."

I glance at the time on my phone: 6:30 a.m.

"Please." The word is heartfelt. "We don't have much time. You're the only one who can help."

Defeated, "OK," I sigh. "But I can't get there at seven a.m."

There's a pause, and I hear keyboard tapping. "It's twenty-six minutes to drive to the Plaza from your location."

"Some of us use public transport," I explain to him.

"I've sent a car," he says. "It will be with you in five minutes."

He hangs up.

CHAPTER FOUR

HOLLY

True to his word, the car arrives within five minutes, the uniformed driver looking distinctly uneasy to be in the neighborhood. It's a limousine, an actual limousine. Another first.

When the driver sees me in my fishnet leggings and lacy skull dress with a studded backpack over my shoulder, he does an actual double take.

"It's all right," I tell him, climbing in, tucking blue hair behind my ears. "I only drink blood at night."

To my relief, he laughs, gliding away from the dingy backstreets and overflowing dumpsters.

I take in my surroundings, wondering if my day can get any weirder. The strange remains of the dead bridesmaid keep inserting themselves into my thoughts, macabre and disturbing. What kind of person could have done that?

I focus on my surroundings, letting myself sink into the soft leather seat. It's the first time I've ever been inside a real-life limo. The interior is orange blossom–scented, serene, and bathed in low ambient light. The rich wood door paneling has a complicated-looking array of buttons. I eye them suspiciously.

"First time in a limo?" The driver's voice comes crystal clear.

I track its direction from a small speaker just above my head and try not to feel unnerved that he can see me back here, but I can't see him.

"First time in a chauffeured car of any kind," I admit. "Rich person etiquette is a mystery to me."

He nods. "When I moved to New York, I thought I spoke perfect English," he says. "It took driving limos to teach me there's more to language than just words."

We pass a soaring billboard with an advertisement for Kensington's New York Club, all red carpet and low lighting, with flashes of designer liquor bottles.

"Guess that's the thing about wealth," I say. "It's as much about the story as it is about the reality."

He considers this. "Well, you know what they say about truth, right? There's yours, and there's mine."

"I'm a forensic scientist," I tell him. "There's only one way to present the truth."

We pass by parks and wider streets of Queens, then into deep shade as the car swings under the elevated 7 line—a steel framework of interlacing metal beams forming a soaring train track over the water to Manhattan. On the road, delivery drivers are making early-morning drops. People are hustling to work. Already the city is waking up.

The driver clicks his tongue. "Traffic," he mutters, spinning the car down a side street I never knew existed. "I'll take the lower bridge route."

We break out of the oppressive underside of the train track, with its miles of peeling green paint, and glide up onto the elegant spine of Williamsburg Bridge. A sudden flash of deep-blue sky and elevation over the East River makes it feel as though we're flying.

In the middle distance, the iconic skyline of Manhattan never fails to make my heart lift. The glass skyscrapers flash blinding slices of early-morning sun, and the Empire State Building and Chrysler Building, with their signature pointed tops, pierce the clouds.

As we descend to the Lower East Side, the density of people on the street has quadrupled that on the far side of the bridge. The streets are closed in tight, dark between tall buildings.

"I grew up here," I tell the driver as we pass by the upscale condominiums and trendy boutiques, "before it got fancy."

The driver gives a good-natured guffaw. "Lot less safe back then too."

"Cops everywhere," I agree. "I used to hang around crime scenes trying to spot things they'd missed."

"Bet they loved that. How do you know Mark Li?"

I hesitate. "I used to work for Simone Walters. The forensic attorney. She has a reality law show on TV."

Through the glass, I see his head bob up and down. "*Wrongly Accused*? I love that show! Solve the puzzle, right?"

I smile. "Right. Simone sees life as one big treasure hunt with a murder at the end. You know she was raised in a trailer park? She won a scholarship to Kensington Manor Boarding School. Lost her Kentucky accent. Learned how to act like one of America's wealthy elite." I sigh. "She was always trying to teach me how to do the same, but it never stuck."

Unease ripples through me. Simone is bound to be at the crime scene already. Meeting my former boss is going to be awkward to say the least.

We've left the huddled streets of the Lower East Side for the wider roads and skyscrapers of Midtown, its metro stations disgorging teeming clumps of people into the morning sun. The flow thins as we break into the tree-lined grandeur of the Upper East Side, stately town houses smiling benevolently on the sidewalks of boutiques and glittering glass restaurants. The river of arterial traffic on Madison runs yellow and black with cabs and chauffeured cars.

Ahead, rising majestically from the manicured sidewalk, is the timeless elegance of the New York Plaza, stretching up into the clouds like a fairy-tale castle. It has an iconic vista all its own, turreted with a regal facade, a thousand rectangular windows detailed in intricate stone carving, and deep-blue awnings at street level.

"You know the Plaza was built on a murder scene?" I tell the driver, trying to quell the unease I always feel entering grand places with well-dressed people.

A pause. "For a pretty girl, you sure talk a lot about death," observes the driver, slowing the car.

"Occupational hazard," I admit. As he pulls to a stop, I see a broad-shouldered man standing by one of the white Grecian pillars that frame the carpeted steps and gold balustrade leading to the Plaza's iconic art deco glass doors. I recognize him immediately. Mark's mix of Chinese and European heritage is distinctive. The brown hair, light eyes, and angular cheekbones are model handsome. To my relief, Simone isn't waiting with him. She must be inside.

"No tip, ma'am," the driver says as I rummage in my purse for bills. "It's all taken care of by Mr. Li."

Second time in one day. The familiar feeling of having breached some unseen formal protocol descends.

"Well. Thanks for the ride," I say, sliding out of the car without waiting for him to open the door.

Fancy buildings always put me on edge, and nerves are getting the better of me. Whatever Mark Li called me in to do, I may as well get it over with.

CHAPTER FIVE

HOLLY

With the Plaza behind him, Mark Li could be a poster boy for New York City. Immaculate in his designer suit and polished leather shoes, sporting the kind of shave and haircut that likely cost more than my entire outfit. He is holding a briefcase—an actual real-life shiny leather briefcase—which he places on the ground when he sees me.

As I walk across the broad sidewalk to the hotel, the humid New York summer morning is working to stick my blue hair to my neck. The polyester black lace sections of my skull pattern dress feel like they're generating their own heat. Glancing at Mark's delicate handmade brogues, I'm aware of my heavy-soled shoes clomping across the floor.

"Ms. Stone!" Mark steps forward, enclosing my hand in both of his and shaking it in a way that should be warm but feels strangely detached. "Thank you for coming. I apologize for the strange circumstances," he adds, not sounding sorry at all and giving me a slightly loaded once-over. I'm guessing he's not used to doing business with women larger than a size six.

"You're telling me it's strange." I look up at the hotel, its American flags hanging above us. "Those pictures you sent—"

Mark nods. "It gets stranger," he says, lifting his briefcase.

"The nineteen eighties called," I joke to disguise my nerves, "They want their luggage back."

He blinks twice in confusion, then continues walking as if I hadn't spoken.

"What's with the briefcase?" I add to hide my discomfort of the joke not landing. "Don't billionaires use man bags nowadays?"

He frowns slightly. "I'm a millionaire, not a billionaire," he says, as if the distinction would mean anything to a girl who survives on Cup Noodles in a shared Queens walk-up. "And I always carry a briefcase. Since I was a boy." He clears his throat. "Before we go inside, I wanted to bring you up to date. What do you know about my future wife?" As he talks, he flicks open the catches of his little case.

I hesitate. Questions like this always trip me up. It feels like a test of protocol I'm bound to fail.

"Adrianna is...famous?" I watch his face. "Really famous?" I try. "She is the billionaire heiress to an international nightclub empire. And...um, she's kind of known for being...you know, sort of difficult? Strong-minded," I amend hastily.

He smiles fondly, opening the briefcase a crack and removing a sheaf of printouts. "It's true, Adrianna really is quite something. But it wasn't her charisma I was referring to. I imagine you've seen her platform?" His face glows briefly with pride.

"I'm not really into all that side of social media," I explain apologetically. "Hair, and...stuff." I sweep an explanatory hand. "I'm more a dark-fantasy gaming-type girl."

"Were you aware Adrianna has a stalker?" He looks anxious now. On edge. I catch a glimpse of the papers. They're newspaper cuttings. Old ones, from Adrianna's infamous twenty-first birthday party.

"Well, yes," I say, pointing to the documents in his hand. "Adrianna was kidnapped. It was a huge story a few years ago. Even I couldn't really have missed that." I hesitate, not sure what else to say. The dark details of the kidnapping would stick in anyone's mind.

"It was three years ago," he says. "Before she and I met. At the time, Adrianna was receiving sinister letters and texts. The police didn't take it seriously despite the fact that the messenger seemed to always know exactly where Adrianna would be." He pauses to let that part sink in. "Then she was snatched from her twenty-first birthday party. Adrianna's stalker held her captive for three days. You must have read that story."

"I remember parts of it," I say carefully. "The party was held on the family's private island, right? In the end, Adrianna had been held captive in the family panic room."

"Correct." Mark nods, apparently pleased with my accuracy. "It was huge international news. Leopold Kensington flew out to the island to join the search. Poured millions into a global manhunt. But while the whole world was searching, Adrianna was being held in that room by some…sick individual wearing a Halloween mask." His mouth twists in the first recognizably emotional gesture I've seen him make.

There's an awkward silence. Everyone knows what was done to Adrianna in that room. The pictures of her emerging from captivity were splashed over every newspaper in the world.

Mark clears his throat. "There was a lot of speculation that it must have been one of the party guests. Adrianna invited her entire prep school, and relations between those girls are unusual to say the least." He straightens his blazer. "But the stalker was never caught."

I swallow. "Is this why I'm here, Mr. Li? You think the person who kidnapped Adrianna three years ago has returned?"

He nods tightly. "Adrianna's stalker is back. But they've graduated from kidnapping to murder."

A ripple of shock shudders through me. I wonder what Simone has made of this.

"Is Simone already here?" I ask Mark. "Because—"

Mark spins on a shining handmade heel, ignoring the question. "Follow me," he says shortly. "I'm going to take you to the scene of the crime."

CHAPTER SIX

HOLLY

I follow Mark in through the high art deco doors of the New York Plaza, my feet sinking into the deep carpeted steps as we ascend. He swings his strange little briefcase as we walk.

Since Simone isn't here in the lobby, she must already be at the scene, I realize. She'll be immaculately dressed in her subtle take on the latest New York fashions, short hair blown out perfectly, ten thousand dollars of bling at her throat, fitting in the luxurious hotel like a hand in a glove. She has a confidence so blazing you could heat your dinner off it.

"Listen," I tell Mark. "If you want Simone and me to work together...that could be a little awkward."

"When did you last speak with Simone?"

"Um. A few weeks maybe. I'm not really taking her calls right now," I admit. "She left for a trip to Elysium with Leopold Kensington right after a fight we had last week. Sent me a couple of messages the day before yesterday."

We've reached a doorman uniformed in jet-black with gold accent braiding standing behind a red rope. When he sees Mark, he draws it back with a smile. Mark nods his thanks and stands back to let me through the door first, passing the doorman a bill that looks suspiciously like a twenty.

"Did you just tip the doorman twenty bucks?" I whisper as we move through the grand doors.

"I didn't have any fifties," says Mark.

I'm distracted from a reply by the sheer scale of the lobby interior. Long windows framed by velvet curtains in a subtle burnt-orange shade cast portals of morning sun across the marble floor.

My eyes can barely take in all the gold filigree. "It's like someone detonated a stack of bullion," I tell Mark.

"I favor this hotel for meetings and lunch appointments," he says, striding along. "That was why Adrianna and I—" He stops suddenly.

Grief? Or something else? I can't tell.

"It was why we chose it for the demo," he says, collecting himself.

Maybe he does care. He just doesn't show it. Or can't, maybe. I'm still trying to figure him out.

We pass a gold-legged glass table set with magazines. On one of the covers, Swedish supermodel turned photographer Petra Morka lounges on a leopard-print chaise longue in high-heeled ankle boots, baggy cropped jeans, and a loose fishnet vest. Her jaw-length white-blond hair is undercut on one side, and her sea-green eyes hold the reader's gaze. She dangles a camera casually from her long fingers.

"She's one of our bridesmaids," says Mark distractedly as we pass.

"Wait. You're going ahead with the wedding?"

His step slows fractionally, and he frowns. "We decided we should. There's a dress fitting booked here for later today, and it's all going ahead. You'll understand when you see what happened."

He unexpectedly swerves off down an arterial corridor. "The manager is a friend of mine," says Mark. "He's agreed to take you into the ballroom through the kitchen entrance."

CHAPTER SEVEN

HOLLY

The Plaza manager is a tall man wearing an understated suit I suspect is extremely expensive. He is bald with short, expressive brows, a sheen to his black skin that speaks of expensive moisturizers, and a twinkling expression in his deep brown eyes that makes me like him instantly.

He proffers a large hand and encloses mine in it. "Miss Stone. I am Mr. Cohen, manager of the hotel. It's good to meet you in person. I've read about you of course. Goth girl Holly Stone. You find things out from crime scene material that even the best police forensics miss."

I find myself blushing. I guess a manager of such a prestigious venue has to be charming by nature.

Mr. Cohen checks his watch, glances at Mark. "We don't have very long before professional cleanup begins. If you'll forgive the imperative, we should go right away."

He leads us into the ballroom through the kitchen entrance.

It's like stepping inside a giant Grecian temple. Classical stone pillars line the sides, rising to arches of deep intricate carvings that curve gracefully overhead. The chandelier is a giant undulating river of glass that seems to pour down from the center of the lavish gold ceiling.

I take in the two broad banks of grand tables laid for dinner. They are, in a word, unreal. Thousands of white and black roses have been fashioned into giant globes, hung strategically around the room. The combined effect is otherworldly, a dark fairy tale made real. Blooming foliage is artfully snaking over the deep-colored soft furnishings as though reclaiming them. I'm momentarily swept up in the theater of it.

It must have been spectacular on the day. But now the edges of the petals have begun to fade to brown, there's something haunting about it. My stomach turns, recalling the image of the remains. They must have been found somewhere in the back. Where the shining dance floor reflects the light. My nostrils are hit by a familiar smell. The cleanup fluids used by professionals in death.

The manager's face mirrors my uneasiness. "I'll wait just outside the room. I…would rather not go any farther inside." He checks his watch. "You have fifty minutes."

Mark and I walk alone, farther into the room. At the back is a stage, and I can just make out three shapes hanging. Two dresses. A third with someone inside. I feel my throat constrict by degrees.

The body, shot in close-up in the pictures I saw, can now be seen in all its awful majesty. It's like a bizarre avant-garde setup. An art installation on the wrong side of good taste. But even I'm aware Adrianna Kensington doesn't know any artists that nasty. It's the strangest murder scene I have ever been to.

The victim has been strung up high above the stage of the Plaza inside a bloodied wedding gown. Her hair is hacked and shorn away. As the features of the face come into focus, I freeze, trying to process what I'm seeing. The head is hanging down, but... Shock waves ripple through me.

"Is this...is this some kind of sick prank?" I demand. But as I turn to take in Mark's face, I know it isn't.

The dead woman is my former boss and mentor. The most brilliant and complicated woman in my life.

Attorney Simone Walters.

CHAPTER EIGHT

HOLLY

Simone's body hangs limply inside a long silk wedding dress. Her feet point downward, inches from the ground, a ghostly ballerina, floating. Her head has dropped to her chest, disguising some of the worse close-up injuries the pictures show.

Of all the hundreds of crime scenes I've attended, I've never had an emotional reaction like this. My chest feels like it's closing in on itself. I put a hand out to steady myself and, finding thin air, stagger slightly.

Simone.

Suddenly the circumstances of our broken contact seem...if not unimportant, then, at the very least, surmountable.

If I had known I would never see her again...

Tears prick my eyes. I turn to Mark, fury blazing. "You told me one of your bridesmaids had been murdered," I accuse.

"That's correct." Mark gives a tight nod. "Simone was one of our bridesmaids."

That's too much data to process right now.

"How *could* you bring me here without telling me?" I demand. "How *could* you?"

"You worked for Simone," he says, looking confused. "I thought you would be well suited to help."

I twist around, filled with a sudden burning desire to slap his face.

"What is *wrong* with you?" I'm so filled with anguish, it feels as though there's nowhere for it to go. "We worked high-pressure crime scenes together for two years," I tell him. "*Two years* we were barely apart except to sleep. Simone was the first person to hire me out of college. She was the *only* person in corporate law not to judge me on appearances."

Mark blinks rapidly. "I don't understand," he says sharply. "If you cared so much about her, why did you leave her company? Why did you stop taking her phone calls?"

"Because I was angry with her," I say. "That doesn't mean I didn't *care* about her." The truth of this is hitting home far too hard, far too late. "I cared about her deeply," I say, more to myself than to Mark, who still seems to be struggling with the juxtaposition of anger and caring. "I couldn't have been so angry at her if I didn't."

It's a horrible realization. My argument with Simone tracked back to the day she flew out to Elysium. For months, she'd been meeting up with Adrianna's shady nightclub-baron father, Leopold Kensington, hatching a plan between them to unmask Adrianna's stalker. The final straw came when she began working pro bono on Adrianna's prenup, which involved flying out to the family's private island.

"Since when do you chase Caribbean vacations?" I demanded. "You used to care about injustice." I felt cut out. Simone had always told me we were the same. Neither of us were raised with wealth or society manners. But she'd learned them, and she wanted to teach me how to join that world like she had. Now she was being secretive and excluding me.

My mind slides hopelessly over all the missed calls. The messages I ignored. I was too angry and betrayed to let her in. Now it's too late.

"I'm leaving," I tell Mark. "Find yourself another forensic."

"I should have told you," he says tonelessly. "I don't know. I guess I just didn't know how. But the police will be back soon. Do you really trust them to discover the truth?"

I swing back around, taking in the awful reality of Simone's death. The way she died.

"Don't you think Simone would have wanted you to investigate her murder?" he adds.

My eyes blaze with fury. "*Fuck* you," I whisper, turning on my heel. "You asshole," I spit back over my shoulder. "How could you let me see her like this?" I don't trust myself to say any more. Tears are filling my eyes as I walk from the room.

Memories of Simone are flowing thick and fast. Eating cold pizza on her office floor as we spread out case files, working late into the night, inventing ever more entertaining ways for her to host forensic revelations on her show. Following the clack of her heels as she headed out to court, dressed to the corporate max. She always saw something in me that no one else did. True, she pushed too hard at times for me to pick up on rules that were completely alien to me. Standing straight, speaking clearly. Presenting evidence a certain way. She wanted me to be able to hold my own with the wealthy elite, and I never fit.

"Wait." Mark jogs to my side, grabs my arm awkwardly. "Please."

I stop, about to tell him where to get off, when I see his face.

There is something emotional now in his cold eyes. Something childlike and tragic.

"Please help us," he says. "You're right, I've done this wrong. I'm not very adept with people. But the police aren't to be trusted. Not where Leopold Kensington is concerned."

"They think Leopold Kensington is involved in her death?"

"No," says Mark. "Leopold was out in LA. They just don't like him. The police are wasting time, trying to score points off him. And Adrianna is in danger." He frowns. "Whatever you feel about me, we need to find who did this. To Simone. Surely you want that too?"

Again, his eyes are missing something. Some depth of feeling. "More than anything," I admit.

"Then please," he says, "take a look at the scene. You're good. You might find something the police missed."

CHAPTER NINE

PETRA

When I heard a bridesmaid had been murdered, I was only surprised it hadn't happened sooner.

I'm walking along the marble-floored corridors of Leopold Kensington's downtown Manhattan office in what is widely known as my signature look. Ripped couture and designer shoes busted up with my own additions. White-blond hair flipped to one side, shaved underneath. A trash-punk model style I've aced for over twenty years now. Long enough to transform my runway success into something iconic.

My phone rings, and I flip it from its gold case. The flashing screen shows my magazine editor's name.

"Petra," he says. "We need to talk about the pictures you took. There's been more complaints."

"I can't talk right now," I tell him. "I'm about to get you a hot tip."

He's silent, thinking this over. "Kensington stuff?"

"What else?"

"OK, meet me for lunch," he decides. "One p.m. Usual place."

"Got it." I hang up. When I moved from Sweden to New York, I thought my family had secrets. A few Nazis in the bloodline is nothing, *nothing* compared to the Kensingtons. They really did write the book on skeletons in the closet. Photographing Leopold gave me the inside track on the world's most notorious family. *Everything* the papers say is true.

I reach an oiled walnut door with an outsize gold plaque announcing:

> Leopold Kensington. CEO. The Kensington Groups.

I enter without knocking and am relieved to see Leopold sitting alone at his desk. Naturally, he enjoys a vast corner office with panoramic views of Manhattan. I'll bet he stands here with a whisky at night, gloating over all the buildings he personally owns.

Leopold looks up from his desk. I can't tell if he's pleased to see me or not.

"Hi." I raise a hand.

"You can't be in here," he says, his gravelly voice sounding even more furious than usual.

Behind him is a wall of framed old newspapers declaring him "The Nightclub Baron of New York." Paparazzi photos of him and his first wife, Athena, back in the 1980s. The headlines have been carefully clipped away. I'm guessing they read something like "Society Girl and the Fish Market Boy," or "Heiress Athena's Lower East Bad Boy."

Leopold famously grew up running the family fish stall at Fulton Market. Before he bought a tired old working man's club and charmed Athena into bringing her society friends.

More recent shots are in color. An aging Leopold glares out of *Forbes*'s front cover, holding a golden model of Manhattan in his palm.

"This whole thing is a fucking shit show. I'm trying to manage it." He shakes his head. "I told you not to come."

I walk up to his desk, and just for a second, a flash of uncertainty passes over his usually confident expression. For a moment, I think he might actually physically stop me as I slide onto his lap. He doesn't.

I turn to take in his desk and pick up a photo. "Nice wedding picture." It's him and Athena in the 1980s at the nightclub that made Leopold famous. He wears an eighties' suit that would look good on an Italian mobster. Athena flaunts a dress that taste forgot, accessorized with hideous electric-blue eye makeup, frosted lipstick, and a sky-high frazzle of honey-blond hair.

"All those wives, and you've still got a picture up of the one who died?"

I've gone too far, and I feel his muscles tighten in annoyance. He takes the picture from my hand. Not snatching exactly but with quiet force. "Athena would have wanted to be remembered at Adrianna's wedding."

"Good for you, Leopold." I say, pressing myself tighter against his body. "Marriage is for life." I tried calling him Leo once and never did it again.

I reach into my pocket and pull out the little silver case Leopold is all too familiar with. It's where I keep my coke. He knows I always have the best. I get it from his clubs after all.

"Coffee break?" I ask him, waving it enticingly. "We could go to one of the rooms at the Kensington Club."

"The wedding is in four days," he says, glowering. But I notice his chest is rising and falling fast. "I got work to do—"

"Have you decided who's going to be maid of honor now?" I ask.

Leopold is usually at his most pliable in these moments, but I notice his whole body tense.

"What are you talking about?"

"Leopold." I roll my eyes. "You chose the bridesmaids. Everyone knows that."

He shifts uneasily, not denying it. "What does it matter who the maid of honor is?" His eyes are searching my face, trying to work out if I know.

"You *know* why," I tell him. "Leopold, you think I'm stupid? You didn't appoint Simone a bridesmaid for free legal advice."

He avoids my eye. "One of the bridesmaids had to be a lawyer. It was the right composition for whatever PR campaign they got going on."

I raise an eyebrow. "Simone isn't even the right kind of attorney for a prenup. Don't play dumb with me, Leopold. You sent Simone out to Elysium to investigate Adrianna's kidnapping. You think it's someone close to her." I pause for effect. "And now Simone's dead. Which proves you right."

"Simone told me she found something on Elysium," he says very quietly. "She was going to share it when I got back from LA. You think that's why she died?"

Leopold's face is swathed in troubled and guilty emotions.

I roll my eyes. "Three dresses. Hair cut off. *Leopold*, it's not just a coincidence."

CHAPTER TEN

HOLLY

Something about Mark Li's tone-deaf emotional range pushes a switch inside me. I feel the familiar thought processes slide into place. Data. Details. I seize them gratefully. Data is a lot easier than grief.

In the back of the famous ballroom is a stage. The long tan curtains are partially closed. In front of them is more crime scene tape. Now we've got sufficient proximity to the stage, we can see them.

Three white wedding dresses, hanging. Turning slowly in the partial light.

They are soaked with blood.

"Three dresses," I murmur, glancing at the crime scene image and back again. "Victim in the middle dress." I swallow. Falling into an analytical state of mind is helping. "The killer cut her hair," I say grimly, looking at how Simone's dark hair has been hacked away in clumps. Close enough to the scalp to draw blood in several places.

Emotion rears up. I fight it down, forcing myself to look at the details.

I glance around the stage. "Did they find the missing hair?" I ask Mark quietly.

He shakes his head.

I swallow, nearing the scene. Despite my natural human revulsion, the forensic part of my mind is already whirring. Blood spatter, trajectory. Were the dresses like this when they were hung up or afterward?

Considering how Simone was found, with all her hair cut away, the latter suggestion hardly bears thinking about. I match the picture on my phone to what's been left on the scene. From the looks of things, the pool of blood under her body has been scrubbed, but there is tape marking out where she fell. I take in the wider stage. Forensics have tagged places where blood spatter has been found.

Then I see something that doesn't show in the pictures. Flowers and candles have been arranged in a circle around the stage. Almost like a religious altar.

Interesting...

I turn to Mr. Cohen, who has stepped back into the ballroom. "Did the police compile a list of who could have gotten in and out of this room?" I ask him.

He clears his throat, looking anywhere but the stage. "The ballroom has four different exits. One directly into the kitchen. Another is a loading entrance. Then we have two public entrances, which filter into different parts of the hotel. The ballroom area was closed off for the Kensingtons. But the lobby and other areas of the hotel were in regular use."

"You're saying anyone staying as a guest in the hotel could have gotten inside?"

"Not just hotel guests," he says. "We have several restaurants and bars that are open to the public. Not to mention a high volume of deliveries arriving at the loading entrance. We monitor what arrives, of course, and we have security cameras in the lobby and elevators. But not in the kitchens or outer corridors."

I map the ballroom. Four entrances. "So more or less anyone could have gotten into the ballroom through the staff areas without being caught on camera?"

"Not easily. But it would be possible."

I consider this, tapping my lip piercing thoughtfully and turning my attention back to the hanging dresses.

"Simone was hung up in the first dress," I say, thinking out loud and removing my phone to reexamine the photo and confirm this. I notice something else. "Simone's ring is missing," I say. "She always wore the same gold ring on her little finger." Tears fill my eyes, and for a moment, I can't speak.

Mark is watching me closely. His eyes drop to the circle of candles and flowers around the dresses. "You think that's like a ritualistic thing?" he asks nervously.

"Could be," I admit. I look back at the photograph.

"Could it be...like a warning to Adrianna?"

"Why would you think it would be a warning?" I catch my curving body and darkly painted eyes in one of the many mirrors.

"Dri has enemies," admits Mark.

"Like who?"

He makes a strange kind of laugh. "Let's just say she likes to keep her enemies close." He avoids my gaze.

"Mark," I say carefully. "You called me here to help you. But if you're keeping something from me—"

He shakes his head quickly. "It isn't that," he says. "I just... Sometimes I think Dri isn't telling me everything."

"Do the police have a theory as to how the victim died?" I ask, unable to bring myself to say her name just yet.

Mark nods slowly. "She was beaten with something heavy," he explains. "Multiple times. Close range. Likely she knew her attacker." He pauses.

"What?" I ask.

"The police are working half on facts and half on media hearsay," he continues. "You know how Adrianna is portrayed by the media."

I do. Adrianna Kensington is characterized as bratty, entitled, and difficult, to use some of the nicer words.

Something occurs to me. "The pictures you sent to my phone were official hard copies from NYPD," I tell him. "Do you have their preliminary report?"

He hesitates.

"I won't ask how you got it," I add.

Mark breathes a halting sigh. "In my car. Parked out front."

"Can we get out of here?" I ask. "I need to read the report and take a look at those pictures in daylight. I have a feeling the police have missed something important."

Something about this whole scene doesn't sit right at all, and I'm fairly sure the hard copy images and a shot of caffeine are going to bring it all into focus.

CHAPTER ELEVEN
ADRIANNA

My New York apartment has always felt like a safe space for me. It's so high above Manhattan, I can see all the way to Brooklyn. A few years back, we had a company fit ballistic walls and floors. Maybe a little overkill, but like Dad says, it's more about the message you send out. It's three thousand square feet, with polished resin white floors and panoramic floor-to-ceiling windows, and I've just had a spa room built, where I'm currently soaking my toes with my half sister, Georgia.

I've been scrolling on my phone every minute since the police left.

"Nothing about Simone's death in the news?" Georgia asks. As usual, she is immaculately styled, her Afro hair sculpted in a halo of glossed curls, dewy skin subtly contoured with expensive makeup. Like me, Georgia inherited Dad's patrician nose and large, slightly close-set eyes, but they look prettier in her warm brown shade than my deep blue. Her slender legs are clad in soft gray jeans, rolled up at the ankle, and she wears a V-neck black chiffon blouse, open low to display a clutch of elegantly understated gold jewelry. Georgia's mom is CEO of an African American beauty brand, while mine was a blond socialite. But there's no mistaking we're related, with Dad's strong features and personality to match.

We are the same age—thanks to one of Dad's short-lived affairs, which Mom always gracefully ignored. Georgia started Kensington Manor Boarding School the same year as me. But to everyone's surprise, we looked out for one another from the start.

My eyes track the headlines. I shake my head. "Dad kept it under wraps. The only thing I can find is reruns of the story from three years ago."

Georgia sits up slightly, her narrow frame slanting forward. "From when you were kidnapped? Why are they running that?"

"Because paparazzi are sick individuals, and because my wedding is coming up, they like to remind me of my lowest point."

My finger zooms over the scrolling news tabs. Old stories.

Society heiress kidnapped

Billionaire heiress snatched

Party girl Adrianna taken

"How are the other bridesmaids taking the news?" I ask Georgia.

"They think your crazy kidnapper is on a killing spree, and they're freaking out," she says. "Just like I am. Dri, do you really think—"

"I'm not calling the wedding off," I tell her, holding up my hands. "I'm not letting a murderer *win*."

She nods briefly, accepting the fact but unhappy still. "I just wonder..." She hesitates. "Dad picked Simone to spy on us, right? All those questions she asked."

I nod slowly. "Maybe," I agree. "Simone wasn't exactly part of the crew."

"She was a Kensington Manor School girl," Georgia points out.

"Yeah...but scholarship. And older. Left before we even got

there. She didn't go through what we all did." I give a little shake, dislodging the memories. "Talk work to me," I tell Georgia. "You know that's your happy place."

This elicits a small smile. "True," she agrees. "OK. We got the pictures back from the bridal swim shoot," Georgia says, handing me a sheaf of color printouts. "We edited Simone out. Journalists are bound to wonder why."

"Let them wonder." My bridesmaids and I stand in a perfectly choreographed semicircle with carefully contrasted heights, hair colors, and bathing suits. We look like a bikini-clad girl band, our postures and facial expressions suggesting a varied range of feminine personas.

I'm in the center, naturally. Lean, tanned, in a white bikini with cutouts. My chestnut curls have been artfully tousled to give a carefree beach vibe. I leaf through, noting Georgia's mark-ups.

Five women smile out from the picture. We're all old school friends. In theory at least.

Silky, a dark-haired art house filmmaker, is the only bridesmaid besides my half sister I'd consider a friend. Next to her, freckled Ophelia works a kooky look to match her career as a celebrity makeup artist. Petra's long limbs and sharp cheekbones supply the supermodel credentials. And finally, Georgia. Her voluminous curls are side-parted and captured at an angle that complements her small jaw. She bears the slightly shocked expression of someone who doesn't naturally pose for photos.

I look back at the image. Five bridesmaids. Down to four. Me. All ready for release.

"None of them look as though they like me," I say, putting my finger on what bothers me about the pictures. "But…I guess it's a solid lineup. Let's just get out to Elysium."

Georgia turns to look at me, her large brown eyes owlish. "Dri," she says gently, "pretty pictures don't mean everything is OK. You can't just bury your head in the sand," she adds, lifting her large phone, scrolling social media.

As I glance at her screen, a familiar headline flashes up. The story that went viral all around the world three years ago.

"Georgia!"

She lowers the large screen. "It just popped up," she says. "I didn't search it, I swear."

My eyes are locked on her screen.

THE KILLING CODE—THREE DRESSES

Three bloody dresses found where Adrianna was snatched.

Then the picture. Me. Three years ago.

ADRIANNA ESCAPES TORTURE ROOM

Bloodied, bruised, with her long hair hacked away, Kensington heiress escapes with her life.

CHAPTER TWELVE

HOLLY

New York's tall buildings have retained the slow heat of yesterday. It's only as Mark and I get deeper into the green heart of Central Park that the peanut- and traffic-scented air breaks into something a little fresher.

I settle myself on a bench while Mark gets coffees and open up my cell, scrolling to the last picture I have of Simone. We have our arms around each other, smiling at the camera, celebrating our latest courtroom success in our favorite doughnut shop.

I flip to another photo. Simone and me in Adrianna's latest New York restaurant. She'd been showing me dining etiquette with limited success.

"I don't get why you're trying to make me act like someone I'm not," I told her. "It's fake."

"It's no different from what we do in court, right?" she replied. "Show forensics in a way people want to pay attention to?"

"That's different," I grumbled. "We're telling the truth."

"Truth is perspective, Holly. We're just helping people see the right one."

That was Simone. Presenting forensic material in an engaging way was exactly why she garnered so many court wins—and TV ratings.

I glance up to see Mark's long body returning with coffees. My eyes drop back to my cell. My thumb scrolls over unread texts from Simone:

Holly. Call Me.
Holly. We need to talk.

The last is an audio message, and I click it.

Simone's familiar voice returns from the grave. Her tone is urgent and hushed.

"Holly, something has happened," says Simone. "You were right. I was keeping things from you. About the Kensingtons."

A river of ice flows down my spine. Eyes wide, I fumble to press the phone against my ear, scanning for anyone who might be able to overhear. Mark is getting nearer.

"I thought it was for your own protection," continues Simone's disembodied voice, "but I've left you exposed. I need to tell you the truth. About who kidnapped Adrianna Kensington. It has to be in person, so call me."

I force myself to breathe out, trying to process the content of the message.

Mark is looking in my direction now, and I lower the phone, forcing my expression to be neutral as he closes in.

"Everything OK?" he asks, frowning.

"Absolutely," I say. "Just…letting a few clients know I'll be in late."

He sits beside me. A few passersby do a double take at the strange combination. The expensively suited businessman with model cheekbones and the girl in the skull dress and goth makeup.

His tablet beeps. "The report has downloaded," he says, turning it so I can see.

I lift the tablet from his hands, pushing the mysterious voice message from Simone to the back of my mind. As I start reading, I realize I was right. Part of the murder scene doesn't fit at all.

CHAPTER THIRTEEN

HOLLY

As I finish reading the report, I'm certain of it. Something's off. There's a major omission. I just can't quite settle on whether to trust Mark with what I've seen.

"So what's your opinion?" he asks. "What do the police think happened?"

I blow on my coffee. Best to start from the beginning, I decide. Something about the familiar practice of deciphering forensic reports is comforting. It allows me to rise above my grief. To focus on the details without being dragged down by who those details are about.

"OK. It's only a preliminary report, since they haven't yet been able to remove the body. But their opinion is…she looks to have been beaten to death. With something blunt and heavy."

I scroll more pages. "There's a lot of bleeding from the head injuries. They were severe enough to smash the skull and break the skin. But she doesn't have much in the way of defensive wounds. You'd expect someone defending their head from an assailant to throw their hands up to protect their face. Then you'd see bruising here." I lift my arm to tap the underside of my forearm. "There's not really bruising consistent with that. It's the wrong angle."

"What are you suggesting?"

I swallow. "If I were to compile a working theory," I say, "the attacker landed a blow to her head that left Simone too dazed to defend herself. Maybe from the side. She has injuries to the outside shoulders, suggesting a wild kind of attack, where maybe the weapon missed the head. This blow, here at the front, smashing her temple, that's the blow that would have likely killed her. Then one at the base of the skull and another at the side." I frown, taking more in. "The bruising," I decide. "Something quite odd about how consistent it is. That would suggest someone quite calculated. Measured. There's an almost workmanlike quality to how they've been administered to all sides of the body with similar force. The sheer volume of injuries points to someone out of control. But… the power with which they're administered suggests the opposite."

I glance at Mark. He's looking straight ahead, and the coffee in his hands is shaking.

"Sorry," I say. "You get used to this stuff in my line of work. I know you knew her too…"

"Actually, I didn't," says Mark. "Not in any meaningful way."

"You didn't know your own bridesmaid?"

He shakes his head slowly. "I know it sounds crazy. Adrianna's wedding is a showpiece for the Kensington empire, so the bridesmaids were chosen by Leopold on the basis of who could most benefit the business. Simone was Leopold's lawyer. We barely knew her. But…it's still just horrible."

My mouth is turned firmly downward. "I agree. It doesn't look like a crime of passion. Those three head blows are almost identical in size and heft. And look how they ring the head. Front, back, side. Like the work of someone making a considered job."

"Taller than her?" Mark looks thoughtful. "A man?"

"Depends on the length of the bar. But they would have had to be relatively strong. It takes up to several hundred pounds of pressure to crack the average skull. Whatever she was hit with was most likely heavy and brought down with considerable force."

I think some more. "The dresses," I say. "How did three wedding dresses get inside the ballroom?"

"The dresses are Adrianna's," says Mark. "Or…they were." His eyes cloud.

"All of them?"

"It's a three-day event," explains Mark. "And some of the days, she'll need outfit changes. One dress for the ceremony, another for the reception. Then one for each party afterward. Five in total." He opens his hands as if this made perfect sense.

"*Five* wedding dresses?" I can't really keep the contempt out of my voice. There are people starving in the world, for chrissakes.

A half smile pulls at Mark's mouth. "Not you too," he says. "You sound like Detective Ortiz."

"Sounds like we have similar politics."

Mark is growing on me. His detached demeanor seems less cold now. Maybe his somewhat robotic manner was a defense mechanism. A stress reaction to the crime scene.

"Look," he says. "I appreciate how it looks on the outside, but a wedding on this scale is its own ecosystem. You have to think about it more like a business merger."

"I don't follow."

"It's really a chance for Leopold Kensington to cement potentially lucrative allegiances. Every choice his daughter makes could have major ramifications for certain businesses. Dri didn't just go out and pick out five fifty-thousand-dollar designer dresses because she thought they looked pretty."

"Those dresses cost fifty thousand dollars *each*?" My eyes return to the hanging gowns. How sad and cheap they look, dirtied with blood. Although...they're not sagging out of shape, are they? I pay close attention to how they hang.

"Between twenty and fifty thousand," agrees Mark. "But you're missing the point. The point is the whole wedding. The dresses, the flowers, the cake, the venue. Even the engagement ring. It's all a very carefully curated brand. Whether she likes it or not, Adrianna is part of the Kensington empire. And the entire business is based on a certain luxury lifestyle. If any small part of that slips, if her wedding is seen as...unaspirational...or, God forbid, cheap... Leopold Kensington looks weak. Or tasteless. And the nightclubs lose money."

I think some more. Scan back to the facts. Make the decision to tell Mark what I've seen as I blow on my coffee again. The remains. *Simone's* remains. The slackness of the facial muscles wasn't what I would expect to see on a day-old corpse.

"The body temperature," I murmur. "That's...odd."

"Odd how?"

"Yesterday was hot, right?" I say. "Same as today."

"Right."

I nod. "Did you say the detective working this case was Ortiz?"

"Yes. Why?"

"I need to give her a call. There's something about this scene the police have missed."

CHAPTER FOURTEEN

HOLLY

A troop of police are already at the Plaza when Mark and I arrive. Simone's body is being carefully winched down with a specialist hand crane, and all eyes are fixed on the loud and painfully slow process. My initial shock has changed to something deeper. A fiery desire to get justice.

Two cops are standing a little apart from the others, watching the process with their backs to us.

Even from behind, I immediately recognize Detective Ortiz from previous crime scenes. She's stocky and brown-skinned, her straightened dark hair edged with rogue wisps of white, and I remember her being smart. No-nonsense.

She's speaking with a tall dark-haired police officer who I can't place.

With the noise of the crane, neither Ortiz nor her companion have noticed us arrive. As we close in, I catch my name being mentioned.

"Stone is always muscling her way onto our crime scenes," the male officer is saying, "pointing out things we've missed. She's like a magician for making us look bad." His voice sounds strangely familiar, and suddenly his identity falls into place.

Great. It's Fitzwilliam. I roll my eyes. We met years ago, studying the same law module at NYU, and have disliked one another ever since. He's an egotistical blowhard who values the image of his department over justice.

"The goth?" Ortiz is saying. "Blue hair. Curvy girl. Pretty if you overlook the fact that she dresses like a vampire who shops at Goodwill. Didn't she help us out on a few cases?"

Ouch. I clear my throat loudly, but neither hear me over the sound of the crane.

"If you count making us look like idiots, then she's helped us out on a lot of cases," says Fitzwilliam. "I always thought of her more as one of the boys. Kind of blunt. Lacking social graces. Tattoos everywhere."

"Excuse me," I say in what I hope is an authoritative voice.

Fitzwilliam spins around. His eyes rest on me. His cool blue-eyed stare and square jaw give him a haughty look that exactly matches his country club accent.

"One of the boys, huh?" I eyeball him. "Should I be flattered, or does that category include you?"

Fitzwilliam has the decency to flush. Ortiz looks amused.

"Miss Stone." Fitzwilliam holds out a strong hand. His signet ring digs into the side of my palm.

I wince. "Thanks for the formal greeting. Nice to see you've brought the frat-boy laundry press to the NYPD." I gesture to his pin-neat uniform and coiffed black hair. He honestly couldn't look more groomed if he tried.

"Holly Stone." Ortiz puts out a hand. "First time I've seen Fitzwilliam on the back foot. Didn't think anything could pierce that WASP confidence."

Mark looks between the female detective and Fitzwilliam. In

some ways, the two men could be cousins. Both have the same effortless aura of health that plenty of money brings: confident stance, strong gym-honed bodies, thick dark hair, and piercing clear eyes. But Fitzwilliam's skin is pale to Mark's light brown, and his features have a square-jawed heaviness compared to his counterpart's delicate bone structure.

"You know each other?" asks Mark, looking between Fitzwilliam and me.

"Sadly, yes," I tell him. "We went to the same college," I say. "But Fitzwilliam didn't manage to graduate, so he became a cop to help his future political career."

Fitzwilliam's pale jaw tightens. He shakes his head wearily. "So says the scholarship girl with a big chip on her shoulder."

"Easy to look down on other people when Daddy's paying your school fees."

"For your information…"

"Now now, children." Ortiz has a small smile on her face. "Play nicely. Fitzwilliam hasn't had it as easy as you think, Miss Stone, for all his pressed shirts and shiny shoes."

Fitzwilliam looks down at his shirt distractedly. Since I assume Ortiz has had her own share of hardships, working her way up from a Latina woman cop to detective, I'm inclined to believe her. Though I can't imagine what Fitzwilliam could possibly have encountered in terms of hardship. Falling off his polo horse and landing on his silver spoon, maybe.

"We spoke on the phone." Mark extends a hand to Fitzwilliam, and they exchange a firm downward shake with the easy recognition of two boys from the same club. "Three dresses at the scene. It's the stalker's calling card, right? You checked the old file."

"Those files weren't in our jurisdiction," says Fitzwilliam

apologetically. "Adrianna's party was held on an island off the coast of Colombia. But…you're right. There are a lot of similarities between the two cases. The ritualistic circle of flowers and candles. The…hair cutting." His eyes glide away from Mark's.

"You think it's the same guy?" asks Mark.

"Not necessarily a man," says Fitzwilliam. "Adrianna's kidnapper wore a full-face mask and cloak." He takes a breath and glances at Ortiz, who bears the steady annoyance of a senior woman used to being overlooked in favor of the nearest white male. She raises her eyebrows at him very slightly, and Fitzwilliam's mouth closes.

"Could it be a copycat?" I suggest. "Adrianna's kidnapping was widely publicized, right?"

Ortiz shakes her head. "Not all the details," she says. "No regular member of the public would have known about the kidnapper's obsession with the number three. Or the ritualistic elements. These cases have a lot more in common than we first thought," she continues. "And at this stage, we have reason to believe you might be correct, Mr. Li. Whoever held Adrianna captive three years ago returned to murder her bridesmaid."

There's a loaded silence.

"I'm told you have a theory, Miss Stone," continues Ortiz, "about the body temperature?"

My eyes slide between them. I'm not used to working directly with cops. I tuck blue strands of hair behind my ears.

"Body temperature drops by an average of one and a half degrees an hour for the first twelve hours after death," I say. No one counters this, so I plunge on. "Based on that numeric, I'd expect the deceased to have a rectal reading of approximately eighty degrees." I see Fitzwilliam twitch at the word *rectal* and work hard not to roll my eyes. "The forensic report registered the body at seventy degrees. Ten degrees lower than the likely range. Particularly given the warm weather we've had."

I pause to let them digest this.

"That would leave two possibilities," I continue. "The first is that Simone died earlier than first assumed."

"Not possible given the number of people who saw Simone alive the night before her death," fills in Ortiz.

I nod. "I thought the same. Which only leaves the second option. Simone's body must have been moved from someplace cooler."

CHAPTER FIFTEEN

HOLLY

We're all silent, absorbing my theory that Simone's body was somehow moved unseen into the ballroom. Mr. Cohen has returned, and his face shows scandalized horror and pensive thought. Fitzwilliam speaks first.

"That's simply nonsense," he says. "This is one of the finest hotels in the world. Are you seriously suggesting someone dragged a battered corpse through the corridors and no one saw?"

Ortiz frowns. "What makes you so sure, Holly? We checked all the footage and interviewed staff. Simone's corpse was one hundred and fifteen pounds deadweight. You can't just throw that over your shoulder and walk in."

"True," I admit. "But the body temperature says different. And Simone wasn't the only deadweight in this room." I point to the dresses. "Those wedding gowns must weigh twenty pounds at least. How were they transported into the ballroom?"

"Couture dressmakers provide their own rolling storage containers," explains Mr. Cohen.

"Large boxes, capable of transporting heavy loads," I confirm. "What time did they get wheeled in?"

Mr. Cohen thinks. "My staff would have transported them in at six a.m. on the day of the demo."

Fitzwilliam and I exchange glances. Surprisingly for a person handed his whole life on a silver platter, he looks to have figured it out too.

"You think Simone's body could have been wheeled in here inside the dress container?"

"It would explain how the body temperature was off," I agree. "Simone was killed somewhere else, her body put in along with the dress, then transported here. If it was a member of the Plaza staff, they wouldn't even have had to know what they were moving."

Ortiz's eyes settle on me in something like dawning respect. "OK," she says, turning to Mr. Cohen. "Where would the dress have been prior to being moved here?"

"We have a large storage room," explains Mr. Cohen.

Ortiz is already moving toward the door. "Can we see it?"

"Certainly." Mr. Cohen hitches a key card from a chain on his belt and gestures for us to follow. "It's just this way."

We exit the back of the Plaza ballroom, make a couple of turns, then stop outside a set of wide double doors.

Mr. Cohen flashes his key card and pushes the handle.

"This is *storage*?" Ortiz enters ahead of me. The room is vast. Several times larger than my apartment. It's decorated in a similar style to the rest of the hotel but is mostly empty besides a few stacked gold chairs and tables.

"Wedding parties often have extensive needs," says Mr. Cohen. "We've had clients fly in two hundred full-size Harrods hampers from London to give as wedding favors. Those items can take up quite considerable space."

"It's cold in here, right?" I shiver. My eyes flick up to an air conditioner on the wall. "Jeez! It's been set to fifty degrees. I didn't even know AC could go that low."

I walk deeper into the room. My eyes land on darker patches on the carpet. I see Ortiz follow my gaze.

Ortiz turns to the hotel manager. "Who had access to this room?"

"It was reserved for the bridesmaids."

"Could someone else have gotten in? Staff or—"

Mr. Cohen shakes his head emphatically. "We take VIP security requests extremely seriously. There were security cameras and a twenty-four-hour guard on this entire area."

Ortiz glances at Mark Li, who is temporarily distracted by a message on his phone.

Her eyes slide to Fitzwilliam's, and she lowers her voice.

"If Miss Stone is right, it rules out Leopold Kensington," she says. "Do you happen to know which bridesmaids visited this room?"

"All of them had access," he says. "Apart from the bride. You could check the security camera footage to be wholly certain."

"We will," says Ortiz. "And we need to seal this room," she adds. "Police only. No civilians."

Fitzwilliam nods, glancing at Mark. "What about her?" He shoots me an undisguised look of hostility.

Ortiz hesitates. "She can stay," she decides.

Mr. Cohen and Mark leave. As the door shuts behind them, the atmosphere shifts.

"You smell it too, right?" I ask her quietly as the door closes behind them.

She gives a short, tight nod. Ortiz's been at enough crime scenes to smell blood in the air.

Fitzwilliam is walking to the back of the room, where a clutch of golden chairs are stacked. He stops, then hunches down low, fixing his full attention on something out of view.

"Look at this," he says. "What is a pile of steel poles doing in the corner?"

I cross the thick carpet to take in what he's found.

A large pile of fifty or so long poles with connecting screw-on segments lie untidily on the floor.

"They're scaffold poles," I say. "Maybe someone was building a stage or display of some kind."

Fitzwilliam points. "Does that look like blood to you?"

I look closer, zeroing in where he's pointing. A thick, sturdy, two-foot-long steel pole.

Fitzwilliam lifts his face to Ortiz. "I think we've found our murder weapon."

CHAPTER SIXTEEN

ADRIANNA

I don't know how long I've been sitting in my closet with a pile of press images when my phone starts ringing in my lap.

"Hello?" I catch sight of myself in the long mirror. My deep-blue eyes are bloodshot. I dab carefully at where my mascara has bled. Run a hand through the thick wave of my chestnut hair.

"Dri?"

"Oh. Hey, baby." My voice softens. It's Mark.

"Listen, Dri." His voice sounds urgent. "Are you with anyone else right now?"

"No. Why?"

He hesitates. "Could one of your bridesmaids have had something to do with Simone's death?"

"What?" I am straight-up furious. "Why would you say that? Dad and Georgia picked the bridesmaids. Of course they aren't involved in Simone's death!"

"I was just with the police. They think Simone's body was moved from a room that only your bridesmaids could get into. Some kind of storage room."

"You've been speaking to NYPD?" I rub my temples with my spare hand. "Didn't I tell you, Mark? Didn't I *warn* you? This is *just* what the cops do. Every time. Did it occur to you *why* they are hounding our bridesmaids instead of trying to catch the actual killer?"

"I just thought… Your bridesmaids were all at your twenty-first birthday party on Elysium, right?"

"Mark, stop! The last time I trusted NYPD, a cop sold pictures of my underwear drawer. Can't you see what they're doing? One picture of me is worth more than a cop gets paid in a lifetime. You can't trust them."

"Can you trust your bridesmaids? I know Ophelia is a friend, but you never see Silky anymore."

"My dad hired all the bridesmaids exactly because they *can* be trusted. Each one of them stands to benefit in a big way from our wedding, and they all have links to the family that go way back. There is absolutely no way any of them would try to sabotage that. And in any case, my bridesmaids are all Kensington Manor School girls."

"Which means what, exactly?"

"Loyalty runs deep. I wouldn't expect you to understand it."

There's a pause, and I can sense his annoyance.

"Look." I reposition a brunette curl. "Whoever killed Simone is a sick, sick person who wants to stop us from getting married. We're not going to let them win, right?"

"Dri…"

"Right?"

"Right. It's just…I'm worried about you, Dri. I think you should help the police any way you can…"

"No. One hundred percent no, Mark. We've talked about this. In our family, you don't call the cops. Ever. You call my dad." My voice softens. "Dad will find out more than the NYPD can. Just let him do his thing."

I look down at the picture in my hand. Me, smiling with all my bridesmaids. We're lined up in matching beachwear, holding giant frozen margaritas, with Coney Island behind us. It was cold that day, I remember. They had to edit out our goose bumps. We tipped the iced drinks on the sand.

"I am so mad the police are wasting their time suspecting my bridesmaids," I say. My voice sounds strange, even to me. "Can you imagine one of them holding me captive in a room for three days?" I try to laugh, but it comes out wrong. Because weirdly, when I say it aloud, I kind of can.

"I don't know," says Mark, picking up on my shaky tone. "Could you? The kidnapper wore a mask and a cloak to cover their face, right? They could have been female…"

"I'd have known," I tell him in a very definite tone. "Three days in a room. If it was someone I knew, I'd have known."

"Dri." He hesitates. "Are you sure you don't want to cancel the wedding?"

"For some crazy stalker?" My jaw hardens. "Mark, do you know how many death and rape threats I get every day? It just comes with the territory of being a woman in the public eye. I take a walk on a beach, someone threatens to kill me. I look out a window in Paris, someone threatens to kill me. So naturally, I'm getting married, and someone is threatening to kill me."

There's a pause. "I love you," he says finally. "Keep your security high."

We say our goodbyes, and I hang up, wondering whether I should text Dad this latest evidence of police incompetence. He'll be making his own inquiries. Always does. I open my phone, adjust my face to contain a self-satisfied smile, and snap a picture.

Not bad. I take a breath. Add some text.

Look who's about to get married to the man of her dreams.

I open my social media and post, feeling the anxiety slip back as the picture loads. But as I scroll down my feed, my manicured finger hovers.

Just as I feared, the stories from three years ago are making a resurgence.

NO RANSOM ISSUED FOR ADRIANNA KENSINGTON.
Police fear worst.

My eyes track down several headlines from three years ago. Something about my wedding seems to be affecting the algorithm, giving these old features new life.

DAY 3 HUNT: POLICE LOSING HOPE OF FINDING 21-YEAR-OLD ADRIANNA ALIVE.

The terrible pictures still grab me right in the gut, even now. Me emerging from the room.

My eyes are glassy. Dead eyes. I don't seem to have even noticed the crescendo of flash photography reflecting on my gaunt face. My dehydrated body is clad in a filthy ripped negligee, and I lean heavily on my dad's stocky frame as he pushes aside journalists with an angry, outstretched hand.

I put a hand to my head, feeling my long brown hair. It's grown back now. When I got out, my famous curls had been hacked away. Cleaved to the scalp in places. Elsewhere, what little shreds remained hung in dirty rat tails.

I stare at the broken girl in the picture. My perfectly manicured nails glide over her tear-streaked face.

Another picture shows the room I'd just left. In the three days I was there, I felt like every square inch was familiar. But now when I look, the bed seems smaller. The hanks of my long hair, which I had remembered littering the entire floor, are gathered in one corner.

Taking a breath, I force my gaze back to the pile of photography in my lap. To the images of the lovely girl getting married next week.

I pause on one. My perfect face, healthy, tanned, juxtaposed with the smiling bridesmaids. We are beautiful. Perfect.

Everybody wants to be us.

Before I can stop myself, I rip the picture clean in half and scream.

CHAPTER SEVENTEEN

PETRA

I emerge from the shower in one of the Kensington Club bedrooms. Leopold is on the bed, buttoning his shirt. The mirror with cocaine residue and a rolled-up hundred-dollar bill are still lying on the coffee table. He tucks the gun he always carries into his waistband.

"Good coke, right?" I nod toward the table.

"Only the best for my clubs," he agrees.

"Are you free this afternoon?" I ask him. "It's fun having you back in the city. You were away in LA so long."

He blinks at me for a moment. "Didn't Georgia tell you? The bridesmaid dress fitting got moved to today."

"She didn't tell me." I rub at my hair with the towel, pushing up a wave of blond spikes.

"Probably slipped her mind," he says nonchalantly.

I turn to hide my annoyance. Absolutely nothing slips Georgia Kensington's brilliant mind unless she's deliberately decided it will happen. Beneath the halo of dark curls, she's every bit as smart and slick as her professional appearance suggests. Leopold always takes his youngest daughter's side, so I've learned not to cause drama.

"Why move the fitting?" I ask.

"Keep the media guessing and tighter security. It will be easier to manage the narrative of Simone's murder if Adrianna isn't getting papped at New York dress stores. You're seeing your magazine editor later, right?"

"I am. But I still don't get it, Leopold," I tell him. "You really want me to leak details of Simone's death? You've spent the last day making sure the story doesn't get out."

I pick up a hair dryer and a brush. Start blasting my short hair into its regular punkish style.

He sits on the bed. Checks his phone. "The best press is proactive, not reactive," he says, looking tired. "I can't hide it forever. And you don't leave silences. That causes speculation. Just drip a few details to your magazine editor today. Not too much. Let them dig around and think they're clever. It makes for bigger coverage."

I walk across the room, sit astride him. Kiss his mouth. The cocaine high hasn't dropped away yet, and I want him to stay.

"You're so smart," I say. I can feel his gun digging into my hip.

"Nightclubs are ten percent furnishing and ninety percent PR," he says with a small smile. "Smoke and mirrors." Leopold loves bragging about his business knowledge.

His cell rings, and he stands, literally levering me off. I push the frown away as he takes the call.

"Hello?" He listens for a few minutes, his face growing increasingly dark. "OK."

He hangs up and turns to me. "Goddamn NYPD have decided their lives aren't glamorous enough."

"What do you mean?"

His mouth sets in a tight line. "Those clowns won't admit they can't find the killer, so they're coming after Adrianna's bridesmaids."

"What? Why?"

"Something about access to a storage closet." He hesitates. There's a pained expression on Leopold's face.

"What is it?" I ask impatiently. I hate it when people make me guess their feelings.

"Adrianna's bridesmaids," he says slowly. "They can be trusted, right?"

Is he actually admitting he might have gotten something wrong? I tilt my head.

He twists at the edge of the linen sheet. "It's just. People... girls...they get obsessed with Adrianna," he says. "You've seen it. It's...crazy."

Of all the people who will never understand devoted fandom, Leopold is top of the list.

I put my hands up to cup his face, long white fingers sliding around his smoothly shaved jaw. He lets me take the weight for a moment.

"It's just like you first said," I assure him. "NYPD are messing it up. Looking for clues in the wrong places."

"You're right." He pulls back, nodding. "I picked the bridesmaids. Nothing gets past me." Leopold looks thoughtful. "It'll take the cops a few hours to get warrants. If this wedding has any chance of going ahead, you and the other girls need to be out of the city by nightfall."

"OK," I say. "Then I guess I'd better go. If you want Simone's death story leaked, I have a date with a magazine editor."

CHAPTER EIGHTEEN

HOLLY

The room has been sealed, and Fitzwilliam, Ortiz, and I have gloved up and are hunched over the pile of metal poles. At least a hundred of them at quick count.

Close proximity to Fitzwilliam means I'm forced to inhale gulps of his lemony aftershave. Everything about him is crisp and richly scented. As though wealth has left a physical imprint on him.

"Guess these scaffold uprights must have been part of the wedding demo," says Ortiz. "How sure are you that it's blood on that pole?" She looks at me.

"You'll want to test to confirm," I say. "But…see the way it's dried in striations? There's a weak ionic reaction with the steel in the scaffold pole. That's typical of an iron-rich fluid like blood."

I take off my studded backpack and begin laying out my equipment at careful right angles. My portable spectrometer. A UV light. Bloodstain-detecting reagents and a swabbing kit.

Fitzwilliam's eyes widen. "You carry those in your purse?" He's eyeing the heavy metal box of the spectrometer with its funnel-shaped aperture for analyzing samples.

"I use it for work. It's less weird than carrying a gun," I tell him, wielding my swab and dabbing the pole.

"Ignore Fitzwilliam," says Ortiz. "He's afraid of technology. An AI ate his grandma."

"I'm not *afraid* of it," grumbles Fitzwilliam. "I just believe in honest sleuthing."

I put my sample in the chute. I press buttons. The spectrometer bleeps and whirs as it analyzes.

"Blood," I confirm.

"That thing can detect blood?" Fitzwilliam scowls at it.

"Not directly," I say. "It analyzes the absorption of light by molecules present in blood and—"

"So this could be the murder weapon?" Ortiz sounds hopeful.

"Forensic report said she was beaten to death with a heavy blunt instrument," I say. "Something heavy. Smooth and consistent in shape. I'd say this would be a dead ringer."

We all stare at the thick upright.

I shiver, wrapping my arms around me. "Maybe the killer knew about the forensic process," I say. "They knew to turn the temperature down in here to throw off the time of death."

I pick up my UV light and start walking the room methodically, starting with the entrance, examining the doorway.

"From what you told me about the case," I say, "the three dresses. The hair cut off. Whoever killed Simone is likely the same person who kidnapped Adrianna three years ago. At her twenty-first birthday party. Right?"

"Yes," admits Fitzwilliam. "We are strongly investigating that connection."

"The kidnapper was never caught. No leads?"

"As I told you before, it wasn't our case," says Fitzwilliam. "The kidnapping happened out on the family's private island—Elysium. We've had to get files from the Colombian police. And the paperwork is patchy to say the least."

I consider this, thinking back to the news reports. "Adrianna believed her kidnapper intended to kill her, right?"

"That's what finally drove her to dislocate her wrist and escape the handcuffs," agrees Fitzwilliam. "She was convinced her captor would kill her after cutting her hair."

"Because?"

"There were two dolls in the room," says Fitzwilliam. "Each day, the kidnapper cut the hair from a doll, then strung it up by the neck. The third day, they cut Adrianna's hair. She figured it was her turn next. Question is, why would a kidnapper take Adrianna, then come back three years later and kill her bridesmaid?"

"It's symbolic," I say immediately. "A wedding is symbolic."

Fitzwilliam rolls his eyes. "Save the criminal profiling for court."

"What's your theory?" I ask.

"Money. Or revenge. The Kensingtons are billionaires. This wedding is worth a lot of money to a lot of people," says Fitzwilliam.

I come to a halt where the carpet meets the wall. "Come look at this," I say. "I think this is where she died."

Ortiz moves in close. "I think I see something," she decides. "Looks like an old stain on the wall that's been cleaned off."

I'm opening my bag excitedly. I have a hunch about this.

"What are you doing?" asks Fitzwilliam carefully as I pull a little spray bottle from my bag and shake it. "This is a crime scene. Hey!" He makes a grab for my hand as I spritz the wall.

"Don't you have any decorum at all?" he demands. "This isn't your crime scene."

I ignore him, watching the effect of the spray. It emits a faint bluish glow. "Thought so," I say grimly. I turn to Ortiz. "Luminol oxidizes in the presence of hemoglobin. This is blood. Would you mind turning off the lights?"

"Best find out where she's going with this," says Ortiz.

Fitzwilliam crosses the room and snaps the lights off.

The luminol glows brightly. Just as I thought, the bloody handprints were no accident. Simone has left a message for us.

"It's concentrated here," I say. "A cluster of handprints. Looks deliberate, wouldn't you say? They seem to be leading down."

The handprints form a vertical line of sorts. "Episode seven," I say, speaking aloud. "Simone set up something similar to draw attention to a carpet stain that had been scrubbed."

Simone. Even in death, she's leaving tricks and trails.

I snap on gloves and follow the concentration of handprints to where it ends above the carpet. There's a bulge, I notice, and before Fitzwilliam can stop me, I carefully peel back the carpet.

"Look," I say. "I think Simone hid something for us to find."

It's a silver key. The top is shaped like a chunky cross. There's a tag attached with a name.

"*Holly*," I read, the blood turning to ice in my veins. I look up at Ortiz.

"Looks like your boss left you a key," she observes.

"There's a number etched onto the front," says Fitzwilliam. "Sixteen twenty."

They both look at me hopefully. I have a sudden vivid memory of Simone. The forensic trails we'd set up together to make the factual parts of her show more entertaining.

"Sixteen twenty is a service elevator key," I explain. "Firefighters use them. It opens any elevator panel in the city." I look at the key thoughtfully. "This featured in the show," I explain. "We'd take real-life cases and set parts of them up for entertainment. In this instance, we cleared the name of a foreign ambassador accused of being a spy. He'd leave sensitive documents around the city for his colleagues to collect. Elevators were one of the drops."

Fitzwilliam and Ortiz exchange glances.

"Simone was genius at staging forensics for TV," I tell them. "It was one of the things we disagreed on."

"Guess her ratings won that argument," says Ortiz. "Solving the puzzle was what made *Wrongly Accused* so addictive."

I nod sadly.

"So she left something for you to find?" suggests Fitzwilliam. "In an elevator shaft?"

"Looks that way," I concede.

"Do you know which elevator Simone would be leaving documents in?" asks Ortiz.

I rub the back of my neck. "Simone liked me to work out her dead drop locations on the basis of forensic evidence. But…this one's easy."

"It is?" asks Fitzwilliam.

I nod. "Since she was found in the Plaza," I say, "my guess would be here."

CHAPTER NINETEEN

PETRA

I'm having a liquid lunch at one of Leopold's favorite restaurants. A formal New York place with snow-white linens, wood-paneled walls, and a clientele of wealthy older New Yorkers. Classic and discreet, but not what you'd call hip.

My magazine editor companion, Max, dresses like a skater boy, emphasizing the youthful cast to his narrow face with beat-up Vans, low skinny jeans, and a baggy band T-shirt. But he unfolds his napkin in the way people who have been raised to wealth do and addresses the waitstaff with the same telltale easy confidence. Max comes from a family with so much money, they sent him to a school with no rules outside Seville. He emerged without a conscience or a single qualification, neither of which stopped him from rising up the ranks of *Titan Magazine*—a celebrity monthly with less scruples than even Max was raised with. His reputation for breaking celebrity stories by any means possible has earned it a circulation and advertising revenue that tops all the other monthlies put together.

When I tell him about Simone's mysterious death, the first thing he does is order champagne.

"Here's to bad news," he says with an elfish sideways smile, raising his glass to toast mine.

I throw back the drink in one go. The cocaine is wearing off, and I need something to buffer the comedown. I miss Leopold, I think, miserably.

The waiter delivers our food. A new-to-the-menu quinoa concoction for my companion. Classic mimosa salad for me, which I push around with a fork and don't eat. The waiter pours a crisp splash of champagne, topping off Max's almost-full glass and refilling my empty one. An iced glass of sparkling water is set to my side by the waiter, its straight sides beaded with chilled droplets. I watch how they distort the light, then realize Max has put the pictures I took on the table. Barely dressed models in New York tenements. Tragic expressions on their young faces. I love these images.

"We can't run your pictures," Max is saying.

I feel the sucker punch in a disconnected place.

"Young vulnerable girls," he fans his hands. "This one looks like a rape victim for chrissakes. *Titan Magazine* always skirts the line of shocking, but these are over the edge."

"You were happy to run pictures of me in some very vulnerable situations," I tell him, tight-jawed.

"That was twenty years ago. The world has changed. I had this girl's mom on the phone, threatening to sue the magazine." He taps the gaunt face of a young girl with dark smudges under her eyes. "Said you pressured her to take her bra off."

"What?" I glare at the images. "That fucking ungrateful little bitch. She just got booked by *Vogue* because of me."

"We can't run them," he says. "And I can't pay off any more models who say you bullied and humiliated them." He eyes me sternly. "Which leaves me with a big problem. A big hole in my fall pages. And I have just the story to fill it."

I raise an eyebrow. "Oh?"

"Thanks to your friend Simone, I managed to get hold of some interviews with the Colombian police."

My stomach lurches.

"They interviewed you, didn't they?" He regards me over his champagne glass. "After Adrianna was kidnapped."

He's fishing. He must be.

"Adrianna is kidnapped. Tortured. You're a guest at her party. And when police accuse you of misleading their investigation, you reply, 'No comment.'" He leaves a loaded pause. "Doesn't look good, does it? Particularly when you're sleeping with her billionaire father." He takes a victorious sip of champagne. "If I can't trust you to get me material, I need a backup plan."

My hand holding the glass is shaking. I force myself to set it down and shrug casually, grateful for my childhood training.

The vulnerable girl who was sent to America's most prestigious boarding school left with the strength to overcome anything.

"I'm the photographer for the Kensington wedding," I say. "What if I were to leak some pictures?" I lift the champagne glass and dispose of the contents in one gulp. His eyes follow the movement.

"Pretty girls in perfect dresses? Not our vibe."

"It's not the sponsor's vibe either. They're paying Adrianna Kensington two million, and they want their pound of flesh."

He tilts his head. "I'm listening."

"I'll be doing something more artistic." I look around impatiently for the waiter to refill.

"With Georgia Kensington managing every photo shoot?" Max considers. "I'll believe it when I see it," he decides, leaning back and sipping champagne. "I don't know what's going on with you, Petra. Your pictures used to be good. Seems like the world has moved on and you haven't. Too much white powder, maybe."

"You're one to talk."

He smiles, revealing ill-kept teeth. Pushes my pictures back toward me across the table.

"Can't take these," he says. "But I might have something else for you since you're so close with the Kensingtons."

I'm still negotiating the spike of shock at his previous remarks. It's hard to choose the right reaction with the champagne lunch and cocaine comedown.

"We had a tip-off," he says. "Apparently, there could be some very sensitive documents hidden in an elevator at the Plaza hotel." He pauses for effect.

I raise an eyebrow. "You know there are a lot of elevators in that hotel, right?"

"Eleven," he says. "Not so many for someone like you. Who has every reason to be there today. For Adrianna Kensington's dress fittings."

"How do you know that?" I snap.

"I pay a lot of money to the right people."

"How are these documents hidden, exactly?" I'm picturing the sleek insides of a Plaza elevator and can't think how that would work.

"I'll leave you to figure that out."

I'm confused. This whole situation is confusing. "If I find you these sensitive documents, that is going to fill your fall pages?"

"If you bring me those documents," he says, "I'll destroy the evidence you want destroyed."

I stand. "I have to go," I tell him. "Adrianna Kensington's driver is picking me up."

CHAPTER TWENTY

ADRIANNA

I'm in the leather-scented safety of my car, being driven to the Plaza for my fitting. Ophelia is sitting across from me, keeping a respectful distance, since she has gauged my black mood. Ophelia is my emotional barometer.

"I think my forehead is shiny," I say, catching a glimpse in the window reflection.

She darts across obediently and powders me. I relax under the sweep of the soft brush.

"There," she says proudly. "Beautiful."

Georgia organizes my schedule, and Ophelia organizes my feelings. I should probably treat her better, but something about her is like a puppy wanting to be kicked.

At school, Ophelia was an insipid chatterbox. Freckled pale skin and ordinary features. Somewhere along the way, she reinvented herself as one of New York's most talented makeup artists, with a palette of primary-color makeup and designer jumpsuits. Her hair is a bright orange, faded to platinum-blond tips in an artistry that speaks of a thousand-dollar-an-hour hairdresser.

The makeover never stopped her talking though. Today it's a

high-speed stream of animated chatter about maximizing security that matches her bright-colored geek-chic clothes.

She's clearly freaking out after Simone's death but unable to voice her real feelings.

I nod along to the suggestion of doubling the bodyguards, my thoughts entirely elsewhere.

"It's OK to not be OK," Ophelia says earnestly, her freckled forehead crinkling.

"I'm fine," I snap.

Ophelia nods in deep understanding, ever the willing emotional punching bag. She hesitates. "You're really sure you want to go to Elysium two days early?" Her voice sounds strained.

"We'll be safe there," I repeat. "Ten thousand miles of ocean between us and the crazy person who killed Simone."

But even as I'm saying it, Mark's words are coming back.

"Can you trust your bridesmaids?"

I press my lips together tightly.

Yes. I can trust my bridesmaids implicitly. None of them would want to hurt me. None of them would dare.

I see Ophelia react to something out on the street. Her eyes widen.

"There's Petra Morka," she says. "Outside that restaurant your dad likes."

"We're picking her up," I explain, and I see Ophelia's rainbow fingernails curl inward.

Even when she isn't posing, Petra's striking features draw the gaze. I wonder if Dad bought her the chunky gold necklace at her pale throat. A flash of rage burns and is gone.

"Should we pretend we didn't see her?" I make my tone completely neutral so I can spin it as a joke or not.

She giggles nervously. "Can you *imagine*?" Her amber eyes are sparkling. "How angry she would be?" There's a wistful edge to her tone.

"Let's do it." I press the intercom button for the driver, walled away behind his glass panel. "Could you drive on, please? There's been a change of plan. Petra doesn't need a ride."

"Sure thing, Miss K."

The car accelerates. Petra, who is watching the familiar limo expectantly, takes another step toward the road. Ophelia and I start laughing. Helpless schoolgirl giggles. But as the car reaches the end of the street, Ophelia wipes the corners of her eyes.

"OK, we should go back now," she whispers with a timid grin.

"No way," I tell her. "Let her take a cab." The image of famous Petra Morka being mobbed as she attempts to hail a New York cab is too funny. But Ophelia's face is grave.

"Don't. She'll be *so mad*. You know how she was at school."

"So? I'm not scared of Petra." I fold my arms, look forward, and pretend not to care. In the rearview mirror, I catch sight of Petra's face, screwed up in rage. "Look at her," I say, trying to recapture our earlier moment. "She looks furious."

"Please, Dri." Ophelia is looking over her shoulder. "*Please.* She'll get us back. She always does."

"She's not the older girl anymore. She can't do anything to us." Beside me, Ophelia is trembling. I relent and press the intercom. "Can you turn back around and get Petra?" I say.

Ophelia sinks back, relieved.

We can both see Petra's furious face now as the car loops back toward her.

I take out my cell and angle it toward us. "We should have a picture. Two friends on the way to the fitting," I decide, turning to highlight my cheekbones. As the happy girl smiles back at me, I feel the tension drain away.

"Don't you remember what Petra used to *do*?" insists Ophelia quietly. "Those awful games. Saints and Sinners."

I twist in surprise. It's an unspoken rule that no one ever talks about what happened to us at school. What is she thinking?

I make a fake confused face. Just enough to signal she should drop the subject. Then replace the smile.

"I really don't remember," I say pointedly. "Could you shuffle to the left?" I add. "I actually think it would be better if this picture were just of me."

CHAPTER TWENTY-ONE

HOLLY

Fitzwilliam and Ortiz have closed ranks, muttering about the legality of opening elevator service panels on private property. Fitzwilliam holds the key in a plastic evidence bag.

"We need to get written permission from the hotel," says Ortiz. "And that needs to be applied for through the correct channels. It could take a day. If we're lucky."

"The bridesmaids all fly out to Elysium this afternoon," Fitzwilliam points out. "We'll be too late to make any arrests if whatever Simone concealed helps the investigation."

"The key was left for me," I tell them. "I can open it."

Fitzwilliam glances a little too openly at my blue hair and lip piercing. "This is police business, Holly," he says. "It's a murder investigation."

"First," I tell him, "as a civilian, I can open that panel right now without the risk of losing my job. Second, how many elevators are in the Plaza? You don't even know which elevator panel to open."

"She's right," says Ortiz. "There must be at least twenty elevators in the public lobby. Plus service elevators. Are you saying you do know which elevator panel to open?"

Fitzwilliam's jaw juts forward petulantly. "Because if you do and you withhold that information—"

"Then there's nothing you can do about it without arresting me and wasting a whole bunch of time." I put my hand out for the key.

Fitzwilliam glowers, moving the bag closer to his body. Ortiz snatches it cleanly from his grip and holds it out to me.

"Let's just give her the key," she says. "Holly, I'm trusting you to tell us if there's anything in that panel of use to our investigation."

"I want Simone's killer caught a lot more than you do," I tell her.

Fitzwilliam's eyes widen in annoyance, but Ortiz nods. "All right then. We can give you some cover. Probably stop people from using the elevators for a few minutes. Any longer than that, the hotel is going to start asking questions."

I nod, hoping I've got this right. "I'll be as fast as I can."

"Good, because we have another issue," says Ortiz. "Adrianna Kensington has scheduled some kind of dress fitting here today. Things are going to get crazy with security on the ground floor." She hesitates. "We need to get you in and out before Adrianna and her bridesmaids arrive."

"How long do we have?"

"Under an hour." Ortiz removes a large battered phone from her pocket and taps a few buttons. "But I'm guessing a few might show up early. All the bridesmaids seem to be involved in the logistics of the wedding," she adds. "Mark Li sent me a picture from Georgia Kensington's PR file." She holds out her cell to display a photo of four impossibly beautiful women draped around Adrianna Kensington.

"These pictures sold for seven figures," adds Ortiz. "Enough to staff my entire department for a year."

The bridesmaids wear magenta dresses, each a slightly different style. Custom-made, I assume, by some very important designer I know nothing about. My eyes fix on a tall black-haired woman, so thin her arms are like broomsticks. She has a fifties vintage look, with front-rolled hair and a morose expression.

"Is that the cinematographer who makes those controversial movies?" I point.

"Silky Eversfield." Fitzwilliam nods.

I look closer and read aloud: "*Silky: languid, artistic, intellectual.* Why is there a handwritten comment over her picture?"

"Georgia Kensington's PR notes," explains Fitzwilliam. "They're all annotated if you look past the crack on Ortiz's screen."

I zoom in. Petra Morka, an art form in strong androgenous beauty with a supermodel glare, gets *couture, older female, dynamic*. Georgia Kensington's pose is awkward and her smile forced beneath the words *career woman, professional, reliable*.

Fitzwilliam points to a girl with a round freckled face and orange hair. "That's Ophelia Mills-Herd. She's an interior designer. But I think Adrianna also gets her to do makeup." Bright orange hair and neon stylized makeup gives her bland features more impact than they might otherwise deserve. Georgia has scrawled an arrow, noting *high energy, music lover, creative.*

"Ophelia is the only one whose smile looks real." I say. "And is it my imagination, or are all of them leaning away from Petra Morka?"

"Maybe," says Ortiz. "All Adrianna's bridesmaids went to the same school. Could be old rivalries."

"Half of the New York elite send their kids to that boarding school," Fitzwilliam adds. "It's known for turning out successful young ladies. I can imagine that to be cutthroat. Petra Morka and Simone Waters are older. Would have been...maybe fourteen and eighteen respectively when Ophelia, Silky, and half sisters Georgia and Adrianna started school at age seven."

"Boarding school starts at age *seven*?" I look between the faces of the women, trying to imagine them as tiny girls being sent away from home to be groomed for New York high society. They certainly look the part now.

I take in the array of perfect faces. Could any of these polished women *really* have kidnapped Adrianna and murdered Simone? At first glance, it seems impossible to imagine. But as I look closer at their rictus grins—unsmiling eyes fixed coldly on the camera—my perspective shifts. It suddenly seems very possible indeed.

CHAPTER TWENTY-TWO

HOLLY

Fitzwilliam and Ortiz escort me to the glistening bank of near-silent elevators at the heart of the lobby and do a great job of flashing their badges.

We wait for the disgruntled hotel guests to exit.

"You're sure you know which elevator you need?" asks Ortiz, watching them leave.

I nod. "I think so." I'm remembering one of Simone's many lectures on expected decorum.

"I don't agree with it," I told her. "Acting like someone I'm not. If people judge me badly, that's their problem."

"And also yours, Holly." She looked at me with her intense gaze. "Understanding different cultures isn't the same as faking."

Ortiz is looking at me expectantly. "Simone liked to pass on the etiquette she learned at school," I explain. "Elevators factored in."

"I take it the lessons didn't stick," says Fitzwilliam, staring down a youth trying to double back toward the elevators. "Etiquette is not your strong suit."

"Simone's boarding school raised them all to be nice young ladies," I tell Ortiz, ignoring Fitzwilliam. "She used to speak about it like…a code. So rich people can recognize each other."

"Ain't that the truth." Ortiz shoots a glance at Fitzwilliam. "GQ here looked like he and Mark Li were going to head off to play tennis together."

"GQ?" I frown.

"It's a little nickname we have for him at the station. So what's the elevator etiquette?"

"Ladies use the farthest elevator from the entrance. On the right-hand side. It's the least likely to be used by anyone else. And since prep school boys are taught to take the left-hand elevators, they're the least likely to encounter a man inside."

"Is that true?" Ortiz asks Fitzwilliam. "About taking left-hand elevators?"

"I didn't go to boarding school, so I wouldn't know," says Fitzwilliam shortly.

"*You* didn't go to boarding school?" I'm stunned.

"I went to a private day school just outside New York," he says. "My mother wanted her sons close by."

"Lucky for her," says Ortiz. "Well, let's hope you're right, Holly. OK." She nods to the now-empty lobby, checks her watch. "You've got fifteen minutes until the dress fitting starts."

I head fast for the elevator.

As I cross the threshold, I realize my mistake. The doors stand open, but they'll only close again with a Plaza key card. If I open the panel, anyone walking toward the elevators will see me. And that's not the only problem. Inside, the elevator cabin is lined with sleek glass, with white LED lights shining through the walls, floor, and ceiling like a starry sky. Even if I could shut the doors for privacy, I can't see where the access panel might be. There's not a keyhole in sight.

A video screen flashes up on the opposite wall. It shows a

white sand beach with crystal-clear waters and waving palm trees. *Elysium Beach* announces a large art deco caption in the signature Kensington branding. *Your place to be.* Adrianna's wedding destination, I realize.

Several images flash. The vacant interior of a sumptuous cocktail bar. Swinging hammocks at a rustic beach house. An aerial shot of a jungle-clad island, fringed with powdery sand.

Words ripple artfully across the screen with accompanying images of island activities. *Hot springs* depicts footage of smoking volcanic pools. *Beach box gym* shows an outdoor exercise area with bamboo benches, log barbells, and sea views.

A final screen flashes. A live image of Adrianna twirling in a bridal dress, then text:

Adrianna Kensington's Dress Fitting. July 3.

Guess they must have rented these screens. I chew a fingernail nervously, taking out the elevator service key and glancing helplessly at the open door.

I'm about to exit the elevator and explain the key card situation to Ortiz when I'm interrupted by a voice.

"Excuse me." A strident voice resounds along the bank of elevators. "You'll find we booked the eighteenth floor for today, and I'm not about to miss the schedule."

There's a click of heels, headed straight for the elevator I'm standing in.

"Hold the door!" A well-spoken female voice breaks into the elevator.

I turn and recognize her features instantly. It's Georgia Kensington.

CHAPTER TWENTY-THREE
ADRIANNA

As the limo stops to collect Petra, Ophelia shuffles toward me nervously, the green silk of her signature-style jumpsuit brushing up against my arm. Her makeup isn't concealing as well as it might, I notice. Her freckles are peeking through, the exact same color as her light-brown eyes. Like her irises have exploded across her rounded nose. I can't decide if it's cute or messy.

The door opens, and a crack of Petra's masculine perfume infiltrates our leather-scented cocoon.

Petra climbs in with no thanks or acknowledgment, forcing me to move awkwardly closer to Ophelia. Her green cat-shaped eyes are made up with a pixel-perfect slash of turquoise liquid liner on each side.

"I thought you were going to drive away," she says, her Swedish accent sharp. "Little girls playing games."

There's a dangerous edge to her voice, and suddenly, all my courage leaves me. Somehow, the dynamics of the car have regressed us all right back to being frightened schoolgirls. My hand slides across the seat to take Ophelia's. She squeezes it tightly.

Petra casts a brief look at Ophelia and turns to me. "We're going to be early for the dress fitting," she says.

"Georgia moved it up," I tell her, "so we can get safely to Elysium this afternoon."

Petra's eyes widen fractionally. "This *afternoon*? Does Leopold know we're going early?"

"He wouldn't approve, so don't tell him," I say, knowing she won't. Kensington Manor School girls don't tattle. "Dad wants his armed goons around me at all times." I give a little shudder. "He doesn't realize the world has changed. Like Mark says. The right technology is worth twenty bodyguards, and we have the best."

Petra looks thoughtful. "Leopold doesn't quite understand the crew he put together, does he?" She pauses for effect. "You, me, her." Petra nods disdainfully toward Ophelia. "Little Georgia and crazy Silky. Going a day early to the island where you were held hostage. And no Daddy to protect you."

At the mention of my being held hostage, Ophelia physically jolts in her seat, her face turning in horror toward Petra. I restrain my reaction.

"Well," says Petra, looking carefully at my face, "aren't you the perfect little Kensington Manor School girl? Smiling through adversity."

With effort, I keep my smile perfectly fixed.

Petra leans back, thoughtful. "I just saw the article in *Vanity Fair*," she says. "How you and Mark met." She turns to look at me meaningfully. "I didn't realize you got together on a dating app."

I turn to Ophelia with a "help me" expression.

"They didn't *meet* on a dating app," fills in Ophelia, releasing a waft of her peachy perfume as she leans forward. "Mark *invented* a dating app for wealthy people. A Who's Who of everyone who's anyone. But also very scientific, taking data from happily married people and figuring out who is going to make you happy long term."

"I hadn't even heard of the app," I interject, "but I noticed when it floated on the stock market. Then a friend told me the guy who invented it, his match was me. I just thought that was funny." I nod to Ophelia to fill in her cue for the well-worn story.

"And maybe a little scary, how he'd gotten access to your data," adds Ophelia obediently. "Right, Dri?"

"Right. I thought Mark was a nerd stalker." I nod. "Then we met by chance at a tech gala, and he kind of swept me off my feet." I smile at the memory. "Our first date, he sent me a custom smartphone loaded with apps he knew I'd like. The ringtone was the song we danced to that night. He'd thought of everything."

Petra looks away, annoyed.

"Shall we look at the plans for the island?" Ophelia suggests quickly, flipping a strand of orange hair from her narrow brow.

I turn to her gratefully as she unearths a printed pack from the purse at her feet, outsize neon plastic bangles clacking.

The branding, with its art deco Kensington edge, has been skillfully spun to a beach, Miami style.

"OK, plans for Elysium. It's going to be fab-ul-lous." Ophelia is reenergized, flipping pages, showing mood boards of green jungle leaf juxtaposed with sooty blacks and antique gold.

"We've focused on luxe wellness. Infinity pools," says Ophelia. "And a whole new redesign of the colonial house in fairy-tale gothic gold and exposed plaster walls."

Petra says nothing. I suspect she's quietly seething at how well Ophelia has met the brief.

"I think it's great that you're branching out," I say. "Not just makeup."

She nods. "I've...actually been doing interior design for a while," she explains shyly.

"Really?" I blink. "I should get you to design my apartment."

"Um. You...did." Her smile flip-flops awkwardly.

Petra makes an exaggerated pretense at disguising a laugh with a cough.

Ophelia regroups. "It was months ago now. You've had a lot on your mind." The smile settles to something hopeful, casting about for recognition.

Petra arches a long, skinny eyebrow. "You should be careful, Adrianna," she says with mock concern. "You know what happens when you get super stressed."

Petra's voice is singsong. She's clearly mad about the car swinging past her.

"What are you talking about?"

"You get a little...you know...cheaty."

"*Cheaty?*"

"You know what I mean. Kissy. Whatever."

I really hate Petra.

"Well, there's no one on Elysium to kiss but my bridesmaids." I force a high, awkward laugh. Beside me, Ophelia's body is rigid.

Petra responds with a predatory smile. "That's kind of what I'm worried about."

CHAPTER TWENTY-FOUR

HOLLY

Georgia Kensington steps into the elevator, a small phone clamped to her ear. She looks like a businesswoman from the fashion industry. Designer flats, skinny jeans, and silk top on her narrow frame, with black curls framing her small jawline. I shuffle back, trying not to draw attention to myself.

"No," Georgia says into her cell. "Adrianna doesn't do videos. Ever. Just pictures. Sixty thousand dollars minimum per shoot. Plus expenses." She frowns, ends the call, then picks up another one right after it.

"Dri?" she says. "You're serious? Silky isn't answering? OK. OK. Just...get here. The floor is all ready for us."

I can't stop myself from staring. There's an obvious family resemblance. Lean with a long nose and pronounced lips. But Georgia's dark skin and clouds of hair soften the severity of her famous features. There's a perfection to her skin and body shape that's hard to quantify in words. Georgia veritably vibrates with understated beauty.

She's prettier than her sister, I think. But her earnest face is taut and unsmiling, as though she constantly has something to worry about.

Georgia ends her call and presses the top of her phone briefly to her forehead as though resting a heavy load of thoughts. Her eyes catch me in the reflection of the elevator.

"Are you waiting for someone?" she asks.

"I'm just figuring out the elevator." I've never been good at lying.

Georgia's face shifts to something like disbelief. She produces her own plastic key card and leans forward to press the elevator button, somehow managing to channel that she's worth a million bucks while doing the most mundane of acts.

There's a noise like a power-up on a computer game, and a console of numbers flashes to life behind the glass panel.

"That is so cool!" I can't help but be impressed.

Georgia's brown eyes flash brief shock. "What floor do you want?"

I catch sight of something on her slim little brown finger. A golden crest. To my shock, I realize she's wearing Simone's signet ring. Horror flushes through me.

How did Georgia get that ring? Simone never took it off.

I'm so distracted by this, I say the first floor that comes to mind.

"Eighteen," I tell her, then curse myself.

"That's the dress fitting." She pauses. "I'm sorry. Who are you?" Her eyes linger for just a moment too long on my shoes.

College parties rush back to me. I was always the poor relative. The one who didn't know how to dress or stand right.

I adjust my skirt. "I'm Holly." It comes out slightly squeaky.

"Wait. Are you a *journalist*?" Georgia is fumbling with her phone.

"I *told* Adrianna that Plaza security wasn't good enough," she tells me. "When are you people going to leave her alone?"

"I'm not a journalist!"

She narrows her eyes. "You know my sister was prescribed antidepressants for a year because of women like you? Pretending to be her friends, then selling her out?"

"Mark Li asked me to be here," I blurt. "I work for Liberation Law."

As soon as the words are out of my mouth, I regret them. I probably should have invented some clever excuse. I picture Fitzwilliam and Ortiz's despair.

"You're a lawyer? Oh." She computes something rapidly. "Did Mark bring you in to replace Simone?"

"I…um. Mark wanted an expert," I tell her. "So…I guess…here I am." I let the phrase drift, rubbing the back of my neck uncomfortably.

She's taking me in with new eyes now. "Well, well," she decides. "I guess Mark Li has finally found his backbone. Good for him. I was wondering when he'd finally stand up to my dad. Not sure his judgment is great though."

Georgia scans my figure thoughtfully and extends a hand. "I'm Georgia Kensington. Sorry we got off on the wrong foot. You can't be too careful where Adrianna is concerned. You would be *amazed* what people will do for a single picture."

I shake her hand uncertainly as her fingers close with surprising firmness on mine. "I'm Holly Stone."

I try not to stare at the ring on her finger.

"Nice to make your acquaintance," she says matter-of-factly. "Word of warning: I'd keep out of my dad's way, Holly. Mark choosing a bridesmaid without checking in is going to infuriate him."

"Wait… Bridesmaid?"

"Didn't Mark tell you?" Georgia looks puzzled. "You can't be the lawyer unless you're the bridesmaid too. It's a trust thing," she says as if this is completely regular. "Wait... Adrianna knows you're here, right?"

"I'm not sure." This is mostly true, I decide. "We haven't met," I add, wondering how long I have to keep this untruth going before I can escape with what I came here to find.

"O-kay. So you're waiting to find out if Dri approves you? If we put the right dress on you, you might pass." Her eyes drops to my waistline. "You'll have to fit for the fashion sponsor too... We'll need to see if Dri likes you." Georgia is opening the camera app on her cell and points it at me. "Smile."

The camera flashes before I can rearrange my features.

"Does she not like people in general?" I ask Georgia, wondering what kind of grimacing, shocked expression of me she just captured.

"Would you?" Georgia looks at me pointedly. "If a pack of paparazzi stalked you across the globe and every cab driver and busboy sold your story to the highest bidder?"

"Guess not," I admit. My eyes drift to where the elevator buttons are now lit up. Then I see it. A tiny circle. Glowing.

That's where I need to fit the service panel key.

The doors of the elevator slide open, and Georgia strides out. It's opened onto a vestibule that looks nothing like the rest of the hotel. It's been repainted entirely in black and gold and is eerily devoid of people. The only color is from industrial-style rose-gold clothing racks of colorful garments that are arranged in rows.

"Whoa!" I'm taking it all in, open-mouthed.

Georgia glances back. I close my mouth and try to look sophisticated.

"Silly me," I announce. "I forgot something in the lobby. I'll just go back and get it."

The doors close before I press the button. Someone else must be calling the elevator. The shaft buzzes, and the carriage begins to descend.

CHAPTER TWENTY-FIVE
ADRIANNA

My cell rings just as I arrive at the Plaza. It's Georgia, speaking in hushed tones like she doesn't want to be overheard. I drop back, gesturing for Petra and Ophelia to walk ahead.

"Dri?" Georgia says. "Oh good God, the new lawyer Mark hired. There are just no words."

I frown. "Mark didn't tell me he'd hired a lawyer."

"Her name is Holly. I just met her in the elevator."

"Does she fit the brand?" I ask.

"Maybe with some help. But something's definitely off. She can barely string a sentence together, and she dresses like a guest at Hello Kitty's funeral."

I laugh. "What?"

"I'm serious. Like, punk or something. But not chic like Petra. This girl has zero class, zero taste, and says the first thing that pops into her head without thinking about it."

"I kind of want to meet her." I'm still laughing. But underneath, I'm nervous. Mark wants some low-rent replacement as bridesmaid? Is he making some kind of premarital power bid?

"Mark must have his reasons," I decide. "Maybe she's super smart."

"Dri, she can't work an elevator."

"I guess...Mark wants to make some choices at his own wedding," I decide.

"I just sent you a picture of her. Check your messages."

I glance down. "Jesus." I hiss. "What was Mark *thinking*?"

The girl has hair the color of a Viagra pill and wears a bizarre shocked grimace. She has no blush to contour her chubby cheeks, which makes her round little face even more childlike, exacerbated by big round eyes. She's outfitted in a weird combination of spider-web jewelry, cyber-goth chunky boots with silver buckles, busted fishnets, a skull-motif dress with long lacy bell sleeves, and more black lace at the hem. As if she didn't have enough on already.

"That skirt is way too short for a girl with no thigh gap," I mutter, tilting my head and wrinkling my nose. "She accessorizes like she raided a kid's Halloween bucket."

"I know. We could style her though. She has good ass to hip."

"And we need curvy."

"Yeah, but...she's not going to fit the dress samples."

I draw the phone away and back.

The *makeup*. Like a dime-store goth.

"She's not *so* big," says Georgia. "She's just a little chubby. It's kind of cute up close."

"I think it's a no," I decide. "Don't worry. I'll break it to her."

"OK. I think...she just got back in the elevator."

"Then I'll see her in about a minute. I'm in the lobby now."

CHAPTER TWENTY-SIX

HOLLY

The elevator doors slide shut and make a gentle descent. I figure I've got about forty seconds to get the panel open before it gets to the ground floor.

I glance across at the lit-up buttons, which are zooming through their sequence with alarming speed.

18, 17, 16…

Removing the key from the pocket of my dress, I slot it into the tiny circle of light. It fits perfectly. But when I go to turn it, nothing happens. I try the opposite direction. Still nothing.

Come on, work.

The buttons are flashing faster.

15, 14, 13.

"Please work," I tell the key. Instead, this time when I twist, an alarm button blinks to life.

5, 4, 3…

I make a final twist. But now the key is stuck completely inside the lock.

The doors slide open. I whirl around, trying desperately to think of a reason why I might be traveling up and down in the elevator car with an alarm blinking and a fireman's key jammed in the access panel.

Fitzwilliam's strained face appears in the door.

"Holly," he says, glancing over his shoulder and stepping neatly inside. "Ortiz couldn't stop Georgia from getting in. Did she call security?"

"No. She mistook me for a replacement bridesmaid."

He laughs. "Wait. You're serious."

"Is that so hard to believe?"

His mouth opens and shuts. I guess his preppy good manners don't have a suggested answer for this scenario.

"Did you change your clothes?" I suddenly realize he's no longer in police uniform. Fitzwilliam is wearing a navy Ralph Lauren T-shirt with black pants.

"I took off the hat, shirt, and gun belt," he explains.

"You wear designer shirts under your police uniform?"

"Adrianna Kensington is in the lobby," he says. "We need to be fast."

"The elevator doors won't shut in the lobby without a key card," I tell him, processing this new side to Fitzwilliam. I never pegged him as a rule breaker.

He holds one up. "Turns out the receptionist wants to be a member of my country club."

Fitzwilliam flashes the card to close the door, then holds a finger to the alarm for a few seconds.

"These alarms operate on an override code," he adds. "This should hold the doors for a few minutes." He looks at the key, jammed in the glowing circle.

"Georgia was wearing Simone's ring," I tell him.

His eyes widen. "OK. That's…odd. We'll let Ortiz know." He frowns for a moment, then lifts his hand and turns the key.

"How did you…"

"I have a way with keys," he says. "And humility."

The panel falls open. Inside, wedged to one side of the controls, is a cream envelope.

For a few seconds, we both stare. Fitzwilliam reaches for it, but I stop him.

"Fingerprints," I say, leaning to take the envelope carefully from the void using my lacy bell sleeve.

The envelope is made of heavy paper and stamped with the Kensington crest. It bulges tantalizingly like there's something inside.

There's writing on the front in Simone's looping script:

Holly. If you're reading this, I didn't make it. Unmask Trinity. Simone xx

My heart catches.

"OK. That's kind of…strange," says Fitzwilliam. "'Trinity.'" He hesitates as if uncertain what to tell me.

I glance across, too thick with memories and questions about Simone.

"I don't know who Trinity is," I tell him.

"OK," says Fitzwilliam. "So 'Trinity' was the police nickname for Adrianna's kidnapper, based on her account of her time in captivity. It was never released to laypeople."

Carefully, I reach inside the envelope, my sleeve still covering my hand.

Inside is an ancient-looking ring bearing a crest of an oak and ravens. It's large and bulky, made of old gold. It has an *S* inscribed discreetly on one side.

"It's a signet ring," says Fitzwilliam.

For a moment, I can't speak. "It's Simone's," I whisper. "She always wore it." I frown. "But I don't understand. I'm sure I saw Georgia wearing it. Just a moment ago."

"More than one ring, I guess," says Fitzwilliam. "Simone wore a ring with a crest on it?"

I nod. "She never took it off."

I look closer at the ring. "The shadowed oak and ravens have a motto underneath: *Mors Aeterna*. That's Latin for *eternal death*."

"That's the Kensington ancestral motto," says Fitzwilliam. "Private education," he adds. "I had an English history teacher who made us learn the old society families."

I ponder this. Simone wore a ring with the Kensington crest. Why? I park it as another disturbing mystery about my former boss and concentrate on the issue at hand. Now I see the ring up close, I notice something I couldn't see when it was on Simone's finger.

"The bulky shape could mean it's a poison ring," I say. "They were a thing in medieval times. A poison ring has a secret compartment to hold the poison. Medieval assassinations are kind of a hobby of mine," I admit.

"You're a weird girl, you know that?"

I ignore him, turning the ring over. "If I'm right," I say, "this part should pop open. Or maybe this part…" I'm turning it, trying to figure it out.

Fitzwilliam takes it smoothly out of my hand and, with a single movement, slides back the front panel to reveal a tiny concealed compartment, no bigger than a fingernail.

"How did you…"

"NYPD," he deadpans. "We may not know a whole bunch

about medieval times, but modern-day kids use slider rings like these for drug stashes."

At first glance, it looks packed with a loose brown powder.

"Heroin?" suggests Fitzwilliam. "Let's bag it," he decides. "Take a closer look later."

We're interrupted by the noise of the doors sliding open. Adrianna Kensington's blue eyes come into view. They widen, taking in me, Fitzwilliam, and the ring held guiltily in my hand.

"Are you the new lawyer?" she asks, staring at what I'm holding in my hand. Her eyes zero in on the *S* etched into the gold. "What are you doing with Simone's school ring?"

CHAPTER TWENTY-SEVEN

HOLLY

I'm gazing mutely at Adrianna. Her signature mane of glossy brown hair is even more vibrant in real life, framing a face contoured in dewy perfection. The full lips are the lightest lipsticked pink, and the famous sapphire-blue eyes are framed by thick black lashes and an artfully layered sweep of nude makeup.

But it's not so much her appearance as her manner that is captivating. If Georgia exudes confidence, then Adrianna beams it like a thousand-watt bulb. The way she walks and holds herself is mesmerizing. I feel my mouth go dry. The ring is still clamped guiltily in my sleeve.

Standing behind her are two of the most beautiful women I have seen in real life. One I recognize: Petra Morka. White-blond hair, cropped short in a way that would only flatter a woman with her cheekbones. Next to her is a deep-green jumpsuited woman, every inch of whom screams "wealthy creative." Her vivid orange hair is faded to light-blond tips in a feat of hairdressing that must be as expert as it is expensive.

"This...is a school ring?" I manage. My eyes land back on the crest.

Adrianna nods rapidly. "A lot of Kensington Manor girls wear them. Why do you have it?"

"This is Simone's niece, Holly Stone," fills in Fitzwilliam smoothly. The women exchange glances.

"Georgia said you were a lawyer," says Adrianna, staring at me intently. "For Liberation Law."

"Um. Right," I say, looking desperately at Fitzwilliam for help. "Simone...my...aunt...recently hired me to work at her firm. But then...she died..." I can't say anything else. My voice catches.

Adrianna's face twists in sympathy. She darts forward and puts an arm around me.

"I'm so sorry," she says. "Were you close to Simone?"

I nod, looking up through tear-filled eyes, my body racked with ugly sobs. Her arm at my shoulder feels comforting. She gently takes the ring and eases it onto my little finger.

"Here," she says softly. "Your aunt wanted you to have it. And I am honored that Simone's niece would want to be my replacement bridesmaid."

"Simone never mentioned having a niece," says Petra suspiciously. "I don't see much family resemblance."

Adrianna frowns at her sharply. "*I* think," she says meaningfully, "the bravery of Simone's niece stepping in is good PR. Kensington Manor School girls pass their rings down, mother to daughter," she adds. "Simone must have thought a lot of you, Holly."

I'm assailed by so many emotions, it's difficult to speak. Simone wanted me to have this ring. Did she think of me as her daughter?

"I *knew* Mark would have a good reason to appoint you as the new lawyer," continues Adrianna, grabbing me in a sudden hug. I feel her rigid limbs fold around me. It feels very much like being enclosed in the grip of a praying mantis.

The faces of the two women behind her would make the best wedding photo ever. Assuming you like your bridesmaid photos to channel jealous rage.

"Ophelia." Adrianna turns to the orange-haired woman, whose green jumpsuit and plastic bangles are creatively mismatched. "Can you style Holly for the plane?" Adrianna shoots me an apologetic look. "We have photos on landing in Elysium," she says. "So we all need to coalesce. Not that your skull thing isn't *super* cool."

"Sure thing," says Ophelia, her eyes twinkling. "We can get you some great clothes, Holly. Something to really bring out those eyes."

Ophelia reminds me of a chattering parakeet, all high color and quick little movements. Her porcelain skin is sprinkled with tan freckles the exact shade of her light-brown eyes, and her small mouth is a perfect Cupid's bow of deep pink.

I can't get my head around Adrianna's sudden affection for me, but by the looks of the other women, it's nothing new.

"Is your assistant going to be joining us in Elysium?" Adrianna asks, eyeing Fitzwilliam with open approval. "You know we're flying out this afternoon?"

"Elysium?" I say. "That's not really... I mean, I don't do full sun... Plus, I don't have a passport..."

Fitzwilliam makes a loud coughing sound. "Ms. Stone's passport is being renewed with extra pages," he says. "On account of extensive travel this year."

I glance across at Fitzwilliam. He and Adrianna match, I think. All that exuberant glossy hair, long thick brows, and dense arc of sooty lashes. Excellent natural protein synthesis seems to be a mark of generational wealth. A legacy of having the best of everything. "I have that passport problem *too*," says Adrianna, rolling her eyes.

"Why do they make them with so few pages?" She shrugs, like, *what-you-gonna-do?* "It's OK. We can fast-track your entry for Elysium. Let's just"—her eyes range over me, the bonhomie in them fading a few degrees—"get you some clothes," she decides, sweeping into the elevator with the two women behind her.

Ophelia leans in, a brittle smile on her brightly lipsticked mouth. Up close, I realize she is not as beautiful as she first appears. Her heart-shaped face is rather broad and the light-brown eyes small. Without the makeup and contrasting orange hair, she'd be pretty rather than striking.

"Don't get used to it," Ophelia hisses. "She likes to play favorites."

CHAPTER TWENTY-EIGHT

HOLLY

Fitzwilliam and I have convened with Ortiz in an empty hotel room. There's an excited gleam to her eyes as we tell her what we discovered.

"OK. Well, first, Holly," she says, "I like the makeover. It suits you."

I glower at her. Adrianna's friend Ophelia managed to get to work before Fitzwilliam could drag me to freedom. My face has "barely there" lip color and blush, which leaves me feeling utterly exposed, and my blue hair is set in tidy waves around my face.

"Second," says Ortiz, "between the two of you, we might just have found a way to get a cop out onto Elysium. That's where Simone spent her last week alive, right? We should look for clues there."

Fitzwilliam and I exchange confused glances. "Wait… You don't actually expect Holly to carry on the pretense of being Simone's niece?" he asks. "Adrianna Kensington isn't as dumb as she makes out. She'll put the pieces together."

"Never underestimate a woman's self-obsession in the days before her wedding," says Ortiz. "I'm going to make a few calls."

"I'll take a closer look at the sample in Simone's ring," I decide.

"I've got my spectrometer here somewhere," I add, delving into my purse.

"You carry a spectrometer?" asks Fitzwilliam.

"It's only a handheld one," I explain. "In Simone's offices, we have the latest Thermo Fisher Orbitrap Eclipse Tribrid Mass Spectrometer and an infrared iS50."

Fitzwilliam's brow creases slightly, and his lips part. "OK, but… this handheld one works?"

"Should tell us what the substance is at least. Maybe more."

I produce the sample pot and spectrometer. Fitzwilliam's eyes widen as he catches sight of the interior of my purse, with its candy bars and gaming paraphernalia.

"Is there anything you *don't* carry with you?"

"Ho Hos are a superfood," I tell him. "Edgar Allan Poe is essential reading. Fantasy trading cards are always useful. And you never know when you might need a twenty-sided die." I open the ring carefully, wield my tweezers, and drop a sample of brown powder in the chute. I press buttons. The spectrometer bleeps and whirs as it analyzes.

We watch as a graph begins to slowly populate waving lines on the small screen.

"Any idea why Simone hid her ring for you to find?" asks Fitzwilliam, glancing at my face.

"She was investigating Adrianna's kidnapper," I say. "I guess… she must have discovered something. Made a backup plan in case the culprit tried to silence her." I blink at the reading. "Looks like…dirt," I say. Fitzwilliam's face falls. "But quite unusual dirt," I counter. "High concentrations of sulfur compounds. And see that spike on the chart? That's a very high mineral reading. Quartz, calcite, iron oxides."

"What does it mean?" asks Fitzwilliam.

I think about this. "Calcite often forms the shells of marine organisms," I tell him. "But this sample has a lot of sulfur. I'm not a geologist, but at best guess, I'd say it matches a place with geothermal activity. A volcano. A meeting of tectonic plates."

"Elysium." Fitzwilliam nods. He reaches to the bedside table and lifts a copy of *Vogue*, then opens it on a double-page spread. "The island's new grand opening is in every magazine this month," he says, letting the pages fall open. The headline is *Elysium Beach*. And the images are of luxury amenities. Over-water cabanas, a beach club. A spa area with natural hot spring pools. An aerial shot takes in a sky-high panoramic, sweeping the length of the green island, with its sand-fringed coves and mainland of verdant overgrowth.

"OK," I agree. "That looks likely. We can narrow it down further." I zone in on my spectrometer. Adjust a few settings. Then begin downloading comparable volcanic sites on my phone.

From across the room, I hear Ortiz's authoritative tone. "Yes," we hear her say. "It's important."

"OK," I say, thinking out loud. "We can confirm minerals and ash, consistent with volcanic soil. But we also have..." I lean forward and adjust the lens of my spectrometer to use the microscope function. "A lot of this clear material. Crystalline structured...too pronounced to be glass. That range can only be silica," I say.

"Which means?"

"Silica and sulfur. Together." I nod encouragingly, but he doesn't fill in the blanks. "It has to be right by a water source. A volcanic water source," I add. "Mineral rich." My finger lands on the glossy magazine spread. I tap one of the landmarks. "Hot springs. Let's try testing the thermal properties." I press buttons. "OK. *Wow*."

"What?" Fitzwilliam glances across.

"Crystalline in structure," I explain. "Thermal range that rules out quartz. *But*. When we use scattered light to identify the molecular vibrations, look at this." I point to the graph on my display. "Distinctive Raman peaks in a range of nine hundred and sixty to eleven hundred centimeters, but here we have a range that you would associate with collagen."

I look up at him expectantly.

"Holly, you're going to have to interpret that mic drop for me," says Fitzwilliam.

"It looks like two different soil samples here," I say. "The first is most likely volcanic with mineral waters. The second is high in collagen and hydroxyapatite."

"Which means?"

"Bone," I say patiently. "Human bone." We're both silent.

"I guess the first thing is to get to the hot springs," suggests Fitzwilliam.

"That's where Simone seems to be directing us." I pause. "Only...how would she imagine I could ever get out there? It's not like I could pass for"—I wave my hand wildly—"one of *them*."

Fitzwilliam assesses me with a long look. "Maybe Simone had more faith in your abilities than you do," he decides.

We're interrupted by Ortiz's voice breaking across the room. "Good news! Mark Li has agreed. Kind of."

"Wait. What?" I'm staring at her in confusion.

"Yep," she says. "I'm a genius. No need to thank me. I figured that the Kensingtons are crazy, but Mark Li might be a reasonable man who actually cares about the life of his fiancée. Turns out I was right. He's agreed to cover for you, Holly."

"Cover for me?"

"You and your lovely assistant." She grins at Fitzwilliam.

"Her *assistant?*" Fitzwilliam has turned a shade of green.

"If Adrianna asks, Mark will confirm the story that you are his choice of stand-in bridesmaid and a relation of Simone's." She pauses. "For a while at least. Mark Li wants results. He's given us twenty-four hours. Then you have to leave. Li will tell Adrianna you got sick."

Fitzwilliam and I exchange glances. "One day," I confirm, "to get to these hot springs?"

"One day to deliver concrete evidence," corrects Ortiz. "If you don't find anything in that time, Li wants you off the island."

Fitzwilliam and I exchange glances. This doesn't seem like nearly enough time.

Ortiz grins. "Pack your bathing suits, kids. You're going to Elysium."

CHAPTER TWENTY-NINE

HOLLY

When Fitzwilliam meets me at the New York private airport, he's dressed like he's about to board a yacht. Pressed chinos, preppy deck shoes, a crisp linen Ralph Lauren shirt unbuttoned at the collar, and a ribbed navy sweater thrown around his neck.

His eyes rest on my blue hair with its recent Kensington restyle and toned-down makeup.

"You kept the new look," he says approvingly. "It suits you."

"Where are your socks?" I ask him.

"I thought it best to wear casual clothes. As an assistant."

"*Those* are your casual clothes?"

He frowns. "Mark Li gave us some intel on the hot springs on Elysium. The good news is they're near the main accommodation. We should be able to get to them fairly easily without being seen. Which is fortunate, because there is also bad news." He pauses. "Li says the hot springs are under construction. They're being completely remodeled for Adrianna's wedding, and work starts tonight."

My heart sinks. "Whatever Simone left could be destroyed?"

"Destroyed. Found by someone else. And after sunset, there'll be a twenty-four-hour construction crew. We won't be able to look either way."

"When does our plane land?"

"Midafternoon, Elysium time."

"Our one-day window to find evidence just dropped to a few hours?"

"It should be all we need," says Fitzwilliam. He glances across the luxurious lounge. "The other bridesmaids will be here soon. Ortiz wanted me to brief you on the Kensington case." His expression makes it clear he doesn't wholly approve of freelance forensics being brought in on police files.

"OK," I say. "Shoot."

He nods. "First, we've confirmed on the security footage outside the storage room where we found the murder weapon, the only people who entered the night Simone died were the four bridesmaids. Last in line was supermodel Petra Morka. But—"

"But since the body was hidden in a dress container," I fill in, "it's possible that any one of the bridesmaids came in after the murder and didn't realize there was a body in the box."

He nods. "So there's that," he says. "But we're also strongly investigating the possibility that this murder is linked with the previous kidnapping of Adrianna. How much do you know about that?"

I shrug. "Same as most people, I guess. Just…what I saw in the news. That picture of the panic room with blood and hair on the floor."

His face looks pained. We all saw the images of Adrianna when she exited that room.

"The family had a showy wine cellar, which they also fitted out as a panic room," he says. "On the ground floor of their grand colonial house. The kidnapper somehow got Adrianna into that room unseen. Held her there for three days."

"How come no one looked there?"

"Misdirection. One of the party guests heard a speedboat leaving the island in the middle of the night. Police piled all their resources on locating it. I have the full report from the Colombian police."

He begins summarizing quickly. "Adrianna was drugged. Went to an upstairs bedroom feeling dizzy. Woke up gagged and handcuffed with no idea where she was."

He turns his phone and begins sliding his thumb across pictures. The filthy remains of the panic room with a blood-spattered bed. A close-up of a pair of rusted manacles.

"You said the panic room was on the ground floor, right? She was carried down from an upstairs bedroom?"

"Right. And according to guests, the celebrations went on all night. The only way to the panic room was through that wild party." He thumbs his phone. "And...there's an artist's impression of the person Adrianna saw when she woke up. Stuff of nightmares." He flashes me the screen. I lean closer, then recoil instinctively.

The figure wears a long black cloak and an almost featureless white mask. All the more disturbing for lacking any discernible mouth or face contours. A slightly peaked center hints at an upturned nose, and the eyes are cross-hatched, presumably to indicate some kind of gauze or wire covering. The long cloak, buttoned at the collar, conceals the figure's entire body, and two arms emerging halfway down show gloved hands.

"How does someone dressed like that walk through a party of two hundred people?"

"It was a masquerade ball," he says. "Venetian-style. Everyone wore a mask."

"Even so..."

"We had a few eyewitnesses who said they saw this figure at the party," says Fitzwilliam. "No one knew which guest it was. No cameras anywhere." His mouth twists wryly. "Elysium is one of the few places the Kensingtons can be truly private."

His eyes drop back to his phone.

"Adrianna says her captor never spoke to her. Not once," he continues. "But through gestures and…assaults, they exhibited an obsession or interest in the number three. Adrianna was made to put on three dresses. One each day. Fed three communion wafers and allowed three sips of water. Her hair was hacked off three clumps at a time. Knife wounds were inflicted on her in the manner of the crucifixion. Three to each wrist and three slashes across the ankles. You probably don't need to see the injury detail pictures." His voice catches slightly. "The hospital treated her for multiple cuts, bruising, dehydration, and a dislocated wrist and fractured shoulder."

"So it was like…a religious thing?"

"Maybe sacrificial even. There were also two dolls in the room."

He shows another picture. Two bloodstained rag dolls, slashed through to the stuffing on the arms and legs, wool hair cut completely away.

"Adrianna came to believe she was doll number three. That's when she escaped. The damage to her shoulder and wrist were from her pulling her arm free from the manacles."

We're both silent, digesting this.

"Three dolls," I say. "And there were three wedding dresses hanging in the Plaza. One with Simone inside."

"Right."

"That's why the police used the name Trinity?" I suggest. "Trinity for *three*?"

He nods.

"What about the forensic evidence from the Colombian police?" I ask. "They must have fingerprinted all the guests. Did they match it to any found in the panic room where Adrianna was held?"

"There were fingerprints in the hostage area from all the bridesmaids, along with about a hundred other people. As well as their DNA, hair, and clothing fibers. The Kensingtons were conducting tours that night, showing off their new panic room. There was so much forensic matter in that room, it took the Colombian team two months to process."

I absorb all this. "You're thinking a party guest kidnapped Adrianna, then lay low for three years."

"Until the wedding was announced," considers Fitzwilliam.

"Or until Simone started investigating," I say. "She was obsessed with that case. Ever since she met Leopold Kensington at a wine gala six months ago. I assumed she was just attracted to the TV ratings. Now I'm thinking…maybe Simone had a closer connection to the case she didn't tell me about. Why else would she have risked her life to investigate?"

"Everything points to another bridesmaid," says Fitzwilliam. "All four women were at Adrianna's twenty-first birthday. All four were the only people with access to the storage room the night of the murder."

My mouth twists. "And we're about to board a plane with them."

CHAPTER THIRTY

HOLLY

Being on the Kensingtons' private jet is a surreal experience. When we boarded, the other bridesmaids barely looked at me.

I had been wondering how the hell this was going to work. How does a new bridesmaid arrive without everybody questioning it? Now I see the opposite is true. Mark was right. It's like a job. Someone else left. I've got the position. No one questions it.

Fitzwilliam has been relegated to the back with the cabin crew. I've been seated right across from Silky, who didn't show up at the Plaza. She's famous in New York cinematography circles for dark and haunting works. Up close, she looks dangerously thin, the skeletal lines exacerbated by her height.

Silky has angular features and black hair cut in a bob. She is dressed almost entirely in rather dilapidated vintage pieces. A lace-trimmed slip dress and a jet-black designer suit jacket swung casually over her shoulders. The look would be perfect for a New York It girl in her twenties, but somehow, she is just very slightly wide of the mark. The dress is a shade too short. The baseball sneakers look a few years out of date. And—I realize with shock—she smells. A low unwashed odor overlaid with high notes of incense that I guess come from whichever Greenwich Village flea market she picked up her wardrobe from. Something about her eyes is wrong. Blank. Distant. As if her mind is very much elsewhere.

She introduces herself, shaking my hand in a languid way and holding me in an intense, serious gaze.

"I'm doing the flowers," she explains. "You?"

"Law," I say awkwardly.

She nods. "Be careful around the other bridesmaids. Kensington Manor School girls can be unkind to new arrivals."

Before I can ask what she means, Silky leans against her seat and closes her eyes. Within seconds, she's breathing deeply.

Adrianna has taken advantage of a private room with a queen-size bed and is presumably snoozing out of sight. Georgia has no such luck; her feet, clad in ballerina flats, are crossed at the ankle as she frantically leafs through seating plans for the wedding breakfast.

Ophelia has her cream leather seat set back, a bold-print eye mask pushed up to ruffle her paint box–orange hair, playing a game on her neon-cased phone. The heat of the flight has raised two rosy-pink spots on the freckled skin of her cheeks. Her jumpsuit and heels combo has been switched for a designer velour version matched with Chanel sliders for the airplane.

Across the aisle, Petra's spider-long legs are kicked out in a pair of silver sneakers. She and Ophelia seem to not be making eye contact. Georgia positions herself as far away from Petra as possible.

Silky wakes up as the airplane begins to descend over a patch of azure Caribbean Sea soaked in blazing sunlight. The island below is a hump of dark green; the headland stretches to a thin tip, which frays away into a tattered coast, like a smudged thumbprint. There's a curved bay taking a deep, sandy-edged bite out of the headland.

The plane loops around, and Silky begins frantically sketching in her notepad.

Around the island, the blue sea gives way to the lightest pastel green. Lagoon-like and pretty. Fuzzy dabs of jungle—one hairy thicket from the air—are scarred with rectangles of broken shrub.

"They tried to grow sugarcane here," explains Silky, pointing. "It never took. The English Kensingtons gifted the island to Leopold as kind of a joke."

"How do you gift someone an island as a joke?"

"It was their wedding present," she explains. "When Leopold got here to check it out, he discovered they'd dumped him with a tropical rock with nowhere to land a plane or even moor a boat safely. The early Kensingtons had thrown up a few stone buildings and fled when they realized you couldn't grow anything here but mosquitos, but"—she stretches her arms high, releasing a waft of musty scent, and yawns—"Leopold being Leopold, he took that worthless land and made it worth a fortune. Playground for the rich and famous. It was the place to be a decade ago."

The comma-shaped island spills from the central cone of a verdant dormant volcano. From the air, I can make out a clutch of water-filled square terraces on one of the steep sides. Hot springs.

"That's Fortune House." Silky is pointing to a jungle-swathed peak topped with slabs of gray building. "The Kensingtons used to have big parties there when we were kids." She looks sad.

"You grew up with the Kensingtons?" I say.

"I'm an old school friend of Dri's," she explains. "But"—she lowers her voice, glancing at Petra, who is using her phone as a mirror—"I never really fit in with the family. I was a scholarship girl at the school we all boarded at. Not old money or connections like all the others." She rubs her eyes and scratches at her arm distractedly.

I take this in. She might look the part, but Silky is less of an insider than I first assumed.

"What's down there?" I squint out the window at some dark shapes in the jungle, mostly hidden in foliage.

"That?" She glances. "That's the old schoolhouse. No one goes there anymore. The ground is unstable for building."

Silky flips her sketch pad and adds some detail to a previous image. Three sad-faced little girls in school uniform stare dolefully out of the page.

"My therapist told me to sketch my dreams," she explains, glancing up to see me looking at the haunting sketch.

"Oh, Silks! You're not *still* going on about our boarding school?" Adrianna, now awake and retuning to the main cabin, cuts across cheerfully. "We all went through it. We all came out of it. That's just what boarding school is."

Silky snaps the pad shut and stares straight ahead. She twitches as if she can't keep still.

"How long until we fucking land?" she mutters as the "fasten seat belt" sign flashes.

"Five minutes until landing," announces Georgia. "A few hours before sunset, local time. Plenty of time to get to the house before dark."

I chew my lip. That doesn't leave us nearly as much time as I'd hoped to get to the hot springs.

As the plane descends and hits the runway with a gentle bounce a few minutes later, Silky stands quickly, clearly anxious to be off it. She moves toward the doors, and I notice Georgia moves to speak with her, and Adrianna pointedly shakes her head. Georgia drops back, and as we ready ourselves to leave the plane, the other girls ignore Silky entirely.

CHAPTER THIRTY-ONE

HOLLY

We exit the airplane into the soupy, tropical Caribbean air. It's late afternoon, and the sun is a gentle blast of golden heat. The airport is nothing more than a landing strip with a cinder-block hut attached and thick jungle behind. A line of bright-blue crabs are scuttling across the far end of the runway, making for the coast in a waving army formation.

In readiness for the island weather, I'd already put on my favorite strappy summer dress before boarding. It's white cotton, screen-printed with black skull outlines and piped in black to give a slight bodice effect. I'm already regretting my silver-buckled leather slingbacks, which feel heavy on my feet in the tropical heat.

Fitzwilliam moves to my side on the tarmac. "I think we have an hour until sunset," he says. "Might be enough time to get to those hot springs if we can slip away."

I shift from foot to foot impatiently. The women all seem to be disembarking very slowly, in new outfits for landing. Adrianna is still out of sight, deep in the private jet.

Ophelia has continued the high-color theme. Her orange hair inside a bright tropical-print turban is matched with heart-shaped shades and a turquoise halter-neck jumpsuit splashed with large pink orchids. She seems to feel no fatigue from the flight whatsoever, talking in bright, rapid sentences as the rest of us blink in the sun. As Ophelia's high shoes navigate the steps, she treads awkwardly, and her phone tumbles onto the asphalt. She stoops quickly to pick it up, and I notice pictures of Adrianna open on her screen. She sees me looking and stashes the phone rapidly.

Petra has donned a fishnet body stocking that reveals large panels of her lean white body, silver heels, and narrow little sunglasses that match her stern expression. I notice Georgia taking in Petra's outfit with obvious displeasure. Looks like Adrianna was supposed to steal the show, but Petra is making a bid for the lead.

Georgia steps forward. I'm wondering how anyone can look so immaculate after a long flight. Large sunglasses sit coolly above perfectly made-up brows. There's not so much as a crease on her white silk blouse.

"We're just waiting for Adrianna so we can get a few pictures," she says.

My heart sinks. How long will that take?

"No unauthorized photography or communication equipment is allowed on the island," continues Georgia, her voice ringing with natural authority. "You'll need to deposit your cell phones and anything else that takes pictures on the other side of the runway. You can pick them up when you fly out."

Silky catches my expression. "You can't be too careful when the right picture of you is worth hundreds of thousands of dollars," she explains.

As we deposit our phones, Adrianna finally emerges from the jet.

Her face looks tired from the flight, but as soon as her feet hit the tarmac, she rearranges her features into a dazzling smile. She wears a long sundress in vivid red, with a crochet cutout effect that suggests snatches of tanned skin underneath and a slit to midthigh. Her narrow feet are set in vertiginous wedge sandals with glittering black jewels decorating the straps and soles.

She stands patiently as Ophelia darts forward and begins powdering and adjusting her makeup, fluffing her hair. Petra starts taking pictures.

My stomach growls. The sun is blazing down overhead, and none of us have eaten a thing for the entire flight. I look across to Adrianna, standing passively as she's pulled about like a piece of meat. Do none of these girls get hungry?

Adrianna turns to address us, pausing for Petra to swing the camera in her direction. Tossing her glossy curls over her shoulder, she breaks into a broad smile. She hesitates, then frowns and signals to Georgia. After a moment, we're all furnished with filled champagne glasses.

"Don't actually drink the champagne," warns Silky as I take a sip and wince. "It's lemon juice and baking soda, to give it sparkles in the pictures."

Adrianna smiles, waiting for all eyes to fall on her. "It's so incredible to have you all here," she says. "I am just so grateful you could be with me at this special time in my life. Thank you all so much." She clasps her hands to her heart, still beaming.

Wow. You'd actually think she knew and liked all these people.

"Here's to *Elysium*!" She raises her glass.

I move to touch mine against Silky's, who's standing the nearest to me, but Fitzwilliam subtly holds my arm and shakes his head.

"Just *raise* it," he whispers. "Never clink."

"We've got *so* much to show you," gushes Adrianna. "The whole island has been rebooted for the new generation. There's a beach gym and a whole new restaurant and bar at Fortune House. Ophelia has also masterminded a brand-new detox lounge called Daybreak. So we can get over our little indulgences." She smiles mischievously. "It's equipped with vitamin drips, detox juices, steam rooms, an oxygen bar, and everything you need to get ready for another big night." She brings her pink nails together. "Then our new secret bar. Sepulcrum."

Is it just me, or did Adrianna's voice just catch?

"Every Kensington Club has to have a secret room, right?" She fixes Petra's lens with a beaming smile, then clears her throat and readjusts her sunglasses.

Fitzwilliam and I exchange glances: we can still make it.

Adrianna's manicured hand closes around her own undrinkable prop. She checks the camera is on her, turns to her bridesmaids.

"Welcome to Elysium. We're going to send out a clear message." Adrianna's voice is raised, but the key is slightly off. Forced. "I am Adrianna fucking Kensington! I am getting *married* this week! Murderers are not invited!"

Petra snaps away furiously.

There's a smatter of uneasy laughter. Adrianna lifts her glass to uncertain light applause, and I notice her hand is shaking. Seems the speech is over, but it's a strange moment to stop. It takes Petra a few seconds to realize she can lower her camera. Adrianna's smile falls with it.

Ophelia smooths the awkwardness by whooping enthusiastically, and the clapping intensifies, but the sour edge to the atmosphere lingers.

"Time to go." Georgia gathers up the undrunk glasses.

Finally.

"A little housekeeping," adds Georgia. "We're two days early, so there are some things that are unfinished. We're going to have to travel the first part on foot, since the road isn't ready for vehicles yet. And there's still construction work happening in places, so stay on the grounds. Luggage will go straight to your rooms."

"We're *walking*?" Petra demands. My eyes drop to her high-heeled shoes.

"Yes, and it's very important we stay together." Georgia's slim brown hand is raised for our attention, a discreet scatter of diamond and ruby rings catching the golden sun. "The island is still being developed. Please don't go exploring past the main grounds. There are armed guards protecting the island, and they can be a little… unpredictable. We don't want anyone getting shot by mistake." Her perpetually anxious expression tightens further at the thought of this.

"You're not *seriously* suggesting your guards would shoot a guest?" scoffs Petra.

"I wouldn't take the risk," says Georgia, her owlish eyes earnest. "They're armed mercenaries Dad rustled up last minute from Colombia. Not the nicest of men."

"Leopold got an armed guard here but no transport to the house?" demands Petra. I'm guessing her silver high heels are already killing her.

"We're Kensington Manor School girls," says Adrianna lightly. "We can handle a little hardship, right? Fine metal withstands great heat." But I detect a slight hint of pleasure as her eyes tack to Petra's stricken face.

There's a strange, loaded pause.

"OK," Adrianna trills, "let's get walking."

CHAPTER THIRTY-TWO

ADRIANNA

I'd forgotten how the slow heat of Elysium consumes you a little piece at a time. The walk through the jungle is uphill and humid. Vines and tree branches snake in at face level.

As we hit the peak of the island, a heavy building rises up from the jungle in all its colonial glory. A set of quad bikes, for meeting guests once the roads are complete, sit quietly out of commission to one side of the approach.

I take a steadying breath but can already feel the sweat prickle my palms.

Fortune House. A big gray stone box of memories.

Beside me, Georgia slides a slim, cool hand into mine and squeezes. She always looks great in humidity, her skin glittering with a faint golden sheen, her hair holding its neat ringlets, the blouse and culotte combo crisply immaculate. I reach a hand to check my bouncy chestnut hair has retained its volume.

"The house is still here," she says quietly.

"Until the end of time," I tell her.

We both smile. This is a little joke between us. Dad used to get excited about the single-mindedness of the first Kensingtons. How they built these stocky stone walls with their mean little scatter of square windows and low slate roof and made a tough-bladed lawn of crabgrass in the melting heat.

He'd brag about how smart the shaded undercroft was, perforating the big stone house at the base with even little arches, designed to keep the servants cool and get more work out of them.

And he loved telling guests how the grand curving stone steps, fortress-size door, and hardwood plantation shutters would last until the end of time.

I hear a sigh of annoyance and flick to Petra, dressed, as usual, to steal the show. *My* show.

"I don't get why you love Petra so much," I tell Georgia irritably. "I can think of plenty of girls who could have been the tall blond in the lineup."

"She always shows up on time, always looks good, and never complains on shoots," says Georgia crisply. "If they were all like her, my job would be a lot easier." She glances at me. "And Petra never bothered with me at school."

I make a high little laugh. "I don't dislike her because of *school*. She's trying to get her claws into Dad."

"I'd say she's done a lot more than tried," says Georgia.

"You know Petra doesn't like you, right?" I mutter. "She's jealous because you're Dad's favorite."

Georgia takes in Fortune House with her clear, clever eyes. "Girls like Petra never like me," she says. "Can't say I mind."

We stop outside the house, and as Georgia begins announcing the busy schedule of photo shoots and cake tasting, Holly requests she absent herself to debrief with her assistant.

"We have a *schedule*," says Georgia, razor-sharp brows descending.

"She can take twenty minutes," I tell Georgia. But as Holly and her assistant vanish out of sight, I lower my voice so only Georgia can hear.

"Holly Stone," I say. "Check her out, would you?"

"What's to check out? Mark vetted her, right?"

I wrinkle my nose. "Maybe it's just her dress sense but… something doesn't seem right. It's like she's…looking for something. A Kensington always knows, right? We can sniff out vipers."

Unexpectedly, I feel Ophelia's hot little body move in to the side of me. Her freckled skin is pink in the heat, clashing with the tropical bird color combo of her bright turban and palm-leaf pantsuit.

"You OK?" Her eyes are earnest.

I maneuver a big smile into place.

"Sure!" I tell her. "I'm *so* excited to be back. Petra, can you get a picture of me at the door?"

CHAPTER THIRTY-THREE

HOLLY

As the other girls vanish into the house, I lead Fitzwilliam to the grassy area we arrived on.

"I saw a sign," I tell him. "Hot springs. They're only a mile away. Other side of the volcano, just like in the brochure."

"That doesn't leave us enough time," says Fitzwilliam. "A mile is a half hour's trek through jungle."

"I had an idea," I tell him, pointing to the quad bikes.

Fitzwilliam looks at them dubiously. "I'm not sure if that dress—"

"Get on behind me." I straddle a quad bike, hitching my dress, and Fitzwilliam reluctantly climbs on. The solid shape of his tall body suggests he's the kind of guy who has a daily regimen of pull-ups and squats.

I pull out the throttle and slip a finger under the handlebars, disengaging the speed restrictor. As I pull out on a cloud of sand, Fitzwilliam lurches back, then grips hold of my waist awkwardly. "Where the hell did you learn to drive these things?" he asks as I speed down the partially finished road, bouncing over potholes and jungle debris.

"Summer job, kiddie camp. Looking after snot-nosed brats like you. Leaders had to use these things to round them up. Hold on." I bank hard, taking a corner and throwing up sand and distance between us and Fortune House.

"You've got a real chip on your shoulder about wealth, you know that?"

"That's what all wealthy people think," I tell him. "The rest of us are too busy picking up after you to form an opinion."

We skid onto a straighter piece of track and pick up a spurt of speed.

"You can slow down on the corners," suggests Fitzwilliam. "Better to get there in one piece."

"We need to get there fast," I tell him. "Find out what Simone left for us."

Behind me, Fitzwilliam is silent.

"Is there something you're not telling me?" I ask.

He takes a breath. "OK. Yes," he admits. "Ortiz got access to Simone's office," he continues. "Simone was planning on bringing another court case against Kensington Manor School. Part of the case was around how the school had a tradition of burning the students' possessions, almost like a rite of passage. The new girls would have their favorite items put into a fire shortly after arriving. Along with a chunk of their hair."

I make a grimace. "That's horrible."

"I think it was sort of...symbolic," he adds. "A ritual to be born again as Kensington Manor girls."

"So Simone wasn't looking to benefit from Kensington fame," I say, reframing this. "She was...exposing the school. And she discovered something out here on the island, where the school was founded."

"Maybe," he says. "Think we'll make the hot springs by sunset?"

Fitzwilliam shields his eyes against the ball of red sun, spilling onto the darkening sea.

"Yes."

The quad bike eats up the distance, flying along the twisty island tracks. If we weren't on a mission, it would be fun. I'm thinking about why Simone led us out here. Her mysterious message about unmasking Adrianna's kidnapper. If the answer is in the hot springs, I'm determined to find it.

The evening breeze is warm on our faces, and the naked heat of the day has settled into something demure and beguiling. A whispering embrace of cicada sounds, low birdsong, and floral scents.

"Can I ask you something?" I call back to Fitzwilliam as we bounce along. "Why does your boss call you GQ?"

"I believe it's a reference to *Gentleman's Quarterly* magazine," he says.

"If you want to fit in with the other cops, you should cut down on the exercise," I say. "Eat potato chips. Slouch a little. You know, live it up."

Fitzwilliam doesn't seem to be listening. "Never saw you as a speed freak," he says, his voice strained, gripping the seat tight. "At college, I had you down as a Dungeons and Dragons type."

"The two things aren't mutually exclusive." I spin around a corner. "I still make D and D nights at Mystic Dice Tavern." I pause. "I didn't realize you even noticed me at college. Not that I wanted you to," I add hastily. "No offense, but you and your buddies were kind of jerks."

There's a silence.

"It goes with the territory," he says after a moment. "Frat boy and all that. I'd like to think I've grown up." He pauses. "Why dress like you do if you don't want to be noticed?"

"I think of it more like armor," I tell him. "Keeps the jerks at bay."

We reach the far side of the volcano, and the jungle view falls away to a spectacular beach and sea. Down on the shore, enormous blue-gray stones look to have fallen from the sky, forming crevasses and tunnels, like a giant's teeth sinking into the sugar sand. The sun bleeds a deep crimson lake into the lapping waves.

Hanging on the side of the volcano are a set of square-sided pools, built Aztec-style, with intersecting hand-cut gray stones, and filled with smoky blue steaming water.

I stare for a moment. "This is incredible."

Fitzwilliam gives a small smile. "First time you've seen hot springs?"

"Isn't it yours?"

"I've seen one or two. These are very well landscaped though," he adds generously, gesturing to the giant blocks of granite interspersed with exotic-looking plants, which make it look like there's been a spa here for a thousand years.

Each milky pool is marked with a rustic wooden sign, announcing various temperatures. Cooler toward the bottom, hotter at the top. Joining them together is a series of mazelike suspension walkways, painted deep red.

"This is just about the worst environment for gathering forensic information," I say. "Outdoors, open to the elements. Multiple bodies of water accessed by multiple people. Maybe…we got it wrong," I say. "If Simone wanted me to find something, why would she have left it somewhere so hard for me to find?"

"If she found something worth killing for, she might not have had a lot of time to hide it," Fitzwilliam points out. "Just had to hope you'd figure out a way out here. And you did."

I rub my forehead. "I was never any *good* at the stuff Simone wanted me to learn. Like…that thing with not clinking glasses when we landed. I don't get it. Why pretend to be these super polite people?"

Fitzwilliam considers this. "I think it's more like signaling you're on the same team."

I shield my eyes from the setting sun. On the far side of the clutch of pools is a huge reception area with a floor of jet-black polished volcanic rock and an entrance bordered by a fan of tree branches.

"If I was leaving clues for forensics," I decide, "I'd pick somewhere not so exposed. Less chance of degradation. Let's check out the reception area."

CHAPTER THIRTY-FOUR

ADRIANNA

Passing through the thick studded door of Fortune House brought a wave of emotions. I manage to get five minutes alone to call Mark before we all need to reconvene.

As the call connects, it's such a relief to see his handsome face. "Adrianna." At the sound of his voice, my whole body relaxes.

He's my rock in a sea of illusions.

"How is security out on the island?"

"It's good," I assure him, checking the little thumbnail image of myself in the phone to be sure my face matches the words.

"Not strange to be back?"

"Ophelia has changed all the design," I say, opting for a half answer. "Did she speak to you about the table arrangements?"

He nods. "She also let slip that the bridesmaids had a fight the night Simone died," he says pointedly. "You never told me that."

"Oh." I let out a ringing little laugh. "Ophelia can be a little dramatic. I wouldn't have called it a fight. All the girls together in a hotel on the night of a wedding demo. It can get a little catty." I curl a strand of hair around my finger, wondering what to tell him.

"Particularly when Georgia decides to make the unveiling of

your bridesmaids a big staged occasion and none of them knew who the others would be," says Mark.

"Yeah." I examine a pink fingernail. "Maximum drama, right? It made for good pictures."

"That's what the fight was about?" he suggests. "Some of the girls weren't happy to share space with the others?"

"I *told* you, it wasn't a fight. And we're all Kensington Manor girls. We keep our jealousies hidden." I sigh. "Simone was talking about her latest show is all. She wanted to shoot some scenes for *Wrongly Accused* out on Elysium. Petra and Georgia didn't like the idea."

"They didn't?"

"Of course not. Georgia doesn't want all that old crime stuff raked over. Not unless she's executive producer. And Petra…she's always the one the conspiracy theorists accuse, isn't she?" I hesitate. Flashes of paranoia grip me. Mark can be trusted, can't he? Every last one of my boyfriends sold stories about me to the newspapers.

"I have to go," I tell him. "Cake tasting."

We end the call, and I try to push aside the conversation. But I can't.

My bridesmaids. Diamond-bright Ophelia with her orange hair and wide smile. Troubled Silky, pale and jittery. Platinum blond, long-limbed Petra with her forceful supermodel stare. Buttoned-down Georgia, pin-neat and tightly smiling.

Simone.

And a whole lot of history.

With the exception of Holly, we've all met back in the vestibule after a hair and makeup retouch; it's hard not to feel overwhelmed. The cool air of the reception area smells of scrubbed wood and fresh paint.

Ophelia's designs for Fortune House seemed like a good idea back in New York. Now that I'm actually here...Georgia is going to freak out when she finds out about the new bar.

I fix on my best hostess smile and take in the new decor. The high walls have been stripped back to bare pitted plaster and painstakingly hand-illustrated with vivid, jewel-bright jungle vines. Midnight-blue skirting and dado rails frame the savage wilderness in polished paint. It's a clever contrast. Like a gothic jungle or a midnight tropical garden.

"It's *perfect*," I exclaim in a pitch several notes higher than I intended. I clap my hands together firmly. "*Exactly* on-brand." This time, my dazzling smile lands correctly.

"Remember how it was before?" Petra's voice is languid, as if the whole business of hanging out with us amuses her. "Red flock wallpaper. Fake gold palm trees. Crystal chandeliers." She stands a little apart from the others, I notice with a crackle of annoyance. As if she owns the place, in her rock-singer attire.

Luckily, Ophelia intervenes before I have to wrestle my hatred of Petra down into a polite reply.

"Do you want to see the secret bar?" she asks.

"Sure." Georgia addresses me, not even bothering to look at Ophelia. "Where is it?"

I pause. "We wanted to surprise you," I tell her, even though I know Georgia hates surprises.

"O-kay." Georgia's confusion is evident as she and the others follow me down the hallway. "Why are we going this way?" she asks. "This leads toward the library. Dri shouldn't be here."

"I'm OK," I say, but my voice sounds strange.

As we walk through the library doors, Georgia makes a strange little muted yelp of deep horror. Her fists are tight balls at her sides.

"Ophelia," hisses Georgia, "please tell me this isn't what I think it is?"

Even Petra has a shocked cast to her elfin features.

"I remember this room," she says, her Swedish accent thicker than usual. "Wasn't this…where the entrance to the panic room was?"

CHAPTER THIRTY-FIVE

HOLLY

We head toward the reception area, crossing the swinging bridges, their decadent hue making a vibrant contrast to the slate-blue waters of the pools.

As we approach, I crane my neck to take in the enormous proportions of the atrium. Simone's messages are flittering through my mind.

Unmask Trinity. Is the answer in these caves?

"Quite the approach," I mutter as we pass. Polished tree branches fan out like rays of the sun around the entrance. Living vines curl around them, creating a soft halo of green leaves at their tips. Beyond its grand entrance, the vast roof is a deep black-gray mass of natural rock, bubble-textured like breaking surf.

"Volcanic heat," says Fitzwilliam as we enter. "Can you feel it?"

I nod. There's something otherworldly about the way the air has become superheated and cloyingly humid, scented with a strange overlap of essential oils and struck matches.

A reception desk made from the same polished branches as the entrance sits adrift on the expanse of shining floor. It fronts a row of deep shelves, artistically set with Elysium-branded spa products, carved wood deities, and luxuriant white towels.

"What is this place anyway? Some kind of natural cave network?" I'm tipping my head back to take in the vast textured ceiling.

"Given the volcano, I'd guess this to be a preexisting lava tube," says Fitzwilliam. "A hole cut by lava flow, back when the volcano was active. They built the spa inside it. Rather clever," he adds grudgingly.

"A lava tube? Someone paid attention in geography."

"If your parents throw enough money at your education, some of its bound to stick," he replies, a half smile on his square-jawed face.

"OK." I take a breath of the burned sulfur air and try to set my thoughts in order. "I'm too hungry to think straight," I tell him. "All my sugar hits are in my luggage. I'd kill for a mini muffin or a Ding Dong right now," I add wistfully.

"Any snack named with an alliteration isn't real food," says Fitzwilliam. "Nor is any product from the Hostess cupcake range."

"Essentially, my main food group. OK." I rub my temples, trying to ignore the gnawing in my belly. The vast interior of the reception area is completely overwhelming.

"Entry and exit points," I decide, calling to mind the first principles of crime scene analysis. My eyes drift to the reception desk. There's a logbook, attached to the desk so as to face outward for visitors to sign in. I approach it, delving into my backpack for gloves.

Carefully, I lift the cover. It's filled in with names scrawled hastily in pen, with times in and out, none of which I recognize. Staff, presumably, or contractors.

On a hunch, I pull some fingerprint powder from my pack and dust for prints.

"Maybe Simone has left a clue like in the Plaza," I explain to Fitzwilliam. "Some shape or word that shows up with forensic tools. That would be exactly her style for the TV show. Camera-friendly forensics."

But as I sweep my brush, there's nothing. At all. "Not a single fingerprint," I say.

"Unfortunate." Fitzwilliam casts a nervous look toward the entrance.

"More than that. It's...strange. Look at all these people who signed in and out. You'd expect this page to be covered in prints. Paper can be a challenging surface to fingerprint due to its absorbency, but still...you'd expect *something*."

"You're saying *lack* of evidence is meaningful."

"Absolutely. *Every contact leaves a trace.* Locard's principle. The fact that this page is completely free of oil or sweat transferred from hands means it's been wiped clean." I think for a moment. "Simone won several big cases by proving forensic cleanup. What it signified."

"What does it signify?"

"That you should take a long, hard look at what's been cleaned."

CHAPTER THIRTY-SIX

ADRIANNA

Ophelia's nonstop commentary hasn't slowed. It seems to map my rising heartbeat. The smell of the old library room is so unexpectedly familiar, I actually stagger as I enter, putting a hand out to steady myself on a deep shelf of old leather-bound books.

"Ophelia," says Georgia, her gaze switching to me in concern, "please tell me you didn't put a secret bar in the panic room where Dri was held hostage?"

"We needed something big for the fashion sponsor," I say. And because my voice doesn't come out right, I do it again. "I'm fine," I repeat. Louder. Brighter.

"Is your *entire wedding day* not enough for the fashion brand?" Georgia sounds furious.

"Every Kensington Club has a secret bar," Ophelia explains. "Tantra has the Red Room, Prohibition has the Distillery, and now..." She pauses for effect. "Elysium has Sepulcrum. That's Latin for *tomb*," she adds. "We got some great gothic branding for it."

"They're paying ten million for exclusive pictures," I remind Georgia quietly. "Rich girls get married all the time, and I don't do video, so..." I let the obvious answer trail off.

"They want to dig up your worst trauma for some magazine pictures," she says finally, a miserable look on her face. "Are you not even a person to them?"

"You know I'm not," I say, meeting her eyes. "I'm a brand. A brand that makes us all a lot of money."

"You don't actually have to go inside the room," Georgia confirms.

"That's…still open for discussion," I say.

Petra's eyes cast about the room. "Where is the entrance?" she asks. "How do you get in?"

"That's the best part." Ophelia beams, beckoning us toward a set of floor-length velvet drapes. She reaches up high with her little arms and pulls a golden cord with effort, lifting aside the heavy fabric in one movement.

"Ta-da!" Ophelia throws out a hand.

Revealed is a full-length portrait of my great-aunt Lady Margaret Kensington in a high-necked dress. She is severe-faced and unsmiling with washed-out eyes. Her dark hair is separated by a razor-sharp central part, giving her the appearance of wearing a black skullcap. Three similarly serious schoolgirls in heavy gray pinafore dresses are arranged at the front. Behind them are some jaunty fat palm trees and the sea on the horizon.

We all recognize it. A replica of this portrait was hung in our headmistress's office at our New York boarding school. Painted in waving letters over the tropical sky are the words

Our Trinity: Discipline, Self-Restraint, Godliness.

Silky takes an audible breath, eyes wide, hand at her chest.

"Isn't it *hilarious*?" says Ophelia, oblivious to Silky's near hysteria. "It's a little in-joke for all us girls who went to Kensington Manor School." Ophelia's eyes are hard and bright, like she's proving something to herself. "Our boarding school motto began out here with your great-aunt Margaret."

Silky's eyes are flitting around the room like a hunted animal. Petra also has something beneath her glacial expression that I've never seen before. She's uncomfortable too, I realize—she's just better at hiding it.

"Remember how the headmistress would tell us tortured saint stories?" says Silky. "That stuff in chapel was not suitable for little kids."

"All the saints being burned alive and stuff?" says Ophelia, picking up on the sudden silence. "That was X-rated. For sure."

"What kind of school," says Silky, "appoints a headmistress who loves scaring little girls half to death with stories of torture and sadism?"

There's a pause. She's broken the code. Everyone keeps it light. Makes a joke of it. She's acting like a victim. We want to be survivors.

"You always were such a fucking *baby*, Silky," shoots Petra. "Always whining and wetting your pants. Why don't you get over it and *grow up*?"

It's delivered with such savagery that I physically flinch. Part of me wants to step in. Try to take issue with Petra's surprising attack or at least reassure Silky, whose chest is heaving so fast, she looks on the brink of physical collapse.

But it's like we're all stuck. Trapped in a past version of ourselves that keeps playing out. The frightened schoolgirls.

Something is happening to Ophelia that is hard to understand. Her eyes are bulging; a flush is creeping beneath her freckled skin. Georgia simply looks tired.

Suddenly I'm furious with Silky. Why does she keep doing this to us? Why does she keep taking us back there?

It's Georgia who breaks the tension. "It's cake tasting next," she says, checking her slim gold watch and eyeing my face with concern. "No time to look inside the new bar now."

The strained atmosphere shifts, and I notice Petra breathe a small sigh of relief.

"I'd better go find Holly," adds Georgia. "She's been way longer than twenty minutes."

"Let's…take a few minutes free time, touch up makeup," I suggest, feeling suddenly exhausted. "Look around. Not you, Silks," I add, thinking I need to read her the riot act on digging up the past.

As the others drift away, Silky stands alone, her gaze vacant and fixed on some far-off point.

I close my eyes, placing my hand on my chest.

"I am safe," I whisper. "I am loved. I am safe. I am loved."

CHAPTER THIRTY-SEVEN

HOLLY

In the lava caves, I begin reading the names on the log carefully, assessing each one.

"I think they're all Colombian names," I say. "Spanish-sounding."

I stop reading. One entry stands out.

"Violet Locard," I breathe. "OK. I think we're in the right place," I tell Fitzwilliam. "Look at this name." I point. "Locard." I twist around to share the joke with Fitzwilliam, but he looks confused. "Locard is a reference to Edmond Locard, the famous forensic scientist," I explain. "*Every contact leaves a trace.*"

"I have no idea what you're talking about."

I frown. "Locard is like…the grandfather of forensics. He wrote *Police and Scientific Methods.*"

"That one skipped me by."

"I loved the early forensic cases as a kid," I tell him. "Locard was hired to investigate the Lindbergh baby kidnapping. The way he analyzed the trace evidence was fascinating. *Wherever he steps, whatever he touches, whatever he leaves, even unconsciously, will serve as a silent witness against him.*" I nod happily. "I was pretty much obsessed with death and science from a young age," I explain in answer to Fitzwilliam's puzzled expression.

"What makes a kid love forensics?"

I crinkle my nose in thought. "I guess...I didn't grow up with the most reliable of people. Forensics don't lie. They don't let you down or change their mind or stand you up. They're just *there*. The most truthful constant there is if you spend the time to look for them."

There's a look on Fitzwilliam's face like grudging respect.

"The point is I think Simone wrote this entry," I say. "Like a clue. To tell us we're in the right place. The only trouble is I don't know what she meant by it."

"Why did she write *Violet Locard* instead of *Edmond Locard*?" asks Fitzwilliam. "Was she trying to obscure the name?"

"Maybe..." I dig in my pack and pull out my forensic light. "Ultraviolet," I say. "Ultraviolet light."

I snap on the purplish beam. Almost at once, I see it. The top corner of the logbook. A clear splotch. Deliberate. Forming a shape, glowing green.

"UV paint. There," I breathe as a shape reveals itself. "You see that?"

Fitzwilliam comes to look. "It's...an arrow," he says. "Only detectable under UV light."

"Simone's clue," I say. "The arrow points to the back of the caves." I shine the light in that direction, and my heart lifts. It's another arrow.

"That way!" I point.

Fitzwilliam is standing perfectly still. "You hear that?" he asks. "I think that's an engine sound. In the distance. It's not sunset." He frowns. "Maybe the workers are arriving early. We'd better be fast."

"Fast and careful," I agree.

Fitzwilliam and I move past the spa rooms, shining pods of

black stone laid at intervals on the volcanic floor of the lava tunnel. Carved into the doorways are the various treatments involving mud and water from the nearby hot springs.

Toward the back is a jagged rope with a sign reading *No Access* written across it.

"Somewhere the Kensingtons don't want us to see?" I suggest. "Let's take a look."

CHAPTER THIRTY-EIGHT

ADRIANNA

The other bridesmaids have peeled away to explore the house, leaving me alone with Silky.

"Why do you always do this, Silks?" I demand. "Why do you have to keep making things awkward?"

"*Why* is Petra your bridesmaid?" Silky plants two skinny arms on bony hips. Her black bangs are still plastered to her pale forehead with sweat, I notice, though it isn't hot inside the house, and her red lipstick is slightly smudged.

I sigh. "I'm really sorry," I say. "I didn't know my dad would appoint her, I *swear*."

"You're such a coward." Silky looks straight ahead through the floor-to-ceiling plantation-style doors at the end of the grand library. The sky and sea are framed by Ophelia's choice of navy drapes and dark-gold tiebacks.

"Silky," I say, attempting to pull some bridal authority into my tone. "I'm sorry your court case against the school didn't go how you wanted. But…"

"It's fine," Silky says, sounding surprisingly genuine. "Petra won. I lost. I'm moving on." She sounds less sincere now. "And… your kidnapping certainly sucked all the oxygen out of the case."

I look away, not sure how to manage my emotions.

"Sorry," she adds. "I didn't mean that."

"You were right. What you said back then," I tell her. "I shouldn't have arranged a big party in the middle of your court case." I'm staring straight ahead. "Karma. I got what I deserved." I try for a wry smile, but it goes weird.

Silky puts a hand on mine. "No, you didn't. No one deserves what happened to you. But no one deserves what happened to me at school either."

I feel the familiar emotions detonate. Sympathy. Confusion. But mostly I wish Silky could just forget about it like the rest of us did.

Three years since she took Kensington Manor School to court. It feels like yesterday when Silky brought all that stuff up.

"And," she says, her voice softening, "I'd be lying if I didn't admit I wish just one of my school friends had stood up for me in court. Told the truth about how they treated us at school."

I can't meet her eyes.

"I know what you're thinking," she says. "*What good would it have done?* School was over. Just petty revenge, right? But…more girls will get sent there. The cycle continues."

"Just don't send your kids there," I tell her, trying to lighten the mood.

It works. Kind of.

"None of us will," she says. There's a pause. "You wouldn't, would you?"

I chew the edge of a nail, then lower my hands self-consciously. "I don't know. Maybe. I mean, it wasn't *so* bad. It taught us stuff. Survival."

Silky is looking straight ahead again. "Guess you got treated better than I did. The Kensington heiress. I was just a nobody."

"I'm sorry," I tell her. "I know Petra was mean to you at school..."

Silky's eyes widen in shock. "Dri! Petra was a lot more than *mean*. Didn't you read the court documents?"

"I...no, I didn't." I catch her expression. "I couldn't. It was hard for me too, Silks," I say quietly. "I didn't want to go back to that place either."

"Can't you see that Petra is still doing it? To all of us?" says Silky. "All the sick power games she played at school. Saints and Sinners. She's still playing them."

I hesitate. Work on getting something bright into my tone. "Look, the wedding will be over in a few days. You'll never have to see Petra again."

"You said that before," says Silky miserably. "At your twenty-first birthday. But look how good she is at worming her way in." She hesitates, cutting me a glance. "Did you see Petra's face when Simone was revealed as your bridesmaid?"

I nod my head slowly.

"They knew each other, didn't they?" says Silky. "From school."

"The timings fit," I shrug. "Though Simone would have been older. What does it matter?"

Silky turns the full lamp-like gaze of her dark eyes on me. "Because what Petra did to us," she says slowly, "someone did to her first." There's a burning quality to her eyes that makes me want to step back, but I restrain myself with effort.

My last therapy session in New York leaps to mind. The psychologist. Red-lipsticked and power-dressed, she was firing questions about Silky.

"You say boarding school wasn't traumatic for you," she mused. "But I think you have a lot of guilt for not doing more for Silky.

You mentioned before that you thought the school deliberately kept pupils in a state of fear. In the weekly chapel visits."

"The headmistress would tell us all these stories," I agreed. "Like all the terrible things that were done to the saints. How they had their skin torn off or were pulled apart by horses."

"That frightened you?"

I nodded. "I remember really clearly this thought process," I told her. "Like, if this can be done to adults, if all these awful things can be done to adults, then what chance do we little kids have? Little kids with no parents to defend them."

She nodded sympathetically. "It felt threatening?"

"To a bunch of seven-year-old girls? We took it as a warning."

"What was the warning?" she asked quietly.

My eyes filled with tears. "Never feel safe," I whispered. "Because really, really bad things can happen to you. Even if you're really good."

"You're safe now," she reminded me. "You are safe and loved."

"I know." I nodded rapidly. "I wish... Maybe I would have liked to have been outspoken like Silky. I had Mom and Dad to think of. The Kensington family *founded* that school."

"That was sixty years ago. They don't run it now, right?"

"No. But it's *called* Kensington Manor School. The place is associated with the Kensington name. Speaking out against it would have been a complete betrayal. And in the end, what would I have said anyway? The older girls bullied us, and the school served bad food? That isn't a *crime*."

She leaned back, tapping a pencil to her scarlet lips.

"I think it is a crime," she said, "to leave small children in the care of fourteen-year-old girls. Particularly if those girls abuse their power."

CHAPTER THIRTY-NINE

HOLLY

As we move into the cordoned-off area, deeper into the back of the spa, the grand cave-like surroundings quickly run out. Beneath our feet is a rubble of volcanic rock. There are cracks in between, filled with the same disturbingly bright-colored crabs we saw on the landing runway. They scuttle away as we walk across.

Fitzwilliam digs in his pocket and produces a small flashlight.

"Don't tell me," I say, "you were a Boy Scout?"

"Sea Cadet. But the life skills are similar."

He swings the slim beam. The cave is much cooler here, with a strong odor of sulfur. The light bathes the textured volcanic rock in a ghoulish green glow.

The darkness leads around a corner and to a smell that doesn't match. High and fragrant.

Instantly, Fitzwilliam's beam of light picks something up. It looks like...flowers.

It takes me a moment to process the magnitude of what I'm seeing. This whole part of the cave has been loaded with blooms of all shades. Roses of white, pink, and peach are wrapped in paper and stacked in layers, a pastel rainbow of velvety petals. Buckets are ranged in rows, filled with the sculpted points of designer-shaded lilies. A huge tarp has been laid in one corner and is mounded several feet high with jewel-bright orange marigold heads.

"I guess…they're storing the wedding flowers here."

"Cool. Dark. Humid," says Fitzwilliam. "Makes sense. Check that out." He points.

There's a giant *K*, over ten feet in height, festooned in blooms. It's not quite finished, but you can see the final effect will be spectacular. Fitzwilliam shines the flashlight farther back.

"Turn off your flashlight."

He clicks it off, and we're plunged into total darkness in the flower-perfumed, water-drip echo of the cave.

"Another arrow," I say. "Drawn on the wall in ultraviolet paint."

Fitzwilliam clicks his light back on as we step a little deeper.

"There's something on the back wall," I say, my voice strained. "Iron bars fixed into stone." My breathing hitches. "Is it…prison cells?"

It's an emotional sucker punch, seeing this cruel-looking penitentiary hidden at the back of a luxury spa.

Fitzwilliam blinks. "A lot of prison cells," he says, taking them in. "They're so *small*."

The cells have been cut into the stone, running along the length and height of the back wall. The upper levels are accessed by stony steps and narrow walkways.

There's something insect-like about the way they are arrayed. Like a row of cocoons pressed into the rock. Every oval aperture has a door of iron bars. Like the kind you get in old-fashioned jails. I shudder as Fitzwilliam's flashlight sweeps, picking them up.

"They look old," I say. "Long abandoned." I eye the thick iron bars, gingered with rust.

"Who would build a prison on a remote island off Colombia?"

"Narcos?" suggests Fitzwilliam, matching my thoughts. "Leopold Kensington runs nightclubs. He doesn't make a secret of drug use in his venues."

We look at the tiny prison cells, barely large enough to hold a person. "Click off your light."

He does. In the dark, we see another arrow, pointing out a single cell.

We follow it, and the arrow directs us to the small confines. Inside is a narrow bench, stamped with an ancient Kensington crest, barely big enough for a person to sit on. The distance to the door is so shallow, it would only allow a person to curl into a ball.

"What are they for?" I breathe. "Too small for prison cells, surely?"

"I don't know," says Fitzwilliam.

I shine the light around the rocky walls, and for a moment, there's nothing. Then I see it. The Kensington crest on the planks of the bench has been daubed with ultraviolet paint. My light settles on it. A splash of glowing green in a dark cell.

Fitzwilliam lifts it. Underneath is a kind of compartment. A natural void where curving rock hasn't matched the flat bench above.

Inside, pushed into the void, is a flash of deep gold. It's a flat shape. A rectangle of card, damp-spotted and old, and foiled in what looks like real gold leaf.

It's a birthday invitation. To Adrianna Kensington's twenty-first birthday.

Scrawled across the front, in jagged writing, is one word.

BITCH.

I hear Fitzwilliam make an intake of air.

"See who it's made out to?" he whispers.

I read the name written on the front.

*T*RINITY.

CHAPTER FORTY

PETRA

It feels strange to be back in Fortune House after three years. It has changed. A lot. In Leopold and Athena's day, it was off-the-hook bling. Back in my early twenties, I thought it was the coolest thing I had ever seen, but I get how Ophelia's designs will breathe new life into the place. Less old boys' club, more fresh-faced wellness. I slip out the cell phone I concealed inside my camera equipment and check the time in New York. I'm still good. I make the call to my magazine editor, Max.

"Petra!" He picks up the call after one ring.

"There were no documents in the elevator panel," I say. "I looked. You sent me chasing wild geese."

He's silent for a moment. "I had a tip-off from a colleague. Simone wanted to shoot an episode of *Wrongly Accused* out on location on Elysium. Feature-length."

I turn this over in my mind. "You think Simone solved the case? Who kidnapped Adrianna Kensington?"

"Simone wouldn't pitch for an hour slot just to rework old material. And my sources say NYPD has an undercover cop out on Elysium," he continues. "If Simone found something juicy out there, then we need to find it before they do."

I'm shaking my head. "The only people out here are Adrianna's bridesmaids, and there's no way..." I pause for a moment. Because there is someone else here, isn't there?

Simone's niece.

Thrift-store goth Holly Stone. And her suspiciously well-dressed assistant.

I had felt a lot of things when Holly revealed her connection to Simone.

It was common knowledge that Simone's family weren't the "right people." She got in on a scholarship, so it didn't exactly surprise me that she had some strange relatives hidden away somewhere, breeding bizarrely dressed chubby offspring.

But what I didn't expect was to feel such anger toward Holly. It's not like I have any feelings for Simone. Why do I care if she hired some relative to work for her?

Now I'm wondering something else. Could Simone's niece be here to investigate her death?

And wasn't Holly holding an envelope when the elevator door slid open?

I'm thinking. "I can try to find out."

"You need to do better than try, Petra. Unless that slot is filled in the next two days, I'm running the interview of you with the Colombian police. Those *no comment*s don't paint you in a good—"

"All right!" I snap, trying to think. What could Simone have found out here?

My mind drifts back to the courtroom. Adrianna's twenty-first birthday on Elysium was scheduled for two weeks after the case kicked off. When I was called to the stand on the first day, I was nervous. My attorney had explained that Silky claimed to have proof. Pictures that showed abuse of younger girls. That was uppermost on my mind as I walked into the court...

I shift my attention back to Max on the other end of the phone. "This could bring down the whole Kensington family," he's saying. "We're talking front page, all-around-the-globe viral."

Hot fear spikes in my throat. "Are you saying Simone found some dark secret about the Kensingtons?"

"It's even better than that," he says. "From the pitch that Simone sent to the networks, it isn't just about *who* kidnapped Adrianna. It's about *why* she was kidnapped." He pauses for effect. "That's what you're going to find out."

I hang up the phone, my jaw tightening. "But you're assuming, Max," I say, "that I don't already know."

CHAPTER FORTY-ONE

HOLLY

In the dark of the lava tunnel, Fitzwilliam reaches in to grab the birthday invitation.

"Wait." I shine my light around carefully. "Don't disturb evidence until you've examined the situation, right?"

I pull it out, inch by inch.

"Trinity," muses Fitzwilliam. "Why would that be on an invitation to Adrianna's twenty-first birthday party?"

"I've seen this invitation before," I tell him. "Simone brought it back from a meeting with Leopold. Evidence that Adrianna's stalker began threatening her before the birthday party."

"It wasn't in the police file."

"I don't think the Kensingtons go to the police," I tell him, eyeing the invitation. The turquoise card is thick, but the color has faded from a vibrant blue to something more muted and patchy. I think for a moment. "There's something stagey about this, right? The trail of UV paint. Then this old invitation. Like something Simone might set up to shoot for *Wrongly Accused*."

"I don't watch the show."

"We use real cases," I explain. "But Simone sets up evidence in an engaging way. This birthday invitation is exactly the kind of thing Simone would have the crew film her unearthing. Assuming it relates to the kidnapping case. Forensics," I say. "*Wrongly Accused* always uses forensics. It was Simone's specialty." I hold the invitation up. "I think we need to take a look at this in more detail. I have a full forensic kit in my luggage."

The rumble of an engine resounds through the cave. "We need to go," says Fitzwilliam.

"OK." With a gloved finger, I begin bagging the invitation, avoiding unnecessary contact. The gold catches the light.

"Fancy," I murmur. "I guess Adrianna was more bling back then." I'm thinking of the more muted but decidedly expensive wedding invitation.

Fitzwilliam grabs it. "We need to go *now*." He slides the invitation into the evidence bag, nods, and puts it in the pack still on my back. It's a surprisingly intimate gesture, and he seems to realize this just after he closes the zipper, not quite meeting my eye.

As we head back toward the hot springs, we pass the boxes and buckets of flowers and the giant flower-clad *K*. Approaching it from the opposite direction, I get a clear view of the unfinished back.

"Silky is organizing the floral display, right?" I say. "Look at the display. It's been built out of scaffold." A realization is forming, deep under the sugar-starved thinking part of my brain.

"This isn't the time to admire the flowers, Holly."

"I'm not really a florals kind of girl," I tell him. "But I am interested in murder weapons."

Fitzwilliam pulls at my arm with a gentlemanly hesitation that I suspect masks his underlying panic.

"The room Simone died in," I say. "Do you think it was floristry scaffold?" I'm absorbing the structure of the giant flower-decorated

K. The scaffold is a honeycomb, interlocking poles all fitted expertly together. "Why would the scaffold be deconstructed on the morning of the wedding demo?" I'm voicing my thoughts, trying to piece together a fact that won't sit in alignment.

"Something to discuss later," says Fitzwilliam, leading me with gentle firmness back to the reception area. He stops dead in his tracks, and I follow his gaze to the hot pools outside. Two burly men in uniforms, with guns slung easily over their bodies, are patrolling the base.

I catch a glimpse of the brutal-looking face of one of the guards, and the way he is flicking the safety catch on his gun makes me instinctively duck back out of sight.

"Think they'd risk shooting a wedding guest?" I ask.

"Let's not stick around to find out," says Fitzwilliam. "They haven't spotted the quad bike," he adds, pointing. "If we slip down the back way, they won't see us."

Silently, we creep down the side of the volcano and back to the parked bike.

"Let's go. Fast as you like," breathes Fitzwilliam, climbing on behind me.

At the roar of the engine, we hear shouts from back toward the hot pools, but we're long gone on the sandy trail before the guards see us.

We speed back to the other side of the volcano with the setting sun behind us, all kinds of strange thoughts looping through my head.

As we roll up the last of the sandy track, the invitation and what Simone might be trying to tell us are jostling for position. The clutch of old prison cells, hidden in the back of Elysium's luxury spa. The floristry scaffold. The birthday invitation, addressed to Trinity.

It all points to a dark secret, hidden out here on Elysium.

CHAPTER FORTY-TWO

PETRA

While the other girls are enjoying free time, I slip out for a cigarette. Below me, Holly Stone and her so-called assistant are arriving back at the house. I've had time to check out Adrianna's new goth bridesmaid and confirmed she worked for Simone's law firm.

But her assistant speaks too well and has far too much decorum to be a PA. Not to mention she doesn't seem to have assigned him a single task since we landed. Not so much as a glass of water.

Now that they think no one is watching, it's even more obvious. Everything about how they relate to one another speaks of equals. Friends. Maybe even something more.

Slowly, I dial a number on my cell, sucking thoughtfully on my cigarette, turning everything over. Holly Stone. Simone.

After the court case, I thought I'd never see her again. But when Adrianna was kidnapped, Leopold was smart enough to figure there was some connection between his daughter being snatched and our old school. He set about getting close to Simone to find out more.

What happened next, I should have expected but didn't.

Georgia sent me a formal invitation to the Plaza ahead of the wedding demo the following day. The theme was "bridal sleepover."

One of Georgia Kensington's clever publicity stunts, with a big reveal of Adrianna's secret bridesmaid list to the press.

Weird now to think that was the last time we saw Simone alive.

The idea was we'd each arrive singly in preselected designer pj's and negligees and react with shock and delight as each successive bridesmaid was revealed. Naturally, I'd been asked to show up second to last to capture the drama of Ophelia's and Silky's horrified reactions.

I sauntered into the room, relishing their discomfort.

I'd expected Ophelia to be in the lineup since her makeup business had taken off. Silky was a surprise, though not completely.

But the joke was on me. As I took my place for pictures next to the other girls, the final bridesmaid walked in.

"Simone Walters," announced Adrianna, beaming her camera-ready smile, "will be my maid of honor."

A ripple of shock had gone through all of us. We all knew the maid of honor was Leopold's choice. Why had he picked *her*?

If I hadn't been so blindsided myself, I might have enjoyed watching Silky and Ophelia attempt to hide their horror.

It was common knowledge that Simone wanted to cover Adrianna's kidnapping for *Wrongly Accused*.

"We need a lawyer to determine the prenup," Georgia explained to the girls. "The issue of Elysium's ownership is complicated."

"But property isn't Simone's area of law," said Ophelia, looking betrayed.

I wondered if Adrianna had hinted that she would be maid of honor. We all knew Georgia couldn't do it—she can't pose for a picture to save her life.

The evening passed in a blur as I struggled with all the questions and emotions of being in the same room as Simone. We staged pictures with bowls of popcorn and had a fake pillow fight. When the photographers left, we all excused ourselves to our rooms along the same corridor. Simone grabbed my wrist as I pressed my gold key card to the door.

"Bunny."

"It's Petra now," I snapped. "I'm nothing like the girl you knew at school."

"I hate what happened between us," she said quietly.

I shook my head in disbelief. "You had ten years to apologize. Why are you here, Simone?" It was still strange. Saying her name aloud after all the years apart.

She glanced back along the hotel corridor. "Penance," she said.

My stomach lurched. "What?" It came out as a whisper. As a grown woman, Simone was tiny to my model height. But somehow, I still saw her as the bigger, older girl.

"Why would you owe Adrianna Kensington penance?"

She shook her head, frowning. "Bunny. Don't you see? The kidnapping. Silky's court case. It's all connected."

The call to my editor, Max, connects, breaking my thoughts. "Petra? What's up?"

"I think I found the undercover cop."

"OK."

"He's with the new bridesmaid. Pretending to work as her PA. She must be in on it too."

"Did they find anything yet?"

"I don't know." I raise my camera and take a snap of Holly and her assistant. Then zoom in. They both seem to be looking at…

My heart skips. A birthday invitation. I remember seeing those

Tiffany blue cards like it was yesterday. I never got one. Leopold had to make a call to get me on the list.

"Maybe," I correct myself. "It looks like they might have been searching the island. Found something."

"Watch and find out."

I nod, wondering how to use this information to my best advantage. Wouldn't Leopold be interested to know there's an undercover cop? And I was the one to point him out?

Either way, I need to get that invitation.

CHAPTER FORTY-THREE

HOLLY

Back at Fortune House, I'm just in time for the cake tasting. Georgia takes me to a private room to pick a dress from a selection Ophelia has collated, then whisks me past a dining room with a long table at the center in the same lushly decadent style as the reception area. Golden plates have been set among jungle leaves in deep colors. There's a dark fairy-tale feel to it, like dining in a forbidden forest. The hardwood table is set with Roman banquet-style foods, like grapes and whole fish.

"Are we having a late lunch?" I suggest hopefully.

Georgia glances at me irritably, as if I should know better than to let my body get hungry.

"This is photo shoot replica food," she says pointedly. "Laid out earlier today for pictures."

I realize the fish has an unnatural painted gleam, and the grapes are fixed to plastic stems. It's fake.

"There's Ophelia," says Georgia. "She'll take us to the Tower Suite."

Ophelia brings us up several flights of stairs to the grand house, where a huge resort-style modern addition has been built on the back. It opens the entire premises out onto a spectacular cliff top, with rock-clad walkways spilling over like bridges, connecting the old house with a new glass and stone structure behind.

We cross over, admiring a chasm of verdant tropical cliff below. Ophelia points to a glass-sided tower right at the top, commanding a view of the entire island.

"That's the grand Tower Suite," she explains. "Leopold Kensington's design, but we've brought it up to date."

"This part was an old fort originally," explains Georgia. "Dad fixed it up. I think that's a man thing," she adds. "Always wanting high-up views of your territory."

As we ascend a glass elevator to the suite, I'm getting an idea of just how high she means. The fiery sun is setting, spilling vivid colors over the darkening sea. Georgia pushes the door to the honeymoon suite open.

"Wow," I say. One side of the room is open to the sheer cliff, with vertiginous views of the entire green island beneath us, curled as if asleep on a bed of gentle waves. My eyes fall on the stony black peninsula, spilling out to sea in a clutch of round black rocks like tipped-out peppercorns.

An infinity pool gives the impression of trickling its contents onto the ocean below, wrapping around a curved deck seating area that juts out directly over the cliff.

"I think my jaw just dropped open all by itself," I tell Georgia. She manages a little smile.

"The Tower Suite is actually a bank of interconnected suites," she explains. "Elysium always brought out Dad's overprotective side." She looks sad. "He didn't want us girls sleeping down in the beach cabanas."

"Isn't it stunning?" Ophelia says, pleased. "We modernized, but…you can't improve on that view."

A hummingbird flutters in and out again. Adrianna and Silky arrive as we're admiring the panorama.

"Is the waitstaff not here yet?" Adrianna looks around, bemused. "Georgia, can you call them?" Her sister obligingly lifts the Tower Suite phone. "Ophelia, could you…maybe show us the pâtisserie video while we're waiting?"

I chew my lip as Ophelia locates a channel on the TV. We watch dutifully as *Sugar Room* flashes on-screen.

"This is live from New York," explains Adrianna. "The sugar room where they create, like, a hundred thousand candy flowers for my cake. Isn't it cool?"

We dutifully watch the TV. The camera shows a huge commercial kitchen filled with sugar flowers. Rows of confectioners busily shape petals or hand-paint saturated shades onto sugar orchids. My stomach rumbles treacherously.

I glance at Georgia. Her face is taut with stress. She holds the receiver to her chest.

"The staff can't seem to get in," she tells Adrianna. "The security. It's set only to recognize your fingerprint."

Please, I beg silently, *please let the cake arrive.*

Adrianna rolls her eyes and walks nonchalantly to a set of double doors in the wall. I glance at the other bridesmaids. None of them look the slightest bit concerned that the cake is delayed.

Lifting a glossy-nailed finger, Adrianna taps a button. The door beeps, and an electronic lock whirs.

To my huge relief, it opens, and a line of gold-liveried waitstaff enters the room, each holding a plate with four tiny little mouthfuls of cake. They hand them out to the assembled girls.

Expectations of the sugar hit flood my mouth. I'm so faint with hunger, I'm honestly not sure I could stand another moment.

"These look so good," I gush at the waiter, who looks slightly disconcerted at my sincerity. I am so hungry I cram the first slice fully into my mouth, barely pausing to chew. It's apple cake with toffee caramel frosting, so creamy and soft, it's like eating clouds.

It's only when I look up that I realize all the other bridesmaids are looking at me with shocked expressions. A second wave of waiters are handing out dainty golden forks.

"Sorry." I wipe cake crumbs and take a fork. All eyes seem to now be on Adrianna, and I watch as the forks stand poised in unison.

With a regal nod, Adrianna takes the smallest fraction of food and tucks it delicately into her mouth. The girls do the same. I swallow the cake in my mouth with difficulty.

"Isn't that *divine*?" beams Adrianna, handing her plate to the nearest waiter. The other girls are doing the same.

I quickly fork two more pieces of cake into my mouth as the waiter comes by.

"Now, the big moment," says Adrianna. "A sneak preview of the cake before the big day."

Staff move to open a discreet set of double doors, completely hidden in the paneling. I guess these must lead to the interconnected suites Georgia mentioned earlier.

Adrianna spins on a diamanté heel, throwing her arms open, ready to showcase the masterpiece.

I'm tucked behind Petra's tall frame, so for a moment, I don't see it, only hear gasps. It takes me a few seconds to realize they are not gasps of delight.

As I step from behind the crush of girls, Adrianna starts screaming.

She spins back, her face a mixture of anguish, terror, and naked fury.

"Who did this?" she demands, teeth gritted. Her voice lowers to an animal growl. "Who *did* this?"

I crane my neck to see what is behind her. A wheeled golden trolley holds the spectacular ruin of Adrianna Kensington's wedding cake.

CHAPTER FORTY-FOUR

HOLLY

There is dead silence in the Tower Suite as we all take in the ruin of the cake. It's a huge five-tiered structure, almost as tall as the bride, finished in white frosting and a floristry of white sugar blooms. Or at least that was how it was designed to look.

Someone has taken a large knife to every part of the cake, hacking and cutting in what could only have been a frenzy. The perfect frosting is gouged in ugly lacerations, exposing naked cake innards in about a hundred wounded fissures. Sugar paste flowers are scattered like fallen blossoms on the cake board. Words are cut deeply into the bottom layer with the straight blade of a knife: *Trinity Is Coming*.

Petra seems to jerk suddenly to life. She raises her camera and snaps a picture, but her heart doesn't seem quite in it.

Georgia's usually reserved expression is furious. "Petra," she hisses. "Not *now*."

Adrianna is blinking rapidly. She turns to Georgia. "Get Mark on the phone," she says. "I want him here by tomorrow. If this is someone's idea of a prank—" She stops.

From the corner of my eye, I see Silky, her face a picture of wide-eyed terror, begin to sway on her feet. I only just manage to grab her as she falls.

"Silky?" Adrianna steps toward us.

"I think she's sick." As I take her weight, Silky rocks back in my arms, eyes fluttering up in her head.

Georgia puts a hand to the smooth dark skin of her forehead. Her brown eyes, under their arc of neatly defined lashes, track back to the ruined cake.

"Probably too much Valium on the plane," she decides. "Let's just…put her to bed in one of the cabanas. I'll see if we can get a medic."

I help Georgia move the now-staggering Silky out of the Tower Suite. Silky now seems more like a drunk, wavering on her feet and mumbling, eyes half-slitted shut.

"You think she'll be OK?" I ask Georgia as the elevator doors open at the base of the cliff.

A sandy path leads out toward the turquoise sea, meeting with a crescent-shaped wooden jetty. Six more jetties point off it like rays from a sun, each culminating in a straw-roofed wooden hut standing on stilts over the water. Ordinarily, I'd be impressed, but I'm too preoccupied with Silky and thoughts of the mutilated wedding cake.

Georgia nods. "Don't worry about Silky. She's scared of flying. Always takes a whole box of downers. She probably just mistimed it, and they're kicking in now. That's happened before. Every time we take an international flight in fact."

We walk the drooping-eyed Silky toward the beach. She sways from left to right and seems to have little sense of her surroundings.

"What do you think happened back there," I ask Georgia, "with the cake?"

Her mouth sets tight. "Maybe someone's idea of a prank," she decides finally. "Like Dri said."

"Why would they write *Trinity*?" I ask.

"Oh." Georgia stops a moment to redistribute Silky's weight. "Trinity was like...a scary story from boarding school. Kind of. The older girls would freak out the new boarders with tales about Trinity." She catches my confused expression. "Trinity was supposed to come in the night and steal your three best things."

I absorb this. "Like a ghost?" I guess the police had no reason to connect Adrianna's name for her kidnapper with her time at boarding school.

"Kind of. The way the older girls spun it, some of the younger ones took it really seriously. Silky in particular. Dri too, though she'd never admit it."

"What about you?"

Georgia hesitates, looking at me a fraction too long as if deciding whether I can be trusted. "I was never afraid of Trinity," she says finally.

Silky moans. Georgia closes her mouth and sets her eyes on the cabanas ahead.

Suddenly, Silky switches back and begins walking toward the opposite end of the beach, forcing us to switch with her.

"Silky," says Georgia, "that's the wrong way."

"No." Silky lifts her hands and points toward the jungle. "That's the school bell tower. See?"

She's looking in the direction of a large forbidding fence, pasted with signs that warn DANGER. UNDER CONSTRUCTION. KEEP OUT in both English and Spanish.

I lift my gaze to the tall jungle. Is there a building farther back, hidden by leaves and canopy? It's impossible to see with the sun behind.

"We don't use that part anymore," says Georgia, physically turning Silky around. "Come on. It's this way."

But as we turn back along the beach, Silky keeps glancing back, her red-painted lips moving, as though she is deeply disturbed by something.

CHAPTER FORTY-FIVE

HOLLY

It seems to take forever to half walk, half carry Silky down to the beach. Georgia is tireless, putting one foot ahead of the other on the sinking hot sand, taking Silky's weight.

We reach the edge of the jetty adjoining the huts. The view of turquoise waters and deep, green island curving back on itself sparkles in the setting sun.

"Cabana number three," says Georgia, clearly far too distracted to appreciate the location.

Silky's eyes are open now. She is regarding the huts like a marathon runner looks at a finish line. Strands of her black hair are plastered to her face with sweat.

Georgia and I step onto the jetty, and the warm planks squeak beneath our weight. The ocean below is a greenish blue, a few feet deep at most. It teems with fish.

"Oh shit!" Silky switches back with a sudden jolt of energy that comes from nowhere, almost knocking me into the water. "Shark!"

"They're just babies," says Georgia calmly. "This shallow part is a nursery. Just keep it together, Silky. You've caused us enough problems." She sounds exasperated and sad rather than angry.

We reach the rattan door of the hut. Georgia flashes a key card and pushes it open. The shade of the bamboo interior closes around us, and it takes a moment for my eyes to adjust from the light outside.

It's stunning, in the way that any wood hut on stilts over water would be stunning, but also basic in a charming way. There's no TV or fancy features. Just a large double bed with mosquito netting waving daintily in the breeze and an open front leading to an ocean-facing deck with a small plunge pool.

The planks beneath my feet show shining slivers of bright ocean. I can hear lapping waves.

"You should rest," I tell Silky, thinking someone should say it. "It's really hot. None of us have eaten much. Just…drink some water. Lie down."

We set Silky down on the bed and let the mosquito netting fall. Slowly, she closes her eyes. Georgia gently slips off her shoes.

Through the mesh, Silky looks like sleeping beauty. A long-lost princess from another world, waiting to be woken up.

"Trinity," Silky whispers in her sleep. "Why did Adrianna invite her?"

Georgia's mouth twists. "Let's go," she says. "She'll sleep it off."

We get to the door, and I'm overwhelmed with questions.

Georgia must realize this, because she stops and turns to me. Her usual serious expression is even more earnest.

"It's…really sad," she says with feeling. "What happened to Silky. I don't think it's good for her, being around Petra."

Her eyes glide to the sleeping Silky, whose breathing is coming in ragged and deep.

"Why not?" I ask.

"You know Silky tried to sue the school?" says Georgia. "Abuse and neglect and stuff. She even had Petra on the witness stand.

Bullying. Humiliation. They put the older girls in charge of the little ones and…stuff happened. But you can't convict a minor after the fact. Plus, no one would testify. I think it made Silky a little crazy, you know?"

"You were the same year as Silky, right?"

"Right." She nods, eyes earnest. "But my mom didn't raise me to be scared of a few mean white girls." She manages a smile. "It was lonely sometimes, being the only girl who stood up for herself. Luckily, I had Adrianna and Ophelia."

We're interrupted by a knock on the door. Georgia's confiding expression drops away to something more wary.

"Who is it?" she asks.

"I'm looking for Miss Stone?" The door opens to reveal Fitzwilliam. After all the weirdness of the last few hours, it's a huge relief to see him. His striking combination of black hair and pale-blue eyes doesn't look so aloof anymore. I notice Georgia taking in his square-jawed handsomeness with a thoughtful expression.

Fitzwilliam casts the barest glance at Georgia but does a pronounced double take at me. I remember I'm wearing the dress Georgia put me in and tug the hem self-consciously.

"Holly," he says, his eyes roaming up and down the dress distractedly, "you have a phone call from your mom. Do you want to take it in your hut?"

"My mom?" I'm half laughing. "My mom would never…" I catch his expression. "Um. Sure. Yeah. Coming right away."

Georgia checks her watch. "We'll all be dressing for dinner soon," she says. "Yours is hut number seven. Meet us on the southern beach at seven p.m. The staff can show you the way."

Fitzwilliam leads me out in silence, then turns, his blue eyes urgent.

"Mark Li called," he says. "Nice dress, by the way."

I ignore him. "Did Li call about something serious?"

"Depends how you define *serious*. He's arriving tomorrow morning, and he wants us gone before he gets here."

"But…that's not fair! He gave us twenty-four hours."

"Guess he's getting anxious about Adrianna finding out. Unless we can come up with something concrete, he wants us off the island. Staff boat leaves at ten a.m."

I press a hand to my head. "Did you manage to find my luggage?"

"Did you doubt your hardworking assistant?"

I smile. "OK. So let's check out the invitation. If Simone was setting up a shoot for *Wrongly Accused*, there'll be something forensic to uncover. Maybe we'll have something to convince Mr. Li it was worth sending us out here."

CHAPTER FORTY-SIX

ADRIANNA

In the aftermath of the cake destruction, the Tower Suite has been cleared. I'm trying to process what happened to my cake. Who could do that? What freaks me out most is how easily I could imagine any of my bridesmaids wreaking the destruction.

I'm interrupted by the sharp trill of the telephone and will my fingers to stop shaking as I lift the receiver.

"Adrianna?"

I sag in relief to hear Mark's voice. "Mark," I breathe. "Something happened. Someone destroyed my cake."

He hesitates. "Why would someone do that?"

"I don't know," I say. There's a long pause.

"Are you OK, Adrianna?"

"I…I'm frightened." He's the only person I could admit this to. "What if the police were right? What if one of my bridesmaids wants to hurt me?"

Another pause. "Come back to New York," he decides. "We'll postpone the wedding."

"We can't." I shake my head. "Two hundred guests. They're all important people."

"They'd understand." Mark's voice is as calm and reassuring

as usual. It's such a relief to have someone who doesn't do dramatics.

"It's not just the guests," I say. "Dad's entire business relies on us getting married in two days' time. Everything in the entire portfolio is bankrolling our wedding."

"Leopold never told me." Mark sounds bemused. "Why would he need a high-risk strategy like that?"

"It's just…his way. Dad loves adrenaline stakes in business. It always pays off. And the wedding will boost Elysium into the stratosphere. Every wealthy celebrity around the globe is going to want to book it."

"I meant how could he put you under that kind of pressure?"

I pause. I'd honestly never thought of it that way before. "It's just…the price of being a Kensington," I tell him. "Your life is for sale." I sigh. "On that note," I add, "Dad is getting crazy about security. He wants three bodyguards to stand in the *actual* aisle."

"You don't want that?"

"I don't think it's necessary. And no bride wants armed goons lurking on her big day. But Dad is insisting."

I'm distracted by a strange noise out on the balcony. Like a tapping sound.

I frown, lowering the phone receiver slightly.

"Adrianna?"

"I'm here." I step slowly toward the glass doors, expecting to see a bird, lizard, or some other tropical creature. But as the wider balcony comes into view, I notice something strange. Out on the terrace, by the glistening flow of the infinity pool, is a notepad. Silky's notepad.

It's open, showing vivid pencil sketches of dark and unsettling subject matter.

"Wait just one second," I tell Mark. I step out onto the balcony, retrieve the notepad, and return to the phone by the bed.

The drawing shows Kensington Manor School's ornate exterior with a line of sad thin girls shuffling toward the entrance, legs and arms bare. Girls in uniforms, their faces disturbingly overlaid by masks. Religious iconography. Three dolls, their hair cut away, blaze in a fire.

In the center is a figure. A girl. Cut into three pieces.

Trinity.

"Dri?" Mark's voice sounds like it's underwater.

I flip a page. The next is filled with unsettling images of food. Little sketches and ugly vignettes of animal insides laid on white plates with neatly set cutlery. Finely drawn veins and tubes poking from the lumps of meat. Bottles of spilled milk with floating lumps.

My stomach constricts at the memory. The teachers would force us to eat this. Part of learning ladylike manners was being bred to swallow anything on your plate without complaint.

I realize something. Someone must have gotten onto the balcony. And left this notepad for me to find. Was it before or after the cake destruction?

Lowering the phone, I scan the length of the long terrace. I blink once. Twice. I don't want it to be real, but it is.

Standing at the far end is the figure of my nightmares. A darkly cloaked person wearing a featureless white mask.

I don't quite know how the phone receiver drops from my grasp, only that it's on the floor, Mark's voice blaring tinnily across the Italian marble.

I'm screaming so loud, a flock of parrots in the jungle below takes flight as one haphazard flurry of green and red wings.

CHAPTER FORTY-SEVEN

HOLLY

As we head for my hut, I fill Fitzwilliam in on the cake destruction. "The way it was hacked to pieces," I say, "seems way meaner than just a prank."

"Agreed," he says.

"If Simone's killer is one of the bridal party, they've been close enough to Adrianna to kill her for years. Silky is the most likely suspect," I decide. "She's the florist who made the scaffold, and Simone was beaten with a scaffold pole. And from what Georgia just told me, she might be a little crazy."

"If her movies are anything to go by, she's not just a little crazy," says Fitzwilliam. "That is a dark imagination."

"Silky had a freaky-looking notepad on the airplane," I say. "Filled with drawings of schoolgirls. I'm wondering if there's something about Trinity in there."

Fitzwilliam nods. "OK, let's try to get hold of that notepad. I can ask in the staff quarters. Gain access to Silky's room or luggage maybe. The cake said, *Trinity is coming*, right? Like a threat?"

I nod. "Or a curse. Like someone doesn't want Adrianna to get married."

"If that's the killer's motive," says Fitzwilliam, "we're running out of time."

It takes me a few moments to set things up back at the cabana. The faded gold birthday invitation lies neatly on a sterilized tray, ready for examination. I carefully take equipment from my luggage, from under my driver's license, pentagram tokens, and twenty-sided Dungeons and Dragons die.

"Nice picture," Fitzwilliam murmurs, eyeing my ID. "You do Halloween parties?"

I delve into my studded backpack and remove my tweezers, ultraviolet pen, fingerprinting kit, magnifying lenses, and various swabs and collection pots. Having my familiar forensic kit in my hands replaces any anxiety with excitement.

"OK." I look close. "First observation. Someone has already fingerprinted this invitation."

"Simone?"

"That would make sense. You can see where there's fingerprint powder remaining." I point to where the dust clings to a set of little swirls and think for a moment. "If Simone got a match, the results would be on file," I say. "At her office. Could you have Ortiz look it up for us?"

He nods. "Shouldn't be a problem."

"If Simone left the powder on the invitation, it would have been for show," I say thoughtfully. "It would mean she found something worth explaining to the camera. Let's try an alternate light method," I add, flicking on my UV light. "See if there's anything more to notice about these prints."

I look closely for a few moments. "Lot of prints," I say. "But... they seem to be one set. Belonging to one person."

When I look up, Fitzwilliam seems to be watching my face closely.

"What?" I ask.

"Nothing. It's just…interesting to watch you work is all—the focus."

"Let's see what Ortiz comes back with," I tell him. "Maybe Simone got some partial prints that didn't fit Adrianna." Something else occurs to me.

"There's fingerprint access to Adrianna's bedroom," I tell Fitzwilliam. "The kidnapper would have had to override it somehow to get inside. But that never showed up on any of the police reports, did it?"

Fitzwilliam shakes his head. "It was checked," he says. "The night she was snatched."

I look at the birthday invitation thoughtfully. "Maybe someone found a way to switch fingerprints somehow." I frown, not sure what to do with this information. "Can you get Ortiz to run these prints herself? Cross-reference with what Simone put on file? Check that they belong to Adrianna and that the police records of Adrianna's prints match the ones Simone would have taken?"

"I can, but it's eight p.m. in New York. We're unlikely to get answers before tomorrow morning. Mark Li wants us gone by then."

I sigh, taking out a few bottles of reagents and a sterile pad. "I'll swab for DNA," I explain. "And use some reagents to see if there's anything chemically unusual. Drugs. Gun powder residue."

I notice a seam along the edge of the invitation that I didn't see before.

"I think…this invitation opens," I say. "The damp has sealed it together."

Using my tweezers, I carefully pry it apart. I'm right. What looked to be a single piece of card has been folded in two. The edges are degraded with water damage, but the center is unspoiled.

"Look," I breathe. "There's a birthday itinerary inside."

CHAPTER FORTY-EIGHT

ADRIANNA

I lean on the balcony of the Tower Suite, staring out to sea.

After I screamed, the masked figure vanished from sight. Within moments, Ophelia was at the door, hammering to get in. I was so worked up it took me several attempts to place my fingerprint and open the door.

Security flooded the room while I sat on the bed shaking, my arms wrapped around my legs, but they found nothing.

"Dri?"

I turn to see Georgia, practically dressed in ballet flats, navy culottes, and a cream camisole. Her anxious face is framed by a neatly styled Hermès scarf, dividing her mass of curly dark hair into a side part, falling prettily forward over her neat brows.

She puts a hand over mine. "They can't find any evidence of an intruder anywhere," she says softly, watching my eyes. "No one could have gotten in or out. We checked. Are you *sure*—"

I shake my head fiercely. "I saw someone. On the balcony. Someone wearing a cloak and a mask." I'm still breathing hard. Slow, considered breaths.

"I spoke to your therapist," says Georgia gently. "She says it's quite usual to have trauma flashbacks when faced with the same environment. And given the stress of the wedding..."

"What about the cake?" I demand. "Did I imagine that?" Feelings overwhelm me, and tears prick my eyes.

Georgia squeezes my hand. "Dri," she says finally, "is there something you're not telling me?"

I don't answer.

"The secret bar in the panic room. Sepulcrum?" She gives me a loaded look. "I saw the designs. I know it's supposed to have a gothic edge, but...what does our old school crest have to do with a luxury chill-out lounge?"

"The brief for Sepulcrum was eclectic," I say, trying to keep my tone casual. My hand is trembling. Forcibly, I will it to stop.

"Just...all those saints and stuff," she presses. "It's creepy."

"Kitsch is really in," I say, relieved that I've managed to get my voice under control now. "We're just used to seeing it a certain way because of Kensington Manor School. All the tortured martyrs." I can't trust my voice anymore, so I stop talking, looking out onto the island.

Georgia frowns. "Silky's notepad," she says. "Housekeeping took it. We need to get it back."

I glance across at her, confused.

"It wasn't just sad schoolgirls Silky drew," continues Georgia. "There was...this...cloaked figure. Exactly like the person who held you captive." She pauses, watching my face. "Dri, how would Silky know that? You only told police, right?"

My hands tighten on the rail. I can't lie to her, so I don't say anything. There's a long pause.

They all know Trinity. Silky. Petra. Ophelia.

"Would it be a good idea to fly Silky home?" suggests Georgia.

I twist to her. "You think we could?" I can't keep the relief from my voice.

"If she's sick…" Georgia's voice trails off. "I'll call housekeeping," she decides, moving to the bedside phone. "See if they can check on her."

"Have them locate the sketch pad too," I say pressing my fingertips into my forehead. "We should…destroy it. Maybe."

Georgia gives a brief, decisive nod.

It's all too much suddenly. The wedding. The bridesmaids. Trinity. *Who did that to my cake?*

I stare out over the island. The first Kensington Manor School started out here. I'm looking to where the faint outline of the old bell tower can just be seen.

Georgia's conversation with housekeeping fades into the background. It's only when she replaces the receiver that I notice the slant of shock on her face.

"What is it?" I ask. "Are you OK?"

"Silky's not in the cabana where I left her. She's vanished." She adjusts the cream strap of her camisole and pulls at the delicate strands of her gold necklaces. "You don't think she's gone looking for the old part of the island?" suggests Georgia nervously. "Where the old school building is?"

"The bell tower?" Both our eyes swing out toward the hump of jungle where a gray bell tower can just be seen through the foliage. I shake my head sharply. "Silky has no reason to go there."

"You know Simone wanted access to the bell tower too?" says Georgia quietly. "That's what she and Dad arranged. Simone wanted access to film part of the show out there. Dri…why would Simone be scoping for an episode of *Wrongly Accused* on Elysium, unless—"

"No." I say it sharply enough to make Georgia blink. "None of my bridesmaids held me captive. I would have known. And don't worry about Silky. She always shows up." I snatch a look at Georgia and then away again, out toward the ocean.

CHAPTER FORTY-NINE

HOLLY

In the cool of the cabana, we stare at the open birthday invitation. "*Canapés, cocktails,*" reads Fitzwilliam.

"I notice they don't mention dinner," I say ruefully, swiping along the paper slowly with a chemical reagent.

"There's an event at midnight," Fitzwilliam points out. "Midnight feast maybe?"

"*Truth or Dare Firepit at the Old Bell Tower,*" I read. "Sounds... ominous. Where's the old bell tower?" I ask. "I didn't see it on any maps of the island." I look closer. "The reagent is reacting with something here," I add. "It's faint but..." I fish a hand lens from my kit and adjust the focus. "It's making the shape of a number. Six..." I peer through the lens. "*Six feet under.*" I raise my gaze to Fitzwilliam. "Why would Simone write *six feet under?*"

"Sounds like the kind of thing you said she did on her show, right?" says Fitzwilliam. "Showy forensic reveal that leads to the next location."

I nod. "Highlighting some important clue to show up on camera in a forensic test. Made for good entertainment. Real evidence mixed with stagey effects."

"You think Simone wanted to draw attention to this bell tower event? Suggest it was…death related?"

"Maybe. We can assume the party guests were there at midnight, the night Adrianna was kidnapped. What time did she go missing?"

"She was last seen at three a.m.," says Fitzwilliam. "Petra Morka saw Adrianna going up the stairs to her bedroom, but no one noticed she was gone until the following morning."

"Wonder where the bell tower is," I say.

"The bridesmaids are due to attend a beach barbecue tonight at the bar. You think you might convince one of them to tell you?"

I wrinkle my nose. "I can try," I say without much conviction. "I think they know I'm not one of them."

"You should have more faith in yourself," says Fitzwilliam. "Simone did. And…maybe don't hunch your shoulders so much. It makes you look unsure of yourself."

"Thanks for the tip."

Fitzwilliam nods, looking thoughtful. "Not all the luggage has been delivered to the cabanas. If you're all down at the barbecue, I can look through it for Silky's sketchbook. Could tell us something more about this Trinity character. Maybe one of the staff can help locate it," he adds. "If they're not all busy trying to stop the bridesmaids freaking out about what to wear for tonight's event."

I roll my eyes. "What's wrong with these women? They can go two days without eating but lose their shit over some clothes?"

Fitzwilliam's face breaks into a wide smile. "Well, yes," he says. His eyes land on a large bouquet of tropical flowers on the table of my cabana.

"Here." He plucks up a white orchid and pushes it behind my ear. "Softens your hair a little," he explains.

I touch the flower uncertainly. His eyes hover over mine for slightly too long. Before I can reply, he clears his throat uncomfortably.

"You need to get to the barbecue before you're missed," he says. "I'll go hunt for Silky's sketchbook while you're eating."

We open the door to leave my cabana and see balls of fire in the middle distance, toward where the cliff meets the sea behind the house.

"I'm guessing your beach barbecue is there?" Fitzwilliam points to a bluff where torches flare. "You're hungry, right?"

"I've kind of gone beyond hunger," I tell him. "Does that mean I'm a real Kensington now?"

He smiles.

"Don't you need food?"

"I grew up in formal situations, remember? You'd be surprised at how used to being hungry that makes you. Anyway, I'm sure they have provisions for staff. Probably more than what you'll be getting."

I take in the view from the beach hut veranda. The sun has split to the barest slice of pink along the black horizon. A thumb stroke of light, throwing peachy shades on the scatter of clouds above. Darkening jungle paints black leaf shapes at the edges of a navy sky.

"I've just got to hope it's not plastic photo shoot food."

CHAPTER FIFTY

HOLLY

I'm hiking up the beach in the soft warmth of the evening air when I hear an unexpected movement from near one of the beach huts. My heart picks up as I turn in the starlight, tuning my ears against the lapping ocean for the sound.

"Holly?"

I turn to see Adrianna, backgrounded by soft night and diamond-bright stars. She looks her usual million-dollar self, the glossy brown hair blown out in soft waves and an aqua print maxi dress belted flatteringly to her curved torso. But her face is tense beneath the dewy airbrushed makeup.

"Cute flower." She nods to the bloom in my hair, and my fingers brush it self-consciously.

"Thanks." I plumb my mind for the kind of charming thing Simone might say. "You look amazing," I tell her, opting for the truth, then regretting how blunt it sounds. To my surprise, her face breaks into a wide smile.

"Thanks. I wasn't sure the blowout was OK for the beach."

It's strange to see her alone, I realize. "Where's the entourage?" I joke with a half smile. To my great surprise, she lifts a manicured nail to her mouth, then drops it quickly, as if it's a habit she's breaking herself of.

"I'm looking for Silky," she says. "Have you seen her?"

"No," I say sympathetically, since I've never seen Adrianna look so concerned. "She seemed…sick. Do you think she's OK?"

Adrianna's close-set blue eyes range my face for a moment, like she can't decide if I've said the wrong thing.

"I'm sure Silky's fine," she mutters finally. "Maybe she's already at the beach bar."

Huge flaming torches light up the edges as we take the sandy path. "When the sun's up, this is Daybreak, our detox bar," explains Adrianna. "Smoothies, raw foods, vitamin drips brought right to your hammock as you look out on the waves. Cool, huh?"

"Um. Yeah." I try to channel the appropriate response. "Very cool."

"But at night, it's where you get your aperitif cocktail before partying at Fortune House."

The intoxicating scent of barbecue hits the air. "That smells so good," I say, my mouth watering.

"They must have begun cooking the food for the photo shoot already," agrees Adrianna distractedly. Her eyes are roaming the horizon.

Among the torches, Turkish rugs and Thai cushions are laid on the cooling sand. We can just make out Ophelia in an open-backed green sequin jumpsuit and long-legged Petra in a silver dress, lounging with cocktails. Even at this distance, their body language is noticeably awkward.

"Silky's not here," says Adrianna, her voice thick with disappointment.

"Why would she go off alone?" I ask.

Adrianna's eyes flick to the flower in my hair and then down to the ring on my finger.

"You might as well know," she decides. "Silky is into drugs. She got into heroin a couple of years ago. Went to rehab, but...it didn't stick. We're kind of used to her skipping out."

"That would explain a lot." I turn this over, fitting it. "Could Silky have gone to the bell tower? I heard that part of your birthday celebrations were held there," I add in response to her surprised expression. "Thought she might be reminiscing."

"Oh." Her face tightens as if deciding what to say. "Well, I guess the older part of the island isn't really a secret," she says finally. "Margaret Kensington started the school out here. Back in the 1950s or something. An education for proper young ladies." She nods her head as if remembering it word for word. "Elysium events often have...reminders...of that heritage."

"Simone mentioned a game of Truth or Dare," I try.

"Simone?" Now Adrianna looks genuinely shocked. "Oh." She looks thoughtful. "Well, I guess. Silky was trying to get Simone to look over her court case. She never gives up." She sighs. "Silky dared me to testify. Stand up against the school. I guess that's how Simone knew about that game."

"You didn't testify?"

"Well, no. I mean I would have, but the court case was two days after my birthday party."

She waits for the meaning to sink in.

Adrianna agreed to testify against Kensington Manor School at her birthday party. Then she was kidnapped.

"Poor Silks," says Adrianna sadly. "We all let her down. It was awful. School was OK if you were strong, I guess. But Silky wasn't.

Little kids that age, they wet their pants, they get sick. They poop in places they shouldn't. And they're *all* sad and terrified. In my dorm, there was a girl who…" She hesitates. "Never mind," she mutters. "But Silky could never forget all that stuff. Some stupid therapist told her to draw it all out, and she never stopped."

Silky's sketchbook pops back into my mind. I wonder if Fitzwilliam has managed to locate it while we're all distracted with the barbecue.

I shake my head slowly, feeling suddenly grateful for my crazy mom and the colorful neighbors in our Lower East Side walk-up.

Adrianna shakes her head. "Then with what Petra did to her…" Her usual perfect mask has dropped. Her eyes are red and her mouth misshapen. But as we reach the beach bar, Adrianna's vulnerable softness drops away, and the confident society queen takes her place.

"I like to think of my life as a movie," she tells me, adjusting her hair as she takes in the stagey composition of her bridesmaids. "The rape threats, the stalkers, the fact that I need security to wait outside the bathroom when I go out in public. That's just the jeopardy the heroine needs for the audience to care, but we all know she's going to marry her Prince Charming in the end."

She produces her cell and flicks to a picture of herself holding a champagne glass aloft, head thrown back, laughing. The bridesmaids smile in the background. I'm in the shot, I realize with shock. You'd honestly think I was enjoying myself.

"This is the *real* me," continues Adrianna. "And no one can touch it."

I suddenly feel so sorry for Adrianna, I want to wrap my arms around her. Beneath the glossy facade, she's so childlike and uncertain. And as Petra's vulpine expression comes into view, I can't help but feel afraid for her.

"Who wants to hit the club?" says Adrianna in an upbeat tone. "Fortune House is open all night."

"Dri, are you sure?" Ophelia looks concerned. "You must be exhausted. And we've only just gotten the beach photo shoot set up."

For a moment, Adrianna's face flickers, and an expression of glassy-eyed fatigue registers and is gone.

"Let's just ditch it," she says. "We've got enough pictures to work. Maybe Silky is there. Besides, tonight is the only chance we have for club photography, and the sponsors need their pictures. Best we look fresh-faced."

They all stand to leave, and my anxiety rises with them. Fitzwilliam won't be expecting anyone to arrive at Fortune House so soon. If he's caught snooping…

"I'll catch up with you later," I announce. "Just remembered I need to retouch my makeup."

"She's only just realized," I hear Ophelia mutter as I head back down the beach quickly. "You need to retouch makeup?"

CHAPTER FIFTY-ONE

HOLLY

I leave the other girls to their club night, marveling at their stamina. Though I suspect I have committed some terrible faux pas by not going along too. I caught a flash of Adrianna's exhausted face before she quickly rearranged her features into "nightclub excitement."

I head for the kitchen, determined to find something to eat, but it's locked, so I go to my cabana, hoping Fitzwilliam has gotten hold of Silky's sketchbook. Maybe she'll have drawn some answers to my questions about Trinity and boarding school.

There's nothing comparable to the total pitch black of a tropical island. The hum of wildlife is deafening. Night birds, insects, and some kind of nocturnal toad determined to get in on the party. The sky above is inky, dotted with a thousand white stars. My feet feel out the comforting straight lines of the plank walkway leading to back to our offshore huts.

As I break out of the jungle, the sight of the ocean takes my breath away. It's lit up from within, spotted all across the shore with bright-blue lights. Like a starry sky from a distant beautiful planet. The warm sand is scattered with an unfamiliar species of small lizard, racing in and out of the darkening tides.

"Wow," I say softly, taking it in.

A figure steps from the dark.

On instinct, I lurch backward, nearly falling from the wooden gangplank beneath me. Strong hands grasp at my dress.

"Holly?" It's Fitzwilliam. He pulls me back to safety.

"Oh my God!" I put my hand to my heart. "You scared the life out of me."

"Sorry. I just wanted to wait until you got back so you didn't walk alone in the dark." He hesitates. "Holly, didn't your mother ever tell you not to walk around at night on an island with a murderer on the loose?"

"She didn't tell me much, actually," I admit. "My mom wasn't around growing up. She had this whole music scene going on."

"Sounds like my dad. Apart from the music." He follows my gaze out to sea. "Beautiful, right?" he says. "That star-studded effect is phosphorescence. You only see it at certain times of the year. It's the kind of thing wedding proposals are made of."

There's a sudden awkward silence that I swear doesn't come from me.

"Did you find anything out?" he asks hopefully.

I nod slowly. "Adrianna agreed to testify at a court case against Kensington Manor School on the night of her birthday party."

"Really?" He thinks for a moment. "I guess the family doesn't own the school any longer. But still...you think she would have actually done it?"

"I don't know," I say. "I guess the question is did someone believe she would?" I consider it. "And who would stand to lose if she did?" We're both thoughtful. "I take it you didn't get Silky's sketchbook?" I suggest.

He shakes his head. "There's some extra luggage waiting to be delivered, but I couldn't get to it without being seen. I'm going to try and sneak in tomorrow morning. Ortiz is going to get us the fingerprint results back then as well," he says.

"Not much time," I murmur, "if we need to leave by ten a.m. tomorrow." Disappointment sags inside me. And the terrible feeling that time is slipping away.

Fitzwilliam clears his throat and thrusts what appears to be a small cardboard box in my direction. "I…uh…got you something," he adds, completely failing to dissipate the weird mood he's created.

"Is it a five-carat diamond ring?" I suggest.

"I wouldn't propose with anything less than six. And no, it's not."

The box is warm as I take it. I can smell something chargrilled and delicious. "Is it *food*?" I ask hopefully.

"It's nothing much. Just chicken and rice." He hands me a wooden fork. "The staff meals are pretty good. Thought you'd appreciate something more than a shaved-leaf salad or whatever they were serving up on the beach."

"You're a lifesaver." I pop open the lid. "There was nothing," I tell him. "No food *at all*." I'm about to shovel an overloaded forkful into my mouth, but I catch the look in his eye and restrain myself. "You have no idea how hungry I am. These women don't eat." I swallow several smaller bites, savoring the rapidly easing pain in my stomach.

"Maybe breathe between mouthfuls," he suggests with a slightly strained expression.

"OK." I plop down on the sand. Take a demure mouthful, like I've seen Adrianna do.

"Can I ask you a personal question?"

I shrug. "Sure."

"Why did you quit working for Simone?"

I pause, forkful halfway to my mouth, hunger fighting anxiety. "I didn't like the direction she was taking the show. *Wrongly Accused* is supposed to be about justice, but the moment Leopold Kensington dangled the chance of big ratings, it was like Simone forget all about ethics and became obsessed with Adrianna. Just like the rest of the world," I add with a small amount of bitterness.

Fitzwilliam regards my expression. "Maybe it was personal in some way," he says. "For Simone."

I swallow rice with effort.

"I have another question," says Fitzwilliam. "Why are you still working as a forensic scientist?"

"What's wrong with me being a forensic scientist?" I'm relieved he's changed the subject.

"I'd expect you to be running your own company. Your own lab at least. At college, we all assumed you were going to become a forensic lawyer for one of the big law firms."

I almost choke on my rice. "You *did*?"

"You had the highest grades," he says with a slight smile. "But you never started acting the part." He eyes the ruffled dress Georgia gave me. "You could easily have gotten into one of the big law firms, but you're still working as a forensic technician with blue hair and a lip piercing, seven years after graduating."

"Yeah, well." I chew some more. "Those big firms have their entries all sewn up with people like you, all at the same country club."

"Holly," he says, "when the internships came around, I never saw you in the interview room. Did you even apply?"

I scuff sand with my foot. "It's different for you," I say, looking into my rice. "Guys like you bounce back from rejection. People like me don't." I lift my eyes to the stars. "Why did you become a cop anyway?" I ask, keen to move the conversation away from myself. "You didn't seem like the type to flunk out."

"No," he agrees. "There was an incident. At college." He sounds like he's choosing his words very carefully. "Made me realize the importance of good policing. I took some time off, then decided that maybe lawyers weren't changing the world for the good the way I thought. Decided I wanted to try and make a difference on the ground." He looks straight ahead to signal the subject is closed, and I feel a prickle of guilt. I misjudged him, I realize.

"OK, I'm done eating."

Fitzwilliam stands and proffers a hand to help me up. We head down the plank gangway over the water, and I fill him in on the way about Silky's random disappearance and addiction issues.

"Let's just get a good night's sleep," says Fitzwilliam unhappily. "I'll come by first thing."

"See you tomorrow."

After Fitzwilliam leaves, I turn out the lights and flop, fully clothed, on the luxurious, lemon-scented cotton sheets. The dredge of sand being pulled and dropped by the ocean swell sounds rhythmically outside. I imagine the graceful turns of the small sharks beneath my room, flitting in and out of the glowing shallow waters.

My mind drifts to Silky out in the dark. I can't help but imagine her lost and frightened somewhere on the island.

As the exhaustion of the day knocks me into a deep, dreamless sleep, I picture Silky alone, staring out onto a black sea under a starless sky.

CHAPTER FIFTY-TWO

PETRA

We're all trooping obediently to Adrianna's decadent new nightclub, photo faces at the ready. It's the one thing Kensington Manor School girls all seem to excel at—looking good in pictures.

Silky still isn't here, and dark thoughts are tugging at me. I hate Silky. Hate how she drags me back to such dark places. She reminds me too much of the person I was before Leopold. As we file into the nightclub in a line, I'm reminded of the last time all five of us were alone like this. Three years ago. At Adrianna's birthday.

It was midnight. We were shuffling in our masks through a torchlit jungle trail, the palm leaves cutting jagged shapes against the moonlit sky. Adrianna had decided to host a midnight event at the old bell tower just for us. We'd all received special invitations, but none of us could figure out why we were chosen.

"I don't get it," Ophelia whispered to Silky. "Why is it just us? Where are the other guests?"

Silky didn't answer. She was completely wasted, eyes rolling around her head. She kept fending away branches that weren't there.

"Some stupid game of Adrianna's," I said dismissively. But my stomach was churning.

I looked ahead to see a fire had been lit, deeper in the jungle, casting shadows against the stone wall of the bell tower. My pulse kicked up. Kensington Manor girls used to come here in their first year for their ritual ring giving. I'd heard they didn't do that anymore.

Adrianna directed us to settle around the fire on little log seats. Flames crackled.

"What's going on?" I tried to sound bored.

"Truth or Dare." Adrianna's voice came from under her mask. "Do you remember that game, Petra?"

I didn't answer.

"Someone has been sending Dri hate mail," said Georgia. "At first, we thought it was a stalker, but now we know it was one of you."

She held up the invitation we had all received. Flashy gold and made at huge expense, with a publicity campaign to match. This was back when Adrianna was finding her feet as an heiress, and her attempts to garner press attention often fell flat or got the wrong kind of attention. The invite was criticized as vulgar in every fashion magazine.

It had the word *Trinity* in the recipient box and *Bitch* scrawled across. Beside me, Silky jerked slightly.

Ophelia's voice came breathlessly. "That's awful."

"It's addressed to Trinity," said Georgia meaningfully. "Is this someone's idea of a prank or something? You might as well be honest." Her face swiveled toward me. "You were pretty mad not to get an invite, right, Petra?"

I stood up fast. "This is bullshit," I told them. "I'm not staying around for this." My log stool fell as I backed away and retreated into the jungle. No one came after me. I breathed a sigh of relief.

Stupid little girls with their stupid little games. I needed to speak with Leopold.

We'd only just gotten together, but both of us knew there was something special between us. Leopold had opened up to me. Told me how his one and only brother had gone missing at age fourteen. Got on the wrong side of some hoodlums. Leopold told me the police didn't even bother to dredge the river for his body. I knew then there was a lot more to him than he let most people know.

I stepped back into the undergrowth and took out my cell. Leopold answered on the first dial. "Hey, Petra. I miss you."

My smile widened under the mask. "I know."

He laughed. "Where are you?"

"I'm at the old bell tower. On the island."

"Oh."

I loved hearing the depth of his voice when he was thoughtful. I missed him so much, my body hurt.

"I told Adrianna not to go to that part of the island," he says. "I sank just about all my free capital into developing it, and it's still not safe," he concluded ruefully.

"Not *safe*?"

"Never mind. When are you coming home to me?"

I eyed the girls as they settled themselves. There was a rose-gold flask of some kind of cocktail being passed around.

"Tomorrow," I decided.

"I don't know why you insisted on going out there anyway."

"Proving a point, I guess. Keeping an eye on a few people." I hesitated in the dark. "I wish I hadn't. I wish I'd stayed home with you."

There was a long pause.

"Marry me," he said. "Come home and marry me."

I closed my eyes and felt tears bubble up. "I can't," I whispered.

He sighed then, and I felt like my heart was breaking.

"I'm not the kind of guy to have a mistress, Petra. You know that."

I let my gaze fall on the girls sitting around the fire.

"I told you when we got together," I replied, "I'm not the kind of girl who fits in."

CHAPTER FIFTY-THREE

HOLLY

I wake to lapping waves and loud bird calls. Fitzwilliam hasn't arrived yet. Too early, I guess.

Sliding out of bed, I shower groggily and open my wardrobe to find an entire ensemble of outfits has been hung, complete with tags matching them to what I assume are photo shoots planned for the island. My fingers hover on a cluster that read *beach picnic* with today's date.

There's a floaty kind of black dress with spaghetti straps and a sweetheart neckline, which would usually be much too girly for me, but overlapping bias-cut skirts at midcalf give it a gothic feel. After a moment's thought, I rake through a few more outfits, pillage a jungle-print scarf from another ensemble, and hold the two together. *Could work.* There's a pair of designer sandals with studs set for another day, and I pick those out too, dressing with more care than usual.

I eye myself in the mirror, surprised at how much I like the look. My blue hair forms a waving cloud in the humidity, and I pin it back with the scarf. This climate really doesn't suit me, I decide, noticing how my sleepy face is flushed with sun.

Picking out the eyeliner I always carry in my purse, I hesitate.

The subtle makeup look that Ophelia applied yesterday didn't look so terrible. I approximate the toned-down colors with my own kit. *Not bad.* I take in my reflection. Simone would certainly have approved. She always thought I hid behind my makeup. I lift a cobweb necklace from the scattered collection in my purse and opt instead for a more subtle half-moon in silver.

Still struggling to wake up, I manage to get myself a coffee from the high-tech machine and open the doors onto my deck, letting the rosy dawn cast low shadows across my room. The morning ocean is a smoky blue, deepening like a pastel wash farther out to sea.

Beneath my feet, small fish flit between the stilts. The scythe shape of a shark tail flickers in and out of sight. My eyes lift to the strata of dawn colors. I sip coffee. It's beautiful.

There's a knock at the bamboo door, and I cross the room to open it. On the other side is Fitzwilliam, looking sickeningly fresh-faced, eating some kind of tropical fruit. His thick black hair is neatly combed, pale-blue eyes shining with health, and his clear skin is somehow ruggedly bronzed after a single day in the tropics. He wears a designer-logo blue-checked buttoned shirt, cream shorts with a brown belt, and preppy deck shoes. Fitzwilliam couldn't look more at home on an island paradise if he tried.

"Nice outfit," he says. "You're really getting this couture thing."

I stifle a yawn. "Ugh! Can you come back more bleary-eyed?" I tell him. "Don't you even have jet lag?"

"Don't really get it," he says, taking a loud bite of the crimson fruit. "A morning jog tends to chase it away. I take it you're not a morning person?" He's carrying a velvet pouch, I notice. Black and luxuriously deep-textured.

"Correct. What even is that?" I eye the pouch, snatching a pack of plastic-wrapped cookies from near the coffee machine.

"Dragon fruit."

"No. That purse thing."

"Ah, *this*." He smiles. "This might be the thing to buy us more time on the island." He holds it up triumphantly. "I got up early. Managed to take a look in Silky's luggage."

I bite a cookie. "Find the notepad?"

"Maybe something better." He loosens the silken string around the neck and opens the bag. "Manacles," he says, drawing them free and letting them hang. "They're old. Antique. And...they look just like the manacles photographed in the evidence folder. After Adrianna's kidnapping. The ones she was chained to a bed with."

I stare. In real life, the manacles have an even creepier dungeon feel. Dark with age. A key is fitted in the lock, but when I turn it, nothing happens.

"Looks like the mechanism has seized shut," I tell Fitzwilliam. "They kind of remind me of the prison cells in the caves, right?" I suggest. "Old-world jail kind of vibe."

Newspaper images of Adrianna emerging gaunt and filthy, the panic room floor strewn with cut hair, spring to mind.

"There's something very sinister about how Adrianna's kidnapper used manacles from the island," I say. "Kind of suggests a power game. Or an obsession with the Kensingtons."

"Criminal profiling?" says Fitzwilliam dismissively. "It's nothing more than conjecture. Let's look at the actual evidence. The floristry scaffold. Manacles in her luggage. Even better news is we can search Silky's room now. Find the sketchbook if it's there."

I remember how fragile Silky seemed the last time I saw her. "I don't feel right about that," I say.

"She's our prime suspect," says Fitzwilliam. "And I'm NYPD, so I overrule you."

As we approach the hut Georgia and I carried Silky to yesterday, I'm struck with sudden unease.

We walk the gangplank to the rustic door. Fitzwilliam knocks a couple of times. There's no reply.

"Hello?" I call tentatively. "Silky?"

I turn to Fitzwilliam. "No answer."

He nods.

I push the door gently. "It's not locked," I say as the door opens.

There's a waft of something. Perfume and moist water. Like someone just took a shower.

"Hello?" I listen carefully. Nothing. The bed is empty and carefully made.

I scan the room. "Looks like Silky took a shower here this morning and left," I decide. My eyes alight on one of the drapes that hasn't been fully opened. Something about it strikes me as off. "You'd open all the drapes, wouldn't you?" I approach the window. Peek behind.

"What the..." I stop dead, trying to work out what I'm seeing. Fitzwilliam comes to a halt right behind me. I pull back the drape to show the bamboo wall behind.

"Oh my God," whispers Fitzwilliam. "Looks like your criminal profiling wasn't so far from the truth, Holly."

For a moment, my eyes can't compute what I'm seeing. Pictures are pasted all over the wall. Different sizes but the subject matter is all the same.

I swallow. Looks like Silky is obsessed with Adrianna Kensington.

CHAPTER FIFTY-FOUR

HOLLY

I take in the bamboo wall of the beach hut with its corkboard of images. It's…like a crazy person's lair. Adrianna Kensington. Everywhere. Small notes have been stuck beneath several pictures. A fan whirs silently above us, making her images flutter in a smiling dance.

"This is…insane," I murmur. "Silky must have been working on this while we all slept."

It's an unsettling thought. The images all seem to be showing a lot of skin—beachwear, nightclub attire.

My eyes focus on a picture of Adrianna in a bikini, her head thrown back, laughing.

The words Bitch. Mega bitch. have been scrawled over her face. A string connects to another shot. Adrianna at a bar. A man pours her a drink. More words are scrawled. Whore. Unfaithful.

My eyes drift around. Everywhere we look are more images.

"Kind of a theme going on," murmurs Fitzwilliam. "Sexualized images, wouldn't you say?"

I nod. "Social and sexual obsession." My eyes skirt over the images. "Those aren't of Adrianna," I point out. "What's *that* one?" To one corner is a cluster of shots that look like they were taken on the island. Old tumble-down buildings. A swimming pool. A stone tower. Dilapidated and covered in creepers and jungle plants.

"Where is that?" asks Fitzwilliam. "Somewhere on Elysium?"

"Looks that way," I say. "I can make out the Kensington crest on one of the buildings, but we didn't see anything that looked like that on the way in. Could be the old bell tower, right?" I point to the taller building and think some more. "When Georgia and I took Silky to her cabana, she was looking back at something in the jungle to the north of the island. Looked like the top of a stone tower. Georgia guided her away."

I walk a little closer. There's a clutch of pictures showing what looks to be a vast open pit of soft earth surrounded on all sides by jungle. It's hard to see but…

"Is that…bones?" I ask.

I turn my head, trying to understand what I'm seeing. White blurry lines in a dark pit of open soil. They're out of focus, unclear, but…is it skulls and rib cages I'm seeing?

Fitzwilliam moves nearer. "I…I think it could be," he says, his voice soft. "If it is, there are a lot of them. Like a…mass grave."

There's silence while we digest the horror of this.

Skeletal remains? On Elysium? What could it mean?

"The soil sample Simone left in her ring," I say slowly, "contained human bone. And the message on the birthday invitation: *Six feet under*. What do you want to bet this is what she wanted us to find?"

Fitzwilliam nods slowly. "Question is where is this bone pit?"

"There's some kind of building to the side," I say, "just out of the shot." I tilt my head to look. "Is that…the same gray stone Fortune House is built from?" I ask. "Next to the pit?"

"Could be," says Fitzwilliam. "Can't be Fortune House though. There's no land like this anywhere near it."

My eyes drift back around the array of images on the walls. The scrawled, hate-filled words labeling Adrianna. The blurry shots of the dark open earth with bone-like shapes in smudged white relief.

"It looks like Elysium has a secret history," I say grimly.

Fitzwilliam opens his mouth to reply when footsteps sound on the gangway outside the room. Someone is walking up to the door.

We look at each other.

Fitzwilliam grabs my arm. "Hide," he decides, pulling me out toward the deck.

We tumble outside, squinting in the morning sun twinkling on the ocean, scouting fruitlessly for places to conceal ourselves.

"There's nowhere," I whisper, taking in the little private plunge pool and deep-hued hammock.

"The sea," decides Fitzwilliam. "We can hide underneath the hut."

"I'm not a great swimmer."

"It's shallow. Waist-deep." Fitzwilliam takes my hand and pulls me toward the edge.

"There are sharks in there!"

He slides into the silty waters below. The sharks scatter. "Holly!" he hisses from down beneath me. "Hurry!"

I look desperately back at the door. The handle is moving. I close my eyes and plunge into the salty water.

Almost immediately, I hit the sandy bottom and come up spluttering. Fitzwilliam pulls me into the darkness beneath the planks that form the hut floor. They are slick with green seaweed and studded with barnacles. Even at this early hour, the water around my hips is the temperature of a warm bath.

From the gaps in between, I can see the red underside of a pair of designer wedge shoes. They walk out onto the deck where Fitzwilliam and I stood moments ago, then return to the room.

The designer undersoles pass back into the room and out again. I let out the breath I didn't realize I was holding. "Do you think that was Silky?" I say.

"Probably," says Fitzwilliam. "Maybe she forgot something. Came back for it."

Something brushes up against me in the water, and I stifle a squeal. "What is that?"

Fitzwilliam glances across. "Strange. It looks like...paper." He lifts a sopping page from the water. "There's more of them," he says. "Look. They must have drifted in on the tide."

I begin lifting them carefully. "Unreadable," I say. "Water damage."

My eyes settle in the middle distance where a thick clutch of them float as one mass. It's then I see a shape in the water, floating by the rocks.

Human proportions. Someone swimming.

But...the shape isn't moving. I squint my eyes against the sun.

A bad feeling is swirling in me, like the sharks in the water.

The shape is rippling at the edges. A cloudy border just under the water.

"Fitzwilliam," I say, "is that..."

"My God," he says. "It looks like a body."

CHAPTER FIFTY-FIVE

PETRA

The cabanas form a semicircle, their balconies overlooking the water. Which gives me a perfect vantage point to watch.

Still no sign of Silky.

Trinity. She comes at night. Takes your three best things.

I force my gaze back out to sea.

Leopold has gambled everything on Adrianna and Mark getting married this weekend. And I really do mean everything. Money. Everything about the Kensingtons revolves around it. Or doesn't. One of the last conversations I had with Simone flashes into my thoughts.

"You think I'm with Leopold for his money?" I demanded. "Surely you've figured it out by now, Simone? You did the prenup, right? Leopold has nothing but debts. Building on Elysium swallowed up every last cent. The only hope he has of his investment paying off is if Adrianna's wedding brings him a whole new set of sponsorship income and high-rolling guests."

I can still see the shock in her large eyes. Hardly anyone knows the truth about the Kensingtons.

"Leopold runs his business on smoke, mirrors, and the drugs

dealt in his nightclubs," I said. "Whenever the police get heavy, the money stops. Adrianna's the only good earner in the entire family."

I'm distracted from the memory by a movement in the ocean. Strange. There's someone in the water.

Holly and her assistant.

There's something unnatural about how they're wading instead of swimming.

My cell rings, and a chill passes through me: Max.

"I told you," I say through gritted teeth. "I didn't find out what Simone was setting up out here yet—"

"You're too late, Petra," he says. "If you want to keep yourself out of a *Titan* exclusive, I need some real dirt on Adrianna Kensington before we go to press tonight."

"They'll know I'm the leak. I'm the only photographer on the island," I say.

"Your problem." He hangs up without another word.

I massage my temples, wondering what the hell I'm going to do. I lift my gaze to Holly and her handsome assistant, far out in the water, and a possibility occurs.

I raise the camera around my neck and zoom in on his determined expression. The chiseled cheekbones. As he turns sideways, I press to take a volley of pictures, then turn the camera to assess. Then I check some pictures I took of Adrianna yesterday, far out in the water in her red bikini.

Maybe, I decide. The light could match. With a little photo editing, something could be done for the magazine.

I take some snaps, then stop. They seem to have taken hold of something in the water. It's long and...human form. As the focus of my camera adjusts, I realize what I'm seeing. I turn and race out of my cabana, heading to the beach.

CHAPTER FIFTY-SIX

ADRIANNA

We're having a light breakfast on the beach. Smoothies for the girls. Lemon water with cayenne pepper for me.

Georgia and Ophelia are giggling about something. I close my eyes. Let the sun warm my face. It's working. The wedding will go ahead.

When I open my eyes, there's somebody in the water, wading onto the beach.

Holly. Her blue hair is hanging in rat's tails. She's dragging something. Some sodden item.

"The guests are arriving today," Georgia explains. "Two hundred handpicked guests. It's going to be…kind of chaos." She looks sad. "I've been changing the table plan since six this morning. I cannot figure out how to get Dad at a table without at least one person who is afraid of him."

I lower my large glasses, noticing Georgia do the same.

"What *is* she doing?" mutters Georgia. "Is that…an air mattress?"

"She's fully clothed," I murmur. "That dress and scarf ensemble is actually a good combination if she hadn't gotten it soaking wet." I take in Holly's rounded limbs and the soft curve of her belly under her soaked clothing. It looks cute, I guess, from a certain perspective. But...why did she jump in fully clothed?

Behind us, I hear a patter of footsteps and turn to see Petra running full speed toward us.

I turn back to the sea. Holly is close enough to make out her expression now. The sea-green eyes wide with shock beneath their skinny brows.

"Oh Jesus!" Bile rises in my throat.

Someone gasps in horror. I think it's Georgia.

Holly is dragging in Silky's battered body.

CHAPTER FIFTY-SEVEN

HOLLY

The beach is a chaos of shocked female faces. Adrianna is making a series of calls on her cell. Petra is standing a little apart. Georgia and Ophelia are to the side, heads resting against each other. I'll say one thing for Kensington Manor School girls: they sure can deal with shock. Not a single one has reacted in the hysterical way many people do when dead bodies are involved.

Fitzwilliam and I kneel quietly by Silky's body. I gently set down the stack of sopping-wet pages we found floating near her.

"Looks like a heroin overdose," I tell him quietly. "Pink-tinged pulmonary secretions around the mouth associated with lung failure. The other injuries could be grazes from her body being washed out to sea and snagged on rocks. We'd need a full forensic examination to be sure though." I'm thinking of Simone's body and can see in Fitzwilliam's face that he's doing the same.

He looks thoughtful, and I realize he must be wrestling with his instinct to be a cop. If this is a murder, he is first at the scene. He should be taking notes and interviewing witnesses. If it's an overdose, then Simone's murder is still the priority, and we shouldn't blow our cover.

"Dad. *Dad*, listen." Adrianna's voice dials up, loud enough for us all to hear. "Forget about the sponsorship. Something happened. Silky's dead."

We don't hear the second part of the call, but we do see Adrianna's face grow gradually less tense and more grief-stricken as the conversation progresses.

She ends the call and looks to Georgia.

"Dad is contacting the Colombian police," she says. "They'll be here in under two hours."

"Why would we call the police?" asks Georgia. "We all know how she died. It's only a miracle she didn't overdose sooner."

Ophelia's amber eyes widen in shock.

"Well, it's *true*," says Georgia, not quite meeting anyone's eyes. "We all knew Adrianna was carrying Silky. For years. And she got nothing but drama. Silky's drug addiction was just one more dirty secret the school forced us to carry. I'm sick of it."

"Quiet! All of you," snaps Petra, her long fingers pushed up to her angular temples, raking fists of platinum-blond hair.

"You don't get to tell us off anymore," says Ophelia, her voice shaky, tears rolling down her freckled cheeks. "We all know you drove her to it. Silky would still be alive if it wasn't for what you did to her."

"There's no need for that," snaps Georgia.

I see Petra glance at her, grateful.

"There's no point turning on each other," says Georgia, running her hands behind the back of her neck. "We need to stay calm. Fine metal, remember?"

They all exchange a long, loaded glance.

"Fine metal," agrees Petra, her face troubled. "Great heat."

CHAPTER FIFTY-EIGHT

ADRIANNA

The plan for breakfast and lunch photo shoots was replaced with a waiting game. Silky's body was removed, and finally, in the early afternoon, initial reports were filed.

But we all knew how Silky died hours before the official verdict came in.

Overdose.

Silky had gone to one of the remote beaches on the island and injected her final shot of heroin. The autopsy—completed at breakneck speed by a Colombian police force with a point to prove—showed that her body forgot how to breathe. She lost consciousness and died of a lack of oxygen. Sometime after, the tide came in and floated her body out to sea, where it snagged on the rocks where Holly found her.

That's what the police say happened. That's what makes sense.

What doesn't make sense is that in the resulting mayhem and calls for urgent online meetings with the various sponsors, I find myself walking out to the beach where Silky took her final breath.

Thoughts and memories are pooling in my head.

I stand on the warm sand and angle my cell phone camera

toward my sapphire eyes, bright and clear, framed by the famous tumble of chestnut curls.

I try a few expressions. Devastated.

Sad and reflective.

Defiant in the face of tragedy.

I put a flattering filter over the image of my sad face and stare at the perfect girl on the screen. The pretty picture no one can hurt. Sending yourself into pieces to survive. My therapist has tried to cure me of it, but old habits die hard.

A sound from the nearby jungle startles me. I stifle the instinct to turn and look. Years of paparazzi trying to goad me into ugly expressions has given me excellent self-control in this regard.

Is someone in the bushes watching me?

An incoming call shatters the image on my cell, sending my disordered nerves in all directions.

"Mark?" I click to answer.

"Your father and I have landed. Leopold is on the runway making calls to the media. I'm headed to the house," he says, direct as ever.

A million thoughts explode in my mind. The arrival of the groom should be a big moment.

"Leopold thinks we should get all the bridesmaids together," Mark is saying. "Make an announcement about staying strong. Leave no doubt the wedding is going ahead."

"Mark," I say, my voice tight in my throat, "I've been thinking. Maybe we should postpone the wedding."

But as I turn to head back to the house, I see something written in the sand in the middle distance. Something that wasn't there before. I was right.

Someone is nearby. Watching. Following.

Mark starts talking, but the words blur into white noise, like I've dipped underwater.

Gouged deep into the sand, in the same ugly writing as was on my cake, is a message:

1,2,3, You're Next

Trinity

CHAPTER FIFTY-NINE

HOLLY

It's several hours later when Fitzwilliam meets me in the enormous catering kitchens, sweating over the sous vide machine. The large vacuum packer is used in high-end kitchens to slow cook, but I've repurposed it for forensic use. I'm processing the papers we found floating near Silky's body in a way I'm hoping will yield results.

"I tried to get a call to Ortiz," he says. "No luck yet."

He has swapped his usual deck shoes for sports sneakers that appear to be new out of the box, and he wears pressed tan shorts and a deep navy T-shirt that fits around his muscular biceps in a way the designer would be delighted by. I can see how the nickname GQ stuck.

"Any word on the autopsy?" I ask.

Fitzwilliam watches as I feed a vacuum plastic pocket into the machine, frowning as if deciding not to attempt to fathom my strange behavior.

He nods. "Only what I heard in the staff quarters. The conclusion is Silky's death was a heroin overdose. Accidental or suicide. No suggestion anyone forcibly injected her, and the drugs she was injecting were very pure."

I nod, pressing another button on the machine. "Sounds right.

I took a good look. Aside from the mouth secretions, there was no abdominal distension or purpling of the skin consistent with drowning." I glance up.

"You seem very sure."

"None of this is my personal opinion. I'm just a translator for data. But...when you see a lot of the same data, it builds a certain picture. And I've seen more than my fair share of overdoses, even before I began work as a forensic." I feed another page through the vacuum packer.

"You have?" Fitzwilliam's pale-blue eyes seem to be struggling with this notion.

"I grew up in a bohemian squat, which is a nice way of saying *opium den*. Silky looked like every other heroin overdose I've seen." I press the vacuum packer button. "But that doesn't mean I don't think Silky was murdered. My hunch is she somehow got close to what Simone meant to film out here. Or someone thought she did. That's what I'm investigating."

"Which is why you came to the kitchens to... What are you doing, by the way?"

I pause to wipe sweat with the back of my hand, noticing he eyes the gesture uncomfortably.

"The documents we found floating in the water near Silky's body. The most likely scenario would be if she was holding them when she was washed out by the tide. They were completely illegible," I conclude proudly. "But take a look." I hold up one of the vacuum-packed envelopes to display a document inside.

"Luckily for us, this is a state-of-the-art catering facility," I explain. "First, I put them in the blast chiller. That took a while," I add. "It only fits seven pages at once. Then I made use of their sous vide machine. That's basically a vacuum packer with heat.

"It expels the frozen water out of the documents as vapor while retaining the print. It's not as good as using the proper equipment, but you can read a lot more than when we first found them."

I glance up, and to my surprise, Fitzwilliam is staring at me with a wide grin.

"Holly Stone," he says, "you're a genius."

"Thanks." I give him a confused smile in return. "I'm just using well-documented forensic processes," I add. "Really, you should thank Mary Louisa Willard."

"Who?"

"She's the first forensic to pioneer… Never mind." I step back from the sous vide machine. "So what do you think?" I ask Fitzwilliam as he leafs through the papers, sealed in their flat plastic. "It looks to me like the transcript from a court case."

"Right." He frowns, turning them. "Or a legal file maybe."

"I've already read a few of the more legible pages," I explain. "It seems to be a printout of the entire court case between Silky and Kensington Manor School."

"Why would Silky have that?"

"I don't know. But from the parts I read, it's an unsettling account of neglect and a culture of institutional bullying."

"But she lost in court, right?"

"Yeah." I sift through plastic pages and lift one. "This is Silky's statement," I explain, reading. "She says: *We lived in fear of the older girls coming. There was no supervision. They did what they wanted to us.*"

Fitzwilliam visibly shudders. "Any mention of Trinity?"

I nod. "Seems like Trinity was…a character, kind of. More like a legend, maybe. Trinity would come and snatch you in the night if you didn't behave. Take your three best things. Cut you into three pieces. But…Trinity was just a story. When the defense asked Silky outright about physical abuse, her answers were bizarre. She talked on and on about a particular piece of graffiti on the wall. Behind one of the beds. Something that had been there since the school began."

"Graffiti? How can that be a case for neglect or abuse?"

"The jury agreed. But in Silky's mind, the school had failed in a duty of care not having this particular wall scrubbed clean. There was a picture on it that scared all the girls, apparently."

"What kind of picture?"

"I don't know. There's a bunch of documents that seem to pertain to it," I add. "They're just coming out of the vacuum packer now."

"That's a statement I never thought I'd hear on a professional scene."

"We're not on a professional scene," I remind him, pulling a document free and turning to look at it. "That's why we're getting results so fast."

"Very funny." But there's a softness to his blue eyes I hadn't seen before.

My gaze drops down to the page that has just emerged. An image with some writing beside it.

"This is…unexpected," I say, reading the text quickly. The court documents depict strangely familiar graffiti, deeply etched into a wall.

Fitzwilliam peers over my shoulder. "I don't get it," he says finally. "Silky's court case took place before Adrianna's kidnapping, right?"

"Right." I nod firmly. "A few weeks before."

"Then why would there be an artist's impression of Adrianna's kidnapper in Silky's court files?"

"It isn't an artist's impression of the kidnapper," I say. "This figure was drawn on the school dormitory wall." I look closer. "Part of Silky's court case was that it was never removed. The school left it up to scare the girls into behaving or something. Look."

Underneath the graffiti image in tiny writing are three scratchy words:

TRINITY IS COMING.

CHAPTER SIXTY

ADRIANNA

When I arrive back at Fortune House, Georgia almost falls over as she rushes to greet me. The silk scarf holding her curls from her face is slightly askew.

"Where have you *been*?" she demands.

"I was on the beach," I say. "Georgia, do you know where Petra and Ophelia were just now? Because there was writing in the sand." I'm caught between not wanting to scare her and ensuring she takes the threat in the sand seriously.

"Dri," says Georgia, "there's been some news—"

We're interrupted by a voice from the stairs. "I came as fast as I could."

"Mark!" I rush toward him, momentarily forgetting the frightening message in the sand. I press my cheek against his chest. I flick my eyes to Georgia, but for once, she doesn't pick up on the cue to leave.

"Mark," Georgia interrupts, "did you check your social media?"

I feel a lurch in my stomach. In the Kensington family, that statement is loaded to say the least.

"What is she talking about?" I glance up at Mark's face, hoping his expression will rescue the moment. It doesn't.

"She doesn't know?" he asks Georgia, dumbfounded.

"Dri." She squeezes my hand. "A video of Simone's death was uploaded onto social media last night. They found the killer."

I'm settled over Mark's laptop with Georgia. I grip her hand tightly. Mark's finger hovers over the button to play Silky's late-night upload.

"It's got half a million shares now," he says grimly. "You're sure you want to see it?"

"I want to see it." I feel as though my eyes are glued to the screen. It holds a frozen shot of the Plaza ceiling, instantly recognizable by its famous cornicing. As the video rolls into motion, a wide-eyed face comes into shot.

Silky. A smear of blood on her cheek. Her dark eyes roll to the camera.

"I did it," she whispers. "I killed Simone." Her face crumples. "It was an *accident*."

The camera goes black. We all sit in silence for a moment.

"The video is time-stamped the night of the murder," explains Mark. "Police verified it."

"Why would Silky upload this?" I whisper. My eyes track to the comments below, which already total 10K and are multiplying before my eyes. "Can we… Is there any way to take it down?"

"I'm sure the police are working on it," says Mark. "But that won't stop people from seeing it. It hit three million views already."

"But why?" I demand. "*Why* would Silky kill Simone? Why would she do that to Simone's body?"

"Why would she say it was an accident?" asks Mark. "You don't accidentally bludgeon someone with a pole."

"Silky was a little crazy," says Georgia. "Maybe it was…some kind of unhinged reaction. Her art was always a manifestation of inner trauma."

"I guess...she just overloaded," I say finally, wondering why the words aren't matching my emotions.

Mark folds his arms around me, and I allow myself one last blissful moment of safety. Because I'm certain of what must be coming.

"I don't blame you if you want to call off the wedding," I say sadly, my eyes searching his face. "My life is crazy. *Crazy*."

"Why would I call the wedding off?" He shakes his head. "I love you, Adrianna. It's sad about Silky, but this is also good news. Simone's killer has been exposed. You can have the wedding you always wanted. No security guards lurking in the aisle."

I lower my voice. "You really still want to go ahead with the wedding?"

"You didn't think I would?"

I shake my head slowly. "No," I admit. "I figured..."

Mark takes both my hands in his. "Do you remember what you told me when I proposed?"

I give him a small smile. "I wanted to know if you really knew what you were asking."

"Right." He nods sagely. "Then you told me what it means to marry Adrianna Kensington. You said I was going to somehow have to manage to live with fear. The knowledge my wife might be kidnapped if she goes for a walk. The fact that if we have children, we'll need a security detail to accompany them to school. The nanny might secretly sell pictures of our babies." He takes a breath. "Remember what I said?"

I smile. "You said, 'I do.'"

"Exactly," he says, still smiling. "And I'm a businessman, remember? I'm used to dealing with high-risk companies."

"I love you," I tell him, taking a breath and trying to push back the tears.

Then I catch Georgia's expression out of the corner of my eye, and reality crashes in. This wedding is far bigger than Mark and me. Georgia knows more than I do what this wedding is worth to the family fortunes.

"It's OK to cry, Dri," says Georgia, a strange look on her face.

"No, it isn't," I tell her wanly. "We have a photo shoot for the sponsor in half an hour."

Georgia's eyes switch to mine, stricken.

"Dri, the fashion sponsor canceled," she says quietly. "Silky's confession—it's too strong for their brand."

"*What?*" The word rings out like a gunshot in the luxe dining room.

CHAPTER SIXTY-ONE

HOLLY

Having pored over the recovered court documents, Fitzwilliam and I have circled back to the depiction of the graffiti on the dormitory wall. It depicts an otherworldly figure, a ghost or a ghoul. I can't help but draw back slightly at the unsettling image.

"Adrianna Kensington's kidnapper styled themselves based on graffiti drawn on the school dormitory wall?" I confirm.

"More than styled themselves," he says, eyeing the court document. It's a sad hunched figure, etched in black pen. "Black cloak enclosing the shape of the body and fitting all the way to the neck. It's an exact copy."

My eyes land again on the scratchy words under the image.

"*Trinity is coming*," I say. "And now Silky is dead."

"Maybe Silky went looking for the bell tower," says Fitzwilliam thoughtfully. "Discovered something she wasn't meant to."

"When we found Silky's body, I noticed there was a lot of sand in her hair that hadn't washed out in the ocean," I say. "Sand grains are hugely varied. It's incredibly interesting, actually. You could make an entire study…" I notice the glassy cast to his eyes. "In any case," I say, "flatter grains of sand tend to adhere very well to skin and particularly hair. Under a microscope, you can see how they almost hook under the overlapping layers of the hair cuticle."

"Holly," says Fitzwilliam in a tired voice. "What's your point?"

"Grains of sand shaped like that have usually been subject to a high degree of water movement. I could maybe narrow it down to the beach she died on. Assuming Silky went looking for that bell tower the night she died, we could track it that way."

"Or," says Fitzwilliam, "there's a large fenced-off area that reads, DANGER, UNDER CONSTRUCTION, with a tall building just visible through the top of the jungle canopy. Do you think that might be an easier place to start?"

I tuck strands of blue hair behind my ears, thinking this through. "Right," I concede. "That could also work."

"Good old-fashioned sleuthing," he says smugly. "Not a spectometer in sight."

"It's called a spec*tro*meter." I think for a moment. "On the airplane, Silky mentioned the original schoolhouse was on the island. Schools have bell towers, right?"

He nods. "Particularly if it was a very religious school."

"Maybe," I say, "for all her glamour and charisma, Simone had a devout side to her."

I'm struck by a sudden memory of Simone's obsession with going to Mass, no matter what we were working on. I teased her once about a guilty conscience, and she avoided my eyes.

"*I hurt someone once,*" she said, toying with her signet ring. "*Someone younger than me who didn't deserve it. You could say that mentoring you is part of my making penance.*"

"Nice to know your interest in me is so personal," I quipped.

Her face lit up in a warm smile. "*Of course it's personal.*"

Fitzwilliam's voice breaks into my thoughts. "Kensington

security is all over the island. Not nice guys from what I overheard in the staff quarters. We need to get onto the jungle path unseen."

He stands, making for the door, and as he does, something around his midriff starts vibrating violently.

"What is that?" I ask. "Some tech fitness device?"

"It's...my pager." Fitzwilliam frowns. "But it shouldn't work out here. It only picks up radio frequency." His eyes drift to the ocean. "Maybe...there's a boat with a mast in the vicinity."

Bemused, he lifts it and begins scrolling.

"You have about a hundred messages from Detective Ortiz," I say.

"I think...she's been sending them for hours. They're all arriving now," he explains. "Perhaps some pirate radio out to sea is in the right position to send a signal." His dark eyebrows rise. "OK. Ortiz got a few things back."

"The fingerprints from Adrianna's birthday invitation?" I suggest hopefully.

He nods. "Adrianna's. Like you said. Simone's report and Ortiz both confirmed. No mistakes."

"Really?" Disappointment mixes with confusion. "Why would Simone showcase the fingerprints like that unless there was something TV-worthy about them?" I think some more. "The Tower Suite has fingerprint access," I say. "Do you think that's significant? Adrianna was snatched from that room, right?"

"Said she went to bed alone there," confirms Fitzwilliam. "Was drugged and woke up in the panic room." He glances at his page. "Ortiz got something else too. Forensics on the scaffold found at the scene."

"What about it?"

"Blood was found on more than one pole."

"Show me." I take the pager. My lips move silently as I scan the text. "Blood on four poles… Distribution consistent with contact rather than spatter…" I look up at Fitzwilliam. "The way the blood was distributed, police seem to think it suggests four murder weapons. It seems to suggest…four people all administering blows to Simone at the same time."

Fitzwilliam takes the pager back. "Ortiz thinks more than one bridesmaid attacked Simone?"

"The injuries on the forensic report…that wouldn't make sense," I say. "The bruising on Simone's body was extremely consistent. It would fit with one person making very calculated blows. But different people? There's no way they would land blows with equal force."

The pager beeps again. Fitzwilliam frowns.

"What's happening?" A coil of anxiety is spreading slowly around my stomach.

"This isn't good. Mark Li didn't agree to the deadline extension. He pulled his permission for us to be on the island. And…it sounds like he's just landed."

"Which means?"

"Ortiz wants us on the next staff boat."

My mind trips to the mysterious bell tower hidden in the jungle. "How long does that give us?"

"Ten minutes." He shakes his head. "I'm sorry, Holly. We've run out of time."

CHAPTER SIXTY-TWO

ADRIANNA

Georgia and I have arranged an emergency meeting in the dining room at the main house while Mark freshens up from the flight. It's a strange backdrop for a family crisis. A perfectly laid table of fake food and a picture window with a view out across the island. Storm clouds are on the horizon, and the tropical heat is turning.

Palm trees dance with the heightening wind.

Since I got the news of Silky's social media post, I've been numb. It doesn't feel real. I guess this is what shock feels like.

"We can fix the flowers, right?" I confirm. "Without Silky."

Georgia's forehead crinkles. "Of course we can," she says. "Silky was always just the name we attached. I never expected her to manage the execution in any meaningful way. But…you're really sure this is what you want? A big announcement that the wedding is still on?"

I shake my long chestnut hair and fix a smile on my face. "Mark and I are *relieved*. Simone's killer has been exposed. I'm safe…"

The door bangs open, and Dad enters, looking tired and hot, without his usual security entourage. Petra has the decency to stay away for once, I notice.

"I came as soon as I could," he says. "How are you doing?"

It's the first time I've heard anything like sympathy in Dad's tone. He moves closer and kisses me on both cheeks, then moves to kiss Georgia.

"The sponsor pulling out is bad news," he says, instantly reverting to business. "But we can handle it. I'll call the drinks brand," he decides. "Harvey owes me a favor. They can take the main slot."

"Dad," says Georgia. "Do you not think this is too much stress for Dri?" Her eyes scoot back and forth between us. "Shouldn't we call it off?"

"And leave two hundred highly influential guests stranded on the tarmac at Bogotá?" I demand. "The business would never survive it."

Dad's face falls. "Adrianna," he says, "we can find a way…"

"With one sponsor already gone? I've seen the figures," I tell him shortly. "And in any case, I *love* Mark." I close my eyes. "This is *good* news. The killer has been caught. Why wouldn't we go ahead? We can stage a victorious family photo shoot on the balcony."

Georgia cradles her head briefly in her manicured fingers. "Dri, you always do this!"

"Do what?"

"You have this twisted idea that as long as your life looks good in pictures, everything is fine. Real life isn't a TV show. You can't just face your demons and they vanish like smoke. Even if the pictures make it look that way."

We're interrupted by Mark entering the dining room. He looks immaculate as always, clean-shaven, in a geometric print shirt and pressed linen shorts.

"Are we ready to assemble the bridesmaids?" He looks around the room.

I cross the carpet to hold his hand, comforted as always to be around his cool, calm demeanor. "Yes," I say with a nod. "Georgia, can you ask Petra, Ophelia, and Holly to come in here?"

"Holly?" Mark's dark brows dance with anxiety.

I latch on to it immediately. Something's wrong.

"Mark," I say carefully. "Is there something you're not telling us about Holly?"

CHAPTER SIXTY-THREE

HOLLY

Fitzwilliam has maneuvered us both out of the labyrinthine staff quarters and onto the grounds of Fortune House.

More messages have arrived from Ortiz, detailing Silky's social media confession. I don't know what to make of it.

"I just can't see that fitting," I tell Fitzwilliam. "Silky killed Simone? Why?"

"That isn't the point," he says. "Our cover could be blown at any moment. With all the heightened feelings and armed security, that could place you in serious jeopardy, and Ortiz won't risk that. Not after Simone's killer has been identified."

"What about the person who kidnapped Adrianna three years ago? Is that Silky too?"

"It would all fit, right?" says Fitzwilliam. "Just like you said. Someone sexually and socially obsessed with Adrianna."

"And if it doesn't fit?"

"Then the kidnapping was never our case," he points out. "It's the jurisdiction of the Colombian police. Our job was to find Simone's killer, and that's been done."

I'm shaking my head. "It just doesn't feel right," I say. "Like, how could Silky have uploaded a video when she doesn't have her phone?"

"Silky went missing yesterday late afternoon. She probably snuck back to the airport and retrieved her phone from wherever they were holding it."

"Why would Silky do that to Simone's body?" I hold my hands out in frustration. "Cut her hair? Arrange her so ghoulishly?"

"Cover-up," says Fitzwilliam. "Silky's trying to throw police off the scent."

"That wouldn't fit with the whole profile," I point out. "Adrianna's kidnapper was all about power games. I can't picture Silky dragging a corpse into the box either. Then sneaking into the ballroom in the early hours...she just didn't seem organized enough for that."

"She was organized enough to construct an entire creepy pin chart dedicated to semiclad pictures of Adrianna Kensington," Fitzwilliam points out. "And you'd be amazed what addicts are capable of."

I sigh. None of this feels right. "What about the bone pit and bell tower?" I say. "We can't just give up on that, right? I think Simone wanted to lead us to uncovering something out here."

Fitzwilliam sighs. "We're off the case, Holly. It sucks sometimes, but I have to follow orders."

I ball my fists and close my eyes. When I open them again, Fitzwilliam's face is filled with concern.

"Look," I say. "You're right, OK? About college. I didn't have the guts to try out being a forensic lawyer. Harvard was filled with people like you, and it scared the shit out of me. But this is my chance to prove Simone's faith in me wasn't misguided. I'm the only forensic out on this island. We know Simone found something important." I take a breath. "She was my *friend*."

Fitzwilliam regards me levelly. "Holly, this isn't the way," he says. "I admire your determination, but breaking the rules and disregarding protocol isn't the way to do it."

"That's your world," I tell him. "Not mine. People like me have to break the rules to get somewhere."

Fitzwilliam shakes his head. "Ortiz has closed the case. There's a boat off the island now. I need to be on it."

"Then go," I say evenly, not wanting to admit how much this hurts me. "I'm going to find out what Simone wanted to expose."

CHAPTER SIXTY-FOUR

HOLLY

I make it out to be no more than a ten-minute walk to the dilapidated buildings I saw from the airplane, but the minute the jungle closes around me, the muggy heat seems to add lead weights to my ankles. The trail is soft underfoot, littered with creeper roots and glossy oval leaves. Insects flit around. I bat them away, feeling sweat prickle my hairline.

"I'll bet Adrianna Kensington has an outfit for this," I mutter, trying to quell the rising anxiety of exploring the family island alone.

"Holly! Wait up!" I turn around to see Fitzwilliam jogging toward me, black hair in its usual tidy shape and the barest sheen of sweat on his clear skin.

Much as I hate to admit it, relief floods through me. It must show on my face, because Fitzwilliam's angular jaw breaks into a smile.

"Don't tell me you've decided to break the law?" I ask.

"Ortiz and I get along pretty good. She might pretend she didn't see if we get caught," he says. "Besides, you'll probably need help getting in. There'll be security." He pauses, taking in my outfit. I changed from the sopping-wet dress I pulled Silky out of the ocean with and put together an outfit from my new designer closet. "You could probably pass as a guest though," he adds.

"I think I'm getting the hang of putting up with discomfort for fashion." I shield my eyes. "What do you think is on the other side of the 'keep out' sign?"

"Something the Kensingtons don't want us to see," he suggests.

"You should be a detective," I say dryly as we start walking. "Speaking of which, what's your take on Adrianna and Mark going ahead with the wedding? I don't understand why she and Mark don't call the whole wedding off. Marry quietly somewhere."

"She's got a lot of responsibility on her shoulders," says Fitzwilliam. "Probably doesn't want to let people down." Something about the way he says it suggests he knows more about this than most.

"You're from a wealthy family, right? At college, I assumed you were a privately educated trust-fund brat."

He laughs. "Not all wealthy families are like the Kensingtons. But yes, I guess you could say that. Anyway, all I'm saying is it works both ways. You grow up with money and a lot of privilege, but you also have a lot of not-so-good stuff. Like it or not, you're part of this family that someone made a big success of. The pressure is there not to mess that up. You're basically born with a gratitude debt."

I'm quiet, turning this over as we hike through the jungle.

"Let's pick up the pace," says Fitzwilliam, oblivious to the fact that I am at aerobic full capacity. "Now that Mark Li has landed, someone will realize who you are sooner or later. We need to find this grave or whatever it is before they catch us."

CHAPTER SIXTY-FIVE

HOLLY

Fitzwilliam and I are deep into the jungle, swatting an endless cloud of bugs.

"You've been on paradise islands before, right?" I ask him, pushing a branch from my face. "Is there some technique for this?"

"You wouldn't usually trek off into the jungle," he says. "Unless you were on an early-morning nature-spotting excursion with a guide."

"Do you miss it?" I ask. "The luxury lifestyle?"

He considers. "Not so much the lifestyle, but being dropped from the world I was raised for was tiring at first. I had no idea how to act in the police locker room or on the firing range. It was like a whole language I had to learn to speak."

I consider this. "How do your parents feel about you becoming a cop?"

"My dad pretty much cut me off," he says.

"Are you serious?"

He shrugs. "Less yelling. But I get sad about it sometimes."

"Least you know your father," I decide, straightening up and leaning back to fill my lungs. "My mom's family disowned her for running away with a musician to a New York squat, and he repaid her loyalty by leaving her just after I was born."

"Sorry to hear that." His tanned forehead puckers as he sets off at a walk. "Explains your rejection issues." Fitzwilliam is striding ahead.

"What rejection issues?" I stop talking since he has come to a halt in front of me. There's a small cinder-block guard hut, almost out of sight in the jungle. It disgorges an angry-looking man wearing the security uniform of Elysium.

"Hey!" He seems unaccountably furious. "You can't come this way. Miss Kensington told all the guests not to come this way," he continues.

"Sorry," I begin, holding my hands up in a placating gesture. "We didn't—"

"Police," says Fitzwilliam in a highbrow authoritative tone I've never heard him use before. He holds out his NYPD badge. "We're here to look around following the death of Silky Eversfield."

The man's face is caught between anger and confusion. "I need to check with Miss Kensington."

"Go ahead," says Fitzwilliam. "We'll wait here."

The guard nods, turns on his heel, and vanishes inside the hut. As he does, Fitzwilliam takes two strides forward, closes the door, and snaps shut an open padlock hanging on the outside.

"Fitzwilliam…"

"I don't think that will hold him for long," he says. "And he'll call for help. If they don't realize you're loose in the jungle, they will soon. I think we should run," he adds after a moment's reflection.

We pelt off into the trees, me in an ungainly arm-flapping run, Fitzwilliam adopting the controlled jog of a man who runs in his free time.

We stick to the trail and, before long, break into a wider clearing, filled with old dilapidated buildings. I pause for a moment, hunched over, breathing hard, my blue hair falling forward.

"Wow," I say after I catch my breath. "I never heard you use that voice before... That was..." I take in more air. "Kind of scary."

"I based it on how my father used to talk to the housekeeper," says Fitzwilliam, taking in our location. "Not the nicest of men," he adds, coming to a halt where the path splits off in two directions.

"Which way?" he ponders aloud.

I take careful stock of the surrounding jungle. It only takes me a few minutes before my eyes light on a palm tree leaning hard to one side.

"This tree has been struck by something large passing by," I say. "A vehicle. Or something like it."

"Then let's go this way."

I follow him around the next corner, and buildings come into view. "What is this place?" I'm looking around.

"Looks like this was the original resort," he says. "Back when Leopold Kensington ran things. It's dated, but I guess this counted as high-end. Jungle's got it now though," he adds with a note of sadness.

"This is so weird," I say.

We come to a tiled outdoor terrace area, complete with a huge swimming pool. It's still filled with water, but the jungle has reclaimed it. Creepers grow around the edges, and underwater plants bloom on a rotting tree trunk that has fallen into the depths. Chunks of rubble at the bottom have become home to tiny swimming creatures.

I take in the overgrown frontage of a large building. I'm guessing it would have once been white, with faux-Grecian columns standing grandly either side of a large double-doored entrance. But the paint is peeling away, and jungle creepers have forked giant cracks.

I put a hand to the flaking paint on the outside. "This wasn't abandoned so long ago," I say. "In humid conditions like these, you'd expect exterior paint to be entirely degraded after a few years. Should we take a look inside?"

We approach silently, entering through the open doorway. It's cool, with a strong smell of mold and soil. What was once a roof has rained down in broken chunks onto the floor beneath our feet, leaving it open to the elements.

"Is it an old spa complex?" I suggest, taking in the crumbling decor.

The floor is studded with a carpet of tiny mosaic tiles, classical white stone columns punctuating the doorways. We pass archways leading to open pools of water. They are lined with debris and dirt from the fallen roof.

"Roman bath-style," I murmur. "Leopold Kensington?"

"I can imagine him playing the part of Nero," says Fitzwilliam. "Maybe they just let this fall to ruin when the family left after Adrianna's kidnapping."

"Why abandon it though?" I say. "Surely you'd just refurbish?"

Fitzwilliam nods. "It doesn't make sense," he agrees. "It would cost millions more to start from scratch. All the good beaches are here too. Why throw away money for no reason?"

My eyes land on a huge crack on one of the exterior walls. "Maybe some kind of underpinning issue?" I suggest. "Looks like the ground beneath might not be so stable."

A rumbling sound stops us in our tracks.

"It's coming from a little deeper in the jungle," I say.

"Sounds like construction work." Fitzwilliam nods. "Maybe they're rebuilding."

We follow the sound using the outside jungle track, passing more abandoned buildings. Suddenly, Fitzwilliam flattens himself against a wall and gestures I do the same.

"What is it?" I ask.

"Take a look." His eyes are wide. "Just make sure they don't see you."

I follow his lead, snatching a glance. It takes a moment for my brain to catch up with what my eyes are seeing.

It's a huge pit. The width and length of an apartment building. An open chasm of rich tropical soil with a thick loamy scent.

The pit's ragged edges are dotted with spade-wielding men and two small excavators. I count ten workers in all. Streaked with sweat, dressed in grimy construction clothing and heavy boots.

My eyes track to an excavator parked at the edge, engine turned off, its bucket raised high.

Hanging from the teeth of the excavator is a human rib cage.

CHAPTER SIXTY-SIX

ADRIANNA

I'm pacing the wooden boards of one of the beach cabanas while Mark makes successive phone calls. Storm clouds are gathering. It's my bachelorette tonight, and I'm anxious heavy rain might spoil the pictures. When he hangs up, his handsome face is strained.

"Leopold says security thinks they saw two people headed north into the jungle," he says.

"They *think* they saw?" I rub my temples. "It's good to have Dad here managing his security at least," I say. "But I still don't trust his guys not to do something crazy." I catch his expression. "Sorry," I say. "The stress of it all is getting to me."

"Shall we try to relax on our last unmarried day together?" suggests Mark. "Try out the pool?"

As we slip into the water, I'm feeling better. From here, we can see staff laying out tables on the beach for the wedding breakfast. Crates of publicity documents, cutlery imported from Italy, and flowers sit ready to be unloaded. Inside the tent, staff are at work, fixing ten thousand rose heads to the ceiling.

I take a breath. Lie back and intertwine my toes with Mark's under the water.

"If we can pull this off, we can do anything," I tell him. "Think it will all go to plan?"

He smiles. "I'm on it. We've got extra staff to strew the approach with petals when the guests arrive. Chocolate torte for dessert."

I sit up in the water, beaming at him. "You remembered!"

"Giving you my chocolate torte the night we met? How could I forget?" He slides closer and wraps his arms around me. "It was worth it," he adds, moving his face close. "Every bite of that dry soufflé." He kisses me softly.

I close my eyes, trying to let myself be drawn in, but I can't.

"What's wrong?" asks Mark. "Silky?"

I shake my head. "I know I should be feeling bad about her death, and I am," I say. "It's more I just have this nasty feeling, even with Simone's death solved, that someone is out to get me."

"Correct." Mark runs his thumbs along my torso. "It's me."

I manage a laugh. "Mark," I say, my eyes on the organized chaos of the wedding arrangements on the sand. "Remember that week we had, just you and me, holed up playing video games?"

"We're talking about the best week of my entire life, right?" he pretends to frown. "Apart from when you beat me on *Fortnite*."

"Do you ever wish we could just go back to that? Marry quietly?"

His face turns serious. "Of course I do," he says. "But that's not an option for us."

"Don't you wish you'd just met a normal girl?"

"No." He pulls me tight. "Let me show you why." Before I can answer, he kisses me hard. I kiss him back and circle him with my legs, feeling myself melt into him. Mark slides his hands down my body, hooking his thumbs into my bikini bottoms.

"We can't," I breathe. "Literally the whole beach can see us."

"So?" He kisses me again. "It's your private island, right?"

I try to relax, but from the corner of my eye, I see something winking in the sun. A photographer's lens?

I sit up in the pool. It's nothing. Just a sun glimmer on the water. But somehow the mood has gone.

CHAPTER SIXTY-SEVEN

HOLLY

I can't take my eyes off the open pit. Tucked among the coffee-colored soil are bones. Lots and lots of bones.

The excavator fires up, and the claw bucket, with its ghoulish human remains, twists around and dumps its load to the side of the loamy pit beneath. The rib cage rolls onto a pile of discarded soil. Even from this distance, I can see it's not the only bone fragment. Tossed aside, half buried in the pile of dug-out earth, I make out a femur, part of a skull, and the broken pieces of at least one hand. All are bleached gray from years underground.

They vary in size. I see small rib cages. Tiny skulls. Long femurs and large mandibles.

I twist back out of sight, resting against the wall.

"There are children's bones in that grave," I say, my stomach tightening at the thought.

Fitzwilliam's square-jawed face is deathly pale. "Are you OK?" he asks.

I nod. My heart is pounding. It's not the first time I've seen human remains. But so many young skeletons…and there's something about the casual way they're being tossed aside that makes my skin crawl.

By the pit, the whirring sound of the excavator suddenly cuts out. My blood turns to ice. Fitzwilliam and I stand stock-still, pressed against the side of the building. It's a terrible hiding place. We're in plain view of anyone walking in this direction.

There are shouts in Spanish. Then, just as I'm certain we're about to be discovered, the voices recede. We wait several agonizing seconds before Fitzwilliam risks another glance around the corner.

"They're leaving," he says. "Taking a break maybe. We should go before they come back."

"I'm taking a look." Ignoring Fitzwilliam's pained expression, I walk softly toward the pit. With a sigh of despair, he follows me.

Old bones stick out of the soil like pirate treasure. Skulls roll in the dirt. There must be hundreds of bodies in this pit, if not more.

"Why would there be a mass grave on this island?" I ask, thinking out loud.

"Drugs?" he suggests. "Maybe this is some drug-smuggling hideout. Or a narco prison."

"The bones are old," I say. "It takes around ten years for soft tissue to degrade to full skeletonization stage." I think for a moment. "Though the process would be faster on a tropical island," I concede. "Heat. Heavy rainfall. Insects."

"The caves were old too," concedes Fitzwilliam. "And the manacles we found in Silky's luggage. How long ago did Leopold inherit the island?"

"Twenty years ago," I say. As I peer over the edge, I realize something. "It's so shallow," I tell Fitzwilliam. "That can't be more than two feet, right?"

"No markers. No gravestones," he agrees sadly. "Just left to rot." He shakes his head at the lack of humanity.

"The clue Simone left. Six feet under," I point out. "She wasn't referring to a shallow grave."

Fitzwilliam hesitates. "She might not have meant it literally. *Six feet under* is a general expression."

"I know but..." I'm staring at the soil. "This is a working site. You couldn't conceal anything here without risking it being destroyed or discovered. And Simone couldn't have known we'd see the inside of Silky's room with the pictures of the open grave. I think we might have put two and two together and made five."

Fitzwilliam considers this. "If Simone wasn't referring to here, then where?"

"I don't know." Defeat rolls through me. "But I feel like I *should* know. Somewhere underground, I guess." My mind mentally maps the island. Then it hits me. "The panic room where Adrianna was held. That's underground, right?"

"Right." He's nodding fast. "It was built to be kind of a bunker."

"*Sepulcrum*," I say, "is Latin for *burial place* or *tomb*. And the panic room would be practical, right? Easy for Simone to get to unseen but not the kind of place that people go rooting around in either. Let's get back and take a look."

There's a flush of excitement on Fitzwilliam's face, which is kind of cute. I push the thought away.

As we reverse our steps, I notice something. Farther back in the jungle and partially obscured by leafy trees is another building, unlike the others.

"Look," I say. "The bell tower we saw from the ocean."

The stone edifice is stocky and colonial in proportions, like a small fortress. Down low and thick-walled, with square turrets on either side of a large arched doorway. A heavy black bell hangs at the top of the turret, and a round-edged cross shape has been cut in relief out of the thick stone frontage.

"It looks like an old church," I say. "The first Kensingtons must have built it."

A strange feeling washes over me looking at the bell tower. "Trinity," I murmur. "Holy Trinity. Looks like we found the old schoolhouse."

CHAPTER SIXTY-EIGHT

PETRA

We're all due at Adrianna's bachelorette party, but Holly and Georgia have vanished. Which gives me a perfect opportunity to search Holly's cabana for the birthday invitation I saw her find in the hot springs. As I slip inside, my cell rings. I check the display, and my stomach does a flip.

It's Max.

"Hey," I answer, upbeat. "You get the pictures?"

"Petra," he replies, his clipped English accent reminding me horribly of my former headmistress. "What the hell? Did you put the wrong attachment? You sent me a bunch of junk."

"You didn't like the pictures?" I pretend to be shocked. "What about the close-up with Georgia? You could twist that one to look like they were fighting or something."

"Don't tell me how to do my fucking job!" The rage in his voice actually makes me take a step back. "You sent me a load of puff. And what the fuck was the picture-edited crap with Adrianna kissing some dark-haired stud? Did you really think you could get it past me? A child of eight could see it had been spliced together with a picture editor."

"I—"

He interrupts me. "I *told* you. I need something good. *Titan* has a million-dollar ad revenue because we break celebrity stories, not because we publish pretty girls in wedding dresses. You're supposed to send me pictures to sell magazines. Not something that's going to put me in court. Otherwise, you know what I have to do."

"Wait," I tell him. "You didn't let me finish. I'm in Holly Stone's cabana right now. Looking for the old birthday invitation Simone set up to shoot for *Wrongly Accused*."

My eyes land on Holly's battered skull-motif suitcase pushed partially under the bed. I kneel and flip the lid.

Gold foil flashes. The birthday invitation to Adrianna's twenty-first birthday is right on top. I let out a breath, hardly able to believe it.

"I found it," I tell him. "I got the birthday invite Simone hid in the cave." I'm staring. I remember this. The game of Truth or Dare Adrianna played to try and reveal who'd sent it.

He pauses. "You did?"

"Uh-huh. It's got writing on it," I add. "*Six feet under.* I guess this is another one of Simone's puzzles. You watch the show, right?"

"Of course I watch the show." He thinks for a moment. "Sepulcrum," he says. "It's marked on publicity material. *Sepulcrum* means *tomb*. A.k.a. *six feet under.*"

"It's a hidden bar," I explain. "Set in the old panic room where Adrianna was held. It would be the perfect place to shoot a high-drama scene if you could get the lighting. I have to be at the bachelorette now, but we're due at Fortune House later…"

"You need to get there," says Max. "Like I told you in New York, we had a tip-off. Simone had some documents that she planned on revealing. Something that would smash the Kensingtons apart. Sounds like you cracked her hiding place." I can almost hear his grin over the phone.

My stomach lurches. "I can't do that to Leopold," I tell him.

"Then it looks like the world is about to get a very different idea of Petra Morka."

I put a hand out to steady myself, breath catching. I feel like I might actually vomit.

"I can get there," I babble. "Easily. Tonight. I just need to slip away from the party while no one is watching."

There's a long moment where I think he might have just hung up.

"I'll give you until midnight," he decides. "If those documents really do reveal why Adrianna was kidnapped, it will be front page all over the world."

"I'll get them," I promise. "Midnight."

CHAPTER SIXTY-NINE

HOLLY

The schoolhouse is cool and dark inside. Plain wooden desks are set in tidy lines. Everything is old. Heavy. Built to last. My eyes track to the Kensington family crest, cut into the stone at the back. "Kensington Manor School," I say. "This was the first. Before the family founded the famous one in New York."

"How come this one closed?" asks Fitzwilliam.

"Something involving the pit of bones outside?" I suggest.

As we walk toward the back of the schoolhouse, I can see a photograph of a woman looking somberly down on the desks. She stands amid her pupils, wearing black schoolmistress robes and a stern expression.

The inscription beneath reads

MARGARET KENSINGTON. FOUNDER OF KENSINGTON MANOR SCHOOL. 1953

"I recognize that woman," I say, pointing. "She's in a portrait up at Fortune House."

The photograph shows twenty or so young women arranged in unsmiling rows. They can't be much older than sixteen, in heavy fifties pinafores. The schoolmistress stands glowering in the center.

"The girls," I say, looking at their sad faces. "Their heads are shaved." I think for a moment. "Some tropics thing, perhaps? Shaving their heads?"

We exchange wretched glances.

"Silky's court case details haircutting," says Fitzwilliam. "Maybe the two things are linked."

My eyes settle back on the picture. Fitzwilliam is looking at a cluster of little icons set on an altar toward the front of the schoolhouse. Mary and Jesus have been inexpertly carved from wood, decorated with bright colors.

"The Holy Trinity," I tell him. "Father, Son, Holy Ghost." A mahogany triqueta, three interlocking almond-shaped arcs, is painted in deep red on the wall.

"Look at this." Fitzwilliam lifts a painted wooden carving. This one isn't gaudy like the others. It's black cloaked, with a ghostly pale face. "Remind you of anyone?" He holds it up in front of the portrait of Margaret Kensington.

"It's…a schoolmistress," I say. "But it also looks a lot like…the masked and cloaked figure who snatched Adrianna."

"Right." Fitzwilliam nods. "Coincidence?"

I swallow. Something about this whole setup is gnawing at me, and I don't know why.

There's a door at the back of the room, and Fitzwilliam moves to open it.

"You'd better come see this," he says grimly, looking inside.

I take a breath, preparing myself for what he has found. The other side of the door is the last thing I expect to see.

It's an office. The strangest office I've ever seen. A thick-legged table and plain wooden chair function as a rudimentary desk. A large computer screen is hooked up to a laptop, which whirs away, powered by a remote power pack.

The screen has a number of wedding mock-ups open. One shows the floristry tower that Silky would have orchestrated. The giant K. It's made of scaffold, and something about that nudges me but refuses to come together.

Blood on multiple scaffold poles. The tower... It won't coalesce, and I return my attention to the table.

I shift my mind away, concentrating on the desk. It's stacked with neat documents. Press releases, I realize, lifting one.

My lips move slowly as I read it:

> Diva Tantrum. Adrianna Kensington demands fresh sheets HOURLY on her honeymoon.

There's a picture attached. Adrianna walking on a beach in a crimson string bikini.

I turn to Fitzwilliam, confused. "This doesn't make any sense. How would someone know what Adrianna is going to do on her honeymoon?"

"The shot is from here," he says and turns to me. "It looks as though someone is selling stories of Adrianna to the press."

"Or leaking stories to make her look bad," I say. "Who would do that?"

Fitzwilliam leans over to select another paper from the pile.

> Spoiled Brat Snack. Live lobsters from Maine. Just one of Adrianna's thousand-dollar beach snacks.

This time, the picture shows the flame-lit beach bar.

"That was from yesterday," I say. "There categorically was *not* live lobster. I would remember."

Adrianna and her bridesmaids are set in a semicircle, beautiful in their designer beachwear. A platter of seafood has been placed dead center. They're all draped over one another like they're the best of friends, although their expressions are aloof.

This picture has a scrawled red markup:

Rich bitches

I move to pick up another page, still turning over what we've discovered. My hand jogs the keyboard, and the large screen flashes to life.

The screensaver is of Adrianna, her arms slung around her sister, Georgia. It's an unusually natural shot. They're both laughing, goofing around. For once, neither is drilling the camera lens with a pouty stare. It's a cute picture. Two sisters hanging out.

A message pings into the top corner of the screen:

EXCLUSIVE: Adrianna Kensington cheats on her honeymoon.

"Look at the sender," I breathe.

Fitzwilliam looks closer. "Georgia Kensington?"

"Yes. But she's sending it to her own account. Wait," I say. "Silky's hut. I just assumed it was hers, because that's where Georgia put her to rest. What if it wasn't? What if the hut with the pictures of Adrianna was Georgia's?"

"So Georgia had a creepy pin chart with pictures of Adrianna, and she's leaking stories to the press," says Fitzwilliam. "Why?"

"Surely she wouldn't have been doing it for the money?" I say.

The dark chapel is lit suddenly by a window of light. Someone has pulled back the curtain. I turn slowly to see an all-too-familiar figure. Tall, lean, and perfectly made-up. Black cover-up thrown tastefully over her white bathing suit.

It's Georgia Kensington.

She's holding a gun, and it's pointed straight toward us. Her smooth face is drawn in annoyance.

"It's always about the money, Holly," she says. "That's what being a Kensington is all about."

CHAPTER SEVENTY

PETRA

I'm dressing for the bachelorette party, the birthday invitation resting on the table in my cabana. So many memories. That party. Silky's court case was partway through, and the bad feeling of it rippled throughout.

"Soul death." That was what Silky had said in court. "I can remember the exact moment my soul died."

Is that what Kensington Manor School did? Killed the souls of other girls? I bring to mind the point when that soft part of me left. I hadn't been nearly as brave as Silky. My soul death had come that very first penance.

My eyes settle on Simone's curving writing on the birthday invitation: *Six feet under.*

I can still remember how, at school, I'd become fascinated by Simone, looking for her each time we went to church. The confidence she moved with. I wanted to learn it for myself. On Tuesdays, she was one of the older girls assigned to our rooms, making sure the new girls washed and undressed in the right order. Folded our clothes correctly on the chairs by our beds. I'd been at the school ten nights and was still crying myself to sleep when I realized in a panic I couldn't find my toy bunny. We were all allowed one item from home, and this was mine. I carried her everywhere with me, chewing nervously on her ears, to the disgust of the teachers. My attachment to the toy had earned me the nickname "Bunny" from the other girls.

Simone found me curled in a ball, sobbing my heart out. "What's wrong?" She knelt beside me.

"My b-bunny," I sobbed. "Anita. I can't find her."

Simone's expression hardened, and I expected her to tell me to toughen up. I was learning fast that these were the rules at Kensington Manor School.

Instead, she stood. "Whoever took this girl's toy bunny, give it back," she said in a sharp voice. "Now. Or there'll be consequences."

Silence descended over the dormitory. Then from nowhere, my careworn bunny, Anita, flew through the air and landed unceremoniously on my bed. I scooped her up gratefully and pressed her to my body.

"Thank you," I told Simone.

"You should be careful," she said quietly. "You don't really want anyone here to see you have a weakness. They'll prey on it."

I climbed into bed, not really understanding, chewing gratefully on Anita's bunny ear. Simone's face softened, and she tucked the covers around me.

"Shall I come again tomorrow?" she suggested. "Just to check that you're OK?"

I nodded, barely able to believe my luck. Simone felt like a warm beacon in the endlessly cold night of Kensington Manor School. She came most nights after that. For several weeks, I wrote her little love notes. Sometimes she'd even sleep with me if I was scared. For certain, I never, ever thought she would betray me like she did.

CHAPTER SEVENTY-ONE

HOLLY

Georgia walks deeper into the room, gun still trained on Fitzwilliam and me. My eyes flick to her open computer screen, and again the floristry tower pushes for my attention. I tuck it away and concentrate on the situation at hand.

"Georgia," I say. "Have you been leaking stories about Adrianna to the media?"

She frowns again. Adjusts a delicate gold bracelet on the dark skin of her wrist.

"Of course," she says finally. "That's my job. I'm PR."

"All that stuff about Adrianna being hard to work with," I say. "Needing thousand-dollar room riders at luxury hotels. This is where those stories originated?"

"That's right." Georgia looks pleased with herself. "One big PR campaign that starts and ends with me."

"Georgia," I say, stunned. "She's your sister. How *could* you?"

Georgia blinks her almond-shaped eyes several times, very fast. Then she laughs.

"Oh," she says. "Holly, I forgot you are new to all this. OK, I can see how all this might look." She waves a glossy-tipped hand at the press releases. "Dri *wants* me to post these stories. It's all part of the brand. We run nightclubs, Holly. It's all about the vibe. The reputation. Without that stuff, all you've got is a loud room with flashing lights."

"You want your sister to be written up as a bitch and a diva?"

"Absolutely. In the early days of Tantra, we dropped hints about Mafia connections too. Just enough to make us sound edgy. But we moved on. Gangsters went out of fashion. It's all about mean-girl influencers now."

"Adrianna is the mean girl?"

"It's what gets the clicks. We need Dri to seem difficult and demanding. Like she will only accept the best. That's part of the luxury image. And…" She lifts a picture of Adrianna in a skimpy bikini looking coquettishly at the camera. "We need to play a fine line with the sexual imagery. If we feed the newspapers enough sexy stories of Dri—infidelity, bisexuality—stories that we can quickly crush, that means we control the narrative." Georgia shrugs. "The media is like feeding a tiger. Dri needs to be a little bit sexy, a little bit bad. We tried to play her as a nice girl in the beginning, and they started hunting out really nasty, sordid things. Ripped her to pieces. There were times she couldn't get out of bed."

Unexpectedly, she raises the gun again.

"PR is about two things, Holly," she says sadly. "Putting out the right stories and stopping the leaks. And unfortunately, we've got a leak here. You and your assistant are NYPD."

The revelation of our blown cover ripples through the quiet schoolhouse.

"You must know how Dri feels about NYPD," says Georgia. "After that cop sold pictures of her underwear, she was in therapy for months."

"We're just trying to protect your family," Fitzwilliam says, "and find out who murdered Simone Walters." He fans his hands out pleadingly. "There's a crazed kidnapper on the loose," he adds. "Let us protect you."

Georgia's eyes flash rage. "Where were you *three years ago*? When we *needed* you? Dad begged the NYPD for help. You were worse than useless." She looks back and forth between us before coming to a decision. "Holly, did you think you could trust him?"

An uneasy feeling pools in my stomach.

Still keeping the gun trained on us, Georgia steps to reach over and tap her computer.

An image flashes up. It's Fitzwilliam far out in the ocean. It looks like…he's kissing Adrianna Kensington.

My eyes switch to his face, questioning and not a little betrayed. I can't help but feel a deep personal hurt, which seems to come from nowhere. Why should I care if Fitzwilliam is kissing Adrianna? But I do.

Fitzwilliam has blushed a deep shade of red. "I didn't… I mean…it isn't—"

"I intercepted this picture from a rogue email account using our IP," interrupts Georgia. "You were sending it to the press. How much more than the salary of a New York cop were they offering to sell us out?"

"I would never do that," he says, turning to me.

I look away from him. Why should I care what he does?

"Do you want to explain again how you have our best intentions at heart?" demands Georgia. "How you're not here to take advantage of Dri?"

Fitzwilliam has flushed a deep livid red.

Georgia lifts a radio from the desk with her free hand. "Security," she says, "I need you at the schoolhouse."

I shiver in the cool, and my eyes settle on the floristry display on Georgia's computer screen. Several facts are moving in my mind.

The cold. The AC in the storage room. Flowers. Floristry. Silky. It all comes together in a rush.

"Call off your security," I tell Georgia. "And I'll tell you what really happened to Simone."

CHAPTER SEVENTY-TWO

HOLLY

In the cool of the schoolhouse, Georgia's expression has switched from anger to quiet confusion.

"You know what happened to Simone?" she says. "How?"

"Call off your security," I counter.

She shakes her head. "You have five minutes until they get here," she says. "If you really can unmask Adrianna's kidnapper, I won't hand you over to them."

I swallow. Because I still don't know who kidnapped Adrianna, but maybe I can buy us time with what I have just figured out.

"Silky didn't do it," I tell Georgia. "At least not in the way it looks. Simone wasn't beaten to death with a scaffold pole."

Georgia blinks at me.

"What?" Her face twists hopefully.

"The scaffold," I explain, "for the flowers. That's why the AC was set so cold in the storage room. It wasn't to throw off the body temperature, it was to keep the flower display cold. Silky must have set up the structure that night."

The gun in Georgia's hand lowers fractionally as she takes this in.

"And?" She glares.

"The floristry scaffold tower on the wedding plans isn't closed off at the top," I explain. "Just a couple of gangplanks. I think Silky set it up that night and climbed to the top. Simone came up to join her. Maybe they had things to talk about."

This is a guess, and I see Georgia's brows lower at the idea.

"If Simone and Silky got in a disagreement and someone took a wrong step," I continue, "Simone could have fallen right into the insides of the tower. Which was a honeycomb of hard metal."

Beside me, Fitzwilliam is nodding thoughtfully.

"If it was high enough and Simone fell right through the center..." I conclude.

"You knock every bar on the way to the bottom," fills in Fitzwilliam, who seems to have momentarily forgotten Georgia is pointing a gun at him.

"Right," I say, still unable to meet his eye since seeing the picture of him kissing Adrianna. "And each blow would be made with the same amount of force. The same amount of impact. Crisscrossing her body and head in a kind of pattern. You see something similar with fatalities who fall down flights of stairs: the head strikes the hard surface, then whiplashes. Only in this case, the whiplash motion forced the head repeatedly forward and back as it struck successive scaffold uprights."

"Which would explain why such a large force could be exerted repeatedly," fills in Fitzwilliam.

"Silky could have been telling the truth," I conclude. "It *was* an accident. At least so far as she knew."

"If Simone's death was an accident," says Georgia, "then who put her body in Adrianna's dress?"

I don't have an answer to that, but I'm interrupted by the sound of footsteps outside. Security, I'm guessing. Fitzwilliam looks at me with a searching expression. Intuiting his question, I give the smallest shake of my head. I don't know who kidnapped Adrianna. Fitzwilliam nods gravely, then lunges suddenly at Georgia, grabbing for the gun. She holds tight, eyes wide, issuing a cry of shock as they grapple.

Security guards crash though the door, shouting. They pelt toward Fitzwilliam, raining blows on his body and pulling him from Georgia's gun. He folds over in pain.

"Holly!" he gasps. "Run!"

I hesitate for the smallest moment, then run for the door.

CHAPTER SEVENTY-THREE

PETRA

Adrianna's bachelorette party starts with cocktails at Daybreak, her detox bar, with the schedule set for photo shoots at various key locations around the island. I've set up to get pictures.

Under the palm-leaf shelter, lap-dancing poles have been erected, and I'm taking pictures of the bridesmaids posing provocatively in skimpy outfits. Ophelia is taking turns to point the camera at me. Holly is nowhere to be seen, but Georgia dismisses my questions.

Adrianna is whirling around the pole with professional grace, her lithe frame strapped into a liquid-metal string bikini. It would be just like her to have taken pole-dancing lessons and then arrange a bachelorette so the rest of us flounder. Luckily for me, I learned to use a pole for a modeling shoot years ago.

I angle the camera to catch Adrianna's slim physique spin with the appearance of weightlessness, her mane of chestnut hair fanning out as she turns.

I need to get to Sepulcrum, and time is running out. Max saw through the fake images of Fitzwilliam kissing Adrianna and demanded I give him something by midnight.

While I'm thinking over hopeless possibilities, Georgia instructs us to change into bridesmaid dresses for the next photo shoot at Fortune House.

Adrianna wears a tiny glittering silver dress, cut deep to expose her thin tanned back. She zeros in on me, throwing a narrow arm across my shoulders with unconvincing bonhomie.

"You and I haven't spoken much, have we, Petra?" says Adrianna. "Let's go back to Fortune House and get a drink."

Something about the way she says it suggests she means an actual drink. Rather than a lime juice and baking soda mix designed to catch the light in pictures.

We tramp up the path to Fortune House, which is low lit and atmospheric in the evening shade.

Adrianna heads straight to the main bar, which is unmanned since no one was expecting us.

Opium is decorated with a lush colonial grandeur. Broad plantation shutters, raw teak floor, and an artfully selected assortment of wingback and Chesterfield chairs in deep colors.

The drink service area is a contemporary rendition of a wall-length Victorian-style English bar, made of polished wood and contemporary jungle-leaf stained glass, showcasing luxury liquors.

Adrianna claps for our attention. We all turn dutifully to watch. I raise my camera.

"Who wants *tequila*?" Adrianna is suddenly making a loud and unconvincing attempt to be the fun bachelorette.

"You've got a full photo shoot tomorrow," Georgia says, walking toward her.

"Relax," says Adrianna. "It's just for the photos." She reaches behind the bar, grabs a bottle, and holds it aloft. "Could we get some glasses?" she adds to no one in particular.

Ophelia obligingly scuttles behind the bar to fish some out.

Adrianna begins pouring shots with a wild-eyed expression. I think back to my nights out with Leopold, and there's something sad about how disingenuous her partying is. Like she's seen fun in photos and is approximating it. She reminds me more of a prisoner at yard time.

"Who wants one?" Adrianna holds up a glass.

There's an eerie silence. We're all here for photo ops and to work. There's a flicker in Adrianna's light-blue eyes. Like she's suddenly seen her life through the fun-house mirror and realized it's a sham.

I leave for a cigarette. Outside Fortune House, I lean against the heavy stone of the wall and stare out across the island, blowing out a steady stream of smoke. It feels like I'm there for a long time. Thinking.

I don't know how long it's been when I notice three figures in the distance, low down on the side of the mountain, headed for the beach. I squint against the setting sun, trying to figure out the dynamics. From this vantage point, it looks as though two people are manhandling a third.

I suck in cigarette smoke and finger the camera slung around my neck.

Making a decision, I zoom in on my camera. When I check the display, I'm startled. Holly Stone's assistant, dark-haired with good cheekbones, is being dragged toward the ocean by two jittery-looking men in ragged T-shirts and jeans.

My pulse lifts. The two men restraining Holly's assistant are clearly high. There's a deadness to both of their eyes, which I've seen before in dangerous men. Dealers, mainly, who use too much of their own supply.

As I absorb this, Holly's assistant twists in their grasp and runs, hands bound, back toward the house. He doesn't get far. Within seconds, a guard is on him, cannoning the butt of a rifle into his back and knocking him to the ground. The second guard closes in on the prone figure and begins administering a volley of heavy kicks. Both men hook their arms under the now-unmoving form and drag him toward the sea.

I inhale several quick drags of cigarette smoke, my long fingers shaking slightly. Should I tell Leopold? His guards have gotten too rough with people in the past. We don't need any more bodies on the island.

My jaw sets tight. No one ever helped me. Decision made, I turn away.

CHAPTER SEVENTY-FOUR

HOLLY

It's a long slog through hot jungle, avoiding being seen, but I finally manage to get back to the main house, my heart beating fast. I'm trying not to think about Fitzwilliam.

Carefully, I slip through the staff entrance in the undercroft and into the kitchen. I'm about to let out a breath when I see a slim figure in the corner.

"Hello, Holly." Adrianna is standing, watching me.

"Oh. Hi." I touch my hair self-consciously. "I was just fixing my makeup. What are *you* doing here?" I add. She's holding a bottle of tequila, I notice, and there's a hazy cast to her sapphire eyes.

Her eyes follow the movement of mine to the tequila. "Oh, you know," she says. "Just getting away from being me for a while." She lifts the bottle. "Join me?"

I move toward her uncertainly.

"You weren't at my bachelorette party."

"No." I plumb my mind for excuses, wondering what she knows. Surely Georgia would have told her I'm undercover? But she seems clueless. And not a little drunk. "I…ah…went for a walk," I say. "It was intense. Finding Silky."

She nods slowly, like she's turning over my words for impact.

"Drink with me." She holds out the bottle.

I take a nervous little sip.

"No, Holly," she says without warmth. "It's my bachelorette. Have an actual drink."

I take another, deeper sip, feeling the liquid burn.

"Come on." Adrianna beckons me. "Let's get back to the party." Her fingers fasten around my arm, just a shade too tight to be friendly. She walks me up the stairs and back into the luxurious hallway of Fortune House. I glance helplessly back along the corridor, and she escorts me to Opium Bar.

Sepulcrum is tantalizingly close, but Adrianna is leading me past the female voices of her bachelorette party and into a private adjoining room. It's empty. She points to a deep-purple velvet seat.

"Sit." There is a hard edge to her voice. "We need to have a talk."

There are glasses on the table, and she sets her bottle of tequila down but doesn't pour us drinks.

"What about?" My voice comes out strangely. I glance at the door. Two heavyset men have appeared to barricade the entrance.

"About you being a lying little snake." She leans closer. "Here's what's going to happen," she says. "You're going to tell me everything you saw. And I'll let your NYPD friend off the island with the use of his legs."

I stare at her, unable to fit this hard version with the glamorous Adrianna in pictures.

"You don't think I can be tough?" she asks. "Nine years of forbearance and suffering. Kensington Manor girls are brutal when we need to be."

"I don't know anything," I tell her.

She looks hard into my face.

"I'm good at telling when people are lying," she says. "You need that in my family. What were you looking for in the jungle?"

"I...we were trying to find who killed Simone."

Adrianna adjusts her position thoughtfully. The movement causes her momentary discomfort, and I catch a flash of red where her dress has been digging into her underarm. Her shoes must be hurting her feet too, I find myself thinking, and for some reason, this lodges somewhere alongside the discoveries we made out in the jungle. Something about women on this island and at the Kensington school. The burdens and strictures they're expected to carry in the name of appearances.

Adrianna raises an eyebrow and turns her head toward the men on the door.

"Call the offshore boat," she says. "Code forty-six."

"Wait!"

"Oh?" She cocks her head.

I plumb my mind for something, anything to tell her that I can pass off as the truth. The bones. The graves. The old abandoned resort.

The whole puzzle of the open grave is fitting together like pieces of a skeleton.

"There were pictures in the schoolhouse of girls with shaved heads." I take a breath as the final elements slot together. "This whole island used to be a prison," I say. "For girls."

CHAPTER SEVENTY-FIVE

PETRA

I notice with mild amusement that Adrianna has left her own bachelorette party. She never grew up. The spoiled little girl I got a kick out of scaring at school is still in there, buried under couture clothing and designer perfume. I try not to think about those times, but sometimes I can't help it.

Something about being back here is dredging up memories.

Older ones, of the girl I was before. Bunny.

I had been at Kensington Manor School one full term before everything changed. Simone had looked after me, since I often couldn't sleep. I missed home dreadfully, surrounded at night by the wretched sobbing of other homesick seven-year-old girls.

Then came the end-of-term ceremony. All the little new girls had been sent to change for bed and instructed to strip down and brush our teeth. Then, shivering in our undershirts and panties, we were instructed to bring the single toy we'd been permitted from home and follow an older girl to the common room. I brought my soft toy bunny rabbit, who'd been with me since I could remember, clutching her close to my body.

"Quickly." The older girl clapped her hands. Clinging gratefully to comforting toys, we followed her to a dingy basement room, where a fire burned in an old-fashioned grate. In the hall was a line of older girls. One for each of us. They all wore black robes with hoods.

I looked up into the face of the girl in front of me. It was Simone. My heart rose. I gave her a little smile, but her face was cold.

"The older girls are responsible for teaching you Kensington Manor School ways," came the announcement. "Tonight is your First Penance."

I started to doubt my English. Then the older girl first in line wrenched a stuffed toy from the little girl in front of her and tossed it into the fire. The little girl gave a heartbroken shriek.

"You're here to learn to be clean young ladies," the elder said as the owner of the toy convulsively sobbed. "Not disgusting babies." She turned to me, and her eyes narrowed. "You're the one with the pash on Simone," she said.

I felt a slow, hot blush begin to spread over my cheeks. I'd never heard that word before and realized it must be some boarding school term, but I was sure I knew what she meant.

"Simone," said the older girl. "You should be the one to do it." She pointed to Anita, my soft toy bunny, clutched tight to my chest.

"No!" I pulled her close.

Simone stepped toward me and took hold of her ears. I clutched her tight.

"Please," I protested. "She's the only thing I have from home."

To my shock, Simone stepped forward and delivered a ringing slap to my face. For a moment, the surprise overwhelmed everything. Then the pain and humiliation seeped in. I wanted so badly to go home that it was a physical pain in my heart.

"Now you behave better," warned Simone, wrenching the

bunny from me. "We've got all of you to wash and get ready for bed, and we haven't even started the ceremony yet."

I chewed my lip. Simone and the other girls were being so unkind, but they seemed to be in charge of us. My eyes flashed to the fire. I knew Simone would never *actually* burn my toy bunny. It was unthinkable. I wouldn't be able to sleep without her.

But she did. Simone tossed Anita into the flames. Her beaded eyes flashed sadly in the fire as they melted. The fur on her weathered ears caught alight.

I howled like the world was ending.

The next thing that happened, I could never have expected. With sharp silver scissors, Simone grabbed a thick hank of my hair and hacked it off. I brought a hand to the severed ends, horrified. I turned to the girl next to me and saw she had peed in her pants and was standing in a growing wet puddle. The older girls tossed our hair in the fire.

To my shock and embarrassment, I started to cry.

"None of that," said Simone in a cold voice. "Kensington Manor School girls don't cry. You mortify yourselves before God. Fine metal withstands great heat," she told me as the acrid stench of our burning hair and toys filled the room.

I look up to see Ophelia has sat herself next to me. Too close, I realize, slightly annoyed. This is an American habit I never got used to.

"Simone," says Ophelia. "She was your older girl, wasn't she?" The usual irritating bounce has gone from her voice now. It is flat calm. And strangely familiar.

I blink at her. "So what?"

"You used to play sick games with us," says Ophelia. "The

younger girls. Don't you remember? Saint games. You were the sinner. We were the saints. You tied us to the bed. Stole our favorite things. You *hurt* us."

I turn laconically, ready to fall back on the familiar strategies. This is not the first time one of the girls from the younger years has tried to confront me about so-called bullying.

"I remember a lot of little babies," I tell her, fixing her with a glare, "who couldn't deal with being away from their nannies. I *helped* girls like you to grow up. How could you have survived without me?"

Ophelia blinks, but not in a quiet, afraid way like Silky used to. "I survived despite you," she hisses.

I roll my eyes. "You didn't even have the guts to stand up for Silky in court."

Ophelia's steely expression wavers. It really is too pathetic. What did she expect me to do? Run away screaming?

"You didn't know I knew Silky asked you to testify, did you?" I ask tauntingly. "I bet Silky begged you to take the witness stand. The things you could have said about me. But you left her to be humiliated. Because you didn't want it to come out in court that you're in love with Adrianna Kensington."

Her freckled face flushes a deep rosy pink. Ophelia's hard expression vanishes, then resets to something else. A fawning kind of smile.

"You know what?" she says brightly. "Let's just quit talking about school. It never did Silky any good, did it?"

"No," I tell her. "It never did Silky any good."

CHAPTER SEVENTY-SIX

HOLLY

Adrianna assesses me coolly, glancing around to be sure the guards have left.

"Well then, Holly." She smiles. "Aren't you clever?"

"I'm right then?" I say. "Elysium was a former prison island."

"They called it a reform school," she says. "The philosophy was to tame fallen women and wayward girls from wealthy families before they fell into disgrace. Not that they had much success. Margaret Kensington fell apart in the tropical climate. Her regime was so harsh that most of the first wave of pupils died. They covered it up and claimed it was because of cholera. Kept taking on new pupils. Little joke on my dad by the English Kensingtons. This whole island is basically a grave."

Her deep-blue eyes stare distractedly into the distance.

"It's been a nightmare for construction," she adds. "The ground is unstable on the old burial sites. We've had to rebuild, like, so many times. Cost way more than we ever anticipated."

"So that's the big family secret?" I suggest, refilling our glasses and passing her one.

Adrianna sips distractedly, looking confused. "It's more like a history we don't widely disseminate. We don't want guests knowing they'll be sipping martinis on the remains of dead prisoners. And Kensington Manor School is one of the most prestigious in the country. Doesn't look good if the founding headmistress went insane in the tropics, mistreating girls."

I empty my tequila glass. This time, it's Adrianna who refills both.

"Back in Dad's day, the island history was just like a colorful addition. Now it's not something we want to be associated with. The Kensington brand has a dark side. But the violent oppression of women?" She wrinkles her slim nose. "Off-brand. Completely off-brand."

I rub my temples. I feel as though I've been led down a rabbit hole. I've lost a lot of time. But I'm trying to think. Could someone be angry with the Kensingtons for their past cruelties, forty years after the fact? Unlikely.

Which means...I've gotten it all wrong. Put Fitzwilliam in danger.

Adrianna is looking at me coolly. "We're all in the business of stories, Holly," she says. "Even you. Georgia looked you up. You're a forensic. That means putting the right story to the court."

"I tell the truth," I say quietly. "According to the evidence."

"There are different kinds of truth, Holly. Haven't you learned that by now?" She turns back to the bar, a strange expression on her face, then switches her sapphire eyes on me.

"I'm drunk," she says.

"Me too," I admit. Although given her size-zero physique, I'm willing to bet I'm not half as drunk as she is.

I pour us both another measure of tequila. Lift it to clink glasses, then remember Fitzwilliam's earlier advice and raise it high instead.

"Here's to Silky," I say.

Adrianna nods sadly, her blue eyes thoughtful. "Holly," she says, "why do you think Silky did that? To Simone?" She says it with such sudden raw vulnerability, I'm stunned. "Why did she cut her hair? Put her in my wedding dress?"

I consider the question.

"I don't think she did," I say finally.

"Then who?" she says.

"I don't know," I tell her. "But if you help me, I can try to find out."

Adrianna lifts her head to the ceiling, then lets out a deep sigh. "This conversation is over," she mutters. "Time you joined your friend on the offshore boat."

"I think this all comes back to your boarding school," I tell her. "Whatever happened to you all there. It's why you were kidnapped. It's why Silky and Simone died. And I think you know the truth, but you're not telling. There's a lost little girl inside you," I say, "who wants to speak out but is afraid."

Her eyes flash up at me, and she throws back her tequila shot. "No, there isn't. That's the power of the school, Holly. You split yourself into pieces to survive. It was how we got through it. Part of me became Adrianna Kensington, the beautiful girl in the pictures. The girl you're talking about died a long time ago. Back at that school."

Her eyes roll up to me, and she looks so sad, I feel like I'm drowning in her deep-blue eyes. There's a flicker of surprise suddenly. Adrianna is looking at someone over my shoulder.

"Holly?"

The spite in the voice is so strong, I flinch as I turn around.

It's Ophelia, freckled face bared in rage, her whole body stiff with malice. "What the hell are you doing?"

CHAPTER SEVENTY-SEVEN

HOLLY

In the luxurious little room, Adrianna turns to Ophelia uncertainly. She looks afraid, like she's been overheard saying something she shouldn't.

"Why are *you* asking Adrianna about school?" demands Ophelia, glaring at me.

I open my mouth and shut it again.

"We're all so *tired* of outsiders who have never even *been* to the school judging us," she continues. "It might have been hard, but that school taught us to be tough. To deal with any kind of situation. You won't find a single girl who didn't love her time there by the end."

"Apart from Silky," I point out. Beside me, Adrianna almost winces.

"Silky was a *traitor*," says Ophelia. "Bringing all those private things to court. People talk as if something might have come of her court case if Adrianna hadn't been kidnapped. But it's…just not true. Even if Silky had gone in to testify, there was no crime to convict. Her evidence was messy."

"You seem to know a lot about the case," I observe.

"We *all* followed that case," says Ophelia. "Every second of it."

"Silky was putting our childhood on trial. But you don't need to be a legal expert to know it isn't a crime to tell ghost stories to young children or feed them gross food!"

The tirade is such a bizarre contrast to Ophelia's rainbow jumpsuit and primary-color eye makeup, it's almost surreal. She seems to realize this, collecting herself. But then her attention settles on the very obviously drunk Adrianna.

"What did you *do* to her?" accuses Ophelia. "You *know* she can't drink on the night before her wedding." Without waiting for an answer, Ophelia steps forward, beaded sandals jingling, and inserts herself physically between Adrianna's thin body and mine.

"Don't worry," says Ophelia. "I'm always here to take care of you, Dri. Always."

It's weird, the way Ophelia is staring at Adrianna, as if she's trying to channel some deep message. "I'm here for you," Ophelia repeats, reaching out a small hand and tentatively stroking Adrianna's hair. I'm caught between a strange mix of emotions. It's perfectly natural for Ophelia to look out for Adrianna. So why is something about the way she winds her small arms around Adrianna's body...creepy?

"I'll get you to bed," Ophelia tells Adrianna, glancing at me. "You don't need to be here, Holly."

This should be the perfect situation. The door from this room is unguarded. Everyone in the adjoining bar assumes I'm still with Adrianna.

I can slip away without anyone seeing and investigate Sepulcrum. But glancing back at Ophelia's hungry expression, I have the strangest sensation that I'm leaving Adrianna in the care of a predator.

I teeter before making a decision. There's no evidence Ophelia is anything other than Adrianna's friend. The best way to help Adrianna is to find those documents and try to find out who held her captive all those years ago. I need to get to Sepulcrum.

As I head out of Opium, my mind twists to the person who held Adrianna captive. Their obsession with the number three. With power. With dolls and dresses.

It all started years ago. At her boarding school.

CHAPTER SEVENTY-EIGHT

HOLLY

I get to the library room where Sepulcrum is hidden. But it's then I realize I don't know where the entrance is. I'd assumed it would be obvious.

My eyes fall on a large oil painting. It depicts Lady Margaret Kensington in schoolmistress robes with three sad-looking girls. They seem to be staring at me challengingly from their palm-tree and sea backdrop.

I let my gaze drift around the room. Bookcases. OK. Maybe there's some secret entrance that way. I start pulling off books wildly, glancing over my shoulder.

"You know," says a familiar voice from the doorway. "That's no way to treat the classics. Even for a scholarship kid."

I turn, part disbelief, part wild hope. "Fitzwilliam!"

He's standing in the doorway, dripping wet, with what looks to be the beginnings of a serious black eye, but is otherwise unhurt.

I run to the doorway and, without thinking, throw my arms around his neck and kiss him.

"I thought you'd left the island," I say, pulling back. "Your face, it's hurt."

"It's good to see you too. It's not as bad as it looks." He winces as I touch his cheek.

"How did you get away?"

"Ortiz tracked my pager signal to the boat I was on," he explains. "Scared the life out of my captors by taking over their radio and asking to speak with me. I managed to get away in the general mayhem." He hesitates. "Listen," he says. "The picture of me with Adrianna. It wasn't real…"

"It's OK," I say. "Perception and truth are different things. I'm learning that one. You should have gone to get help," I add. "Not come back here."

"And leave you alone on Death Island? Never. Especially not when I can help you out."

He strides over to the family portrait, eyes it for a moment, then curls his fingers around the edge and pulls.

"I think it's a door," he explains, voice strained with effort. "But it seems to be locked."

My eyes track around the portrait. There's a set of discreet cables running from the top.

"It's probably an electromagnet lock," I decide. "Probably some clever way to pop it." I sigh. "I guess when Simone figured this for a hiding place, the painting wasn't blocking the entrance."

I cross the room and begin dragging a chair across. Stepping onto it, I yank the wires. The portrait gives an audible click and peels a few inches from the wall.

"High school diploma in illegal entry," I tell him, hopping down.

"They teach that in public school?"

"No, they don't teach that. I'm joking. One of us should wait here," I add. "I only interrupted the power. The door will probably reseal itself if we don't keep it open."

Fitzwilliam pulls the portrait fully back. It turns on hinges.

We're both silent as a dark row of steps is revealed, leading downward.

The gap seems to loom out at us.

Fitzwilliam swallows. "I'll go," he says, walking forward.

"What happened to ladies first?" I say weakly, trying and failing to lift the sudden awful tension.

"You wait at the top," he says, his face strained. "And keep watch."

The darkness closes around him.

"Fitzwilliam?" I call after a few moments. "Is everything OK down there?"

A disembodied voice comes back from the dark below. "Depends how you define OK," he calls back.

I move nearer to the steps. "This is no time to joke," I tell him, glancing over my shoulder. "Are you OK or not?"

Something inaudible floats up the steps. He must have gone deeper into the panic room. I step forward, putting a hand on the doorframe at the top of the stairs.

"Fitzwilliam?"

More inaudible mumbles. Is he...groaning in pain? A flash of hot adrenaline hits me. Should I go down after him?

"Fitzwilliam?"

He doesn't answer. And before I can decide what to do, I feel a hard shove in my back.

My arms fly up on reflex as I pitch forward. Steps rise up to meet me as I fall headlong into the dark. Behind me, the portrait swings shut.

CHAPTER SEVENTY-NINE

PETRA

The bachelorette party ended in slow chaos. By the finish, we were scouring Fortune House for a drunk Adrianna, who it seemed Ophelia had taken upon herself to put to bed.

I'm back in my beach cabana when Leopold finally comes to see me.

"You've been avoiding me," I accuse.

He shifts uncomfortably. "The wind's picking up," he says. "The wedding guests can't land."

"You need to be careful the police don't crash in," I tell him. "Silky overdosed. Police might put it together that you supplied her with drugs."

"And? So what?" says Leopold tersely. "Of course I supplied Silky's drugs. Third time she got beat up by a street dealer, she nearly lost an eye. Silky couldn't do rehab just then. She just couldn't." He shrugs. "They can arrest me for all I care."

Sometimes Leopold's bravado is frightening, even to someone like me.

"*I* care," I tell him. "I covered for you. Told the police I didn't hear a speedboat the night Adrianna was kidnapped."

He blinks, confused. "What are you talking about?"

"Your *cocaine deliveries?*" I remind him. "You had drugs delivered nightly by speedboat. I told police I heard it, then changed my story when I realized it could get you into trouble."

He runs a hand through his hair. "I've got bigger problems," he says. "Everything Adrianna has been through and now this."

"Everything she's *been* through?" I can't help but sound a little contemptuous. "Leopold," I say, "you do everything for her." I sound bitter because I am.

Leopold shakes his head and sits on the bed. "I messed up when she was a kid. Didn't see her much. That morning, three years ago...when we woke up and Adrianna was gone... You start thinking about all the ways you let your kid down. All the lost time, you know?"

I don't know. But part of my role with Leopold has always been to listen. He isn't the kind of man who would book a therapist.

"When Adrianna started school," he continues, "her mom, Athena, there were things she told me. Like Adrianna was begging to come home. I ignored them." His brown eyes seek mine out, part smiling, part guilt. He sighs. "But Adrianna never liked to be ignored. She somehow got connected to my direct line. Little eight-year-old kid. Don't ask me how. She was smart."

He makes the same little smile of reminiscence that always gives me a nameless ache somewhere. The part of him that will never be mine. Since Athena died, she'll always be on a pedestal. Leopold has conveniently forgotten that their marriage was far from perfect.

"Adrianna was crying," he says. "Like really crying. I could almost hear the snot coming out of her goddamn nose. She said, 'Daddy, you have to get me out of here. Please come get me.'" There's a distant look in his face. "She said a bunch of other stuff I don't really remember. The food was bad or whatever. Other girls were mean." He takes a long shuddering breath. "You know what I did?"

I don't. But I know he's going to tell me, so I keep a dutiful silence, waiting.

"I got mad. Really mad at her. Called her a brat and entitled. Said she was lucky to even have food. Told her she didn't know what mean was. I grew up with guys who'd nail your hand to a park bench 'cause you had a Polish surname." His eyes are on mine now, imploring. "I messed up. First time in my life I didn't know what to do. Honestly. I didn't have any experience with boarding school or any of that stuff. I didn't know what was usual. Hell, I didn't even know what a normal childhood was." He shakes his head. "Wish I go could back now and take her out of there like she wanted me to."

"No, you don't, Leopold." I take both his hands. "We all hated that school at first, but it made us strong. Adrianna is lucky to have a dad like you, even if she doesn't appreciate it."

There are a lot of emotions in Leopold's face. We've always bonded over being immigrants. Being strong. But there's something in his expression I've never seen before.

"Tell me the truth, Petra. Simone got access to parts of Silky's court case. The whole school thing. Did they do that stuff to Adrianna and Georgia?"

I felt my jaw stiffen. "No," I lie. "They didn't."

"It's just… Isn't it weird? What Silky said happened in school. And Adrianna's kidnapping…" He looks at me. It's the first time I've ever lied to him, and he knows it.

"We loved each other once, didn't we?" he says sadly.

"Right up until you asked me to marry you," I tell him. "You might think yourself a New Yorker, Leopold, but having a mistress is part of the look."

He looks at the floor, then back at me.

"I wish I had," I tell him. "I wish I had married you."

"Then why didn't you?" He sounds angry suddenly.

I give him a small smile. "Penance," I say. "I couldn't have done that to your daughters. It wouldn't have done either of us any good. And it's too late now. Besides"—I cut him a small smile—"you don't have any money."

"I gotta go. Need to figure a way to land those guests in a storm."

"And if you can't?"

His face is grim. "I honestly don't know."

I move toward him, sliding my hands around his waist and pushing my body close to his.

"You'll figure it out," I whisper in his ear. "You always do."

He doesn't respond how he usually does, and a flash of shock and hurt echoes through me. I push it back down, concentrating on keeping him distracted as I kiss him goodbye. Leopold doesn't see me reach behind him and slide the gun from the bedside table. He always keeps extra firearms close by on Elysium.

"I'm going for a walk," I tell him. He nods distractedly, and I gauge his lack of interest.

There's plenty of time for me to slip down to the panic room without being seen. So long as I'm back before dawn, Leopold will never even notice his gun was missing.

I'm not about to let Holly get hold of those documents and tear the Kensingtons apart. Leopold will never appreciate everything I do for him.

CHAPTER EIGHTY

ADRIANNA

The Tower Suite bed linens are scented with the outdated florals I requested be modernized. It's dark save for a spray of stars, and the only sound is the ocean as it rakes rhythmically over the white sand.

Where is everyone?

I try to sit and realize with shock that my body feels horribly heavy. There's a pain in my head too. Slowly, I bring the shining edge of the infinity pool into view as it tumbles away into the blackness below.

I'm getting married tomorrow. Or is it today?

We don't put anything as vulgar as clocks in our suites, so I have no idea what time it is. But as I cast around, I see something next to me on the bed. It's a person. So still, I didn't notice them sleeping beside me.

There's a pop of bright orange hair sticking out of the comforter. *Ophelia*, I realize with something amounting to slightly sick shock. *Ophelia climbed into bed with me and fell asleep.*

There's a loud knock at the door, which takes me several seconds to process. My head isn't working right, and my eyes are sore. Dusty.

Slowly, I swing my feet out of the bed, and that's when I realize I'm naked. I grab at a sheet to cover myself, just as the door starts to swing slowly open.

"Dri?" A shadowy figure. Familiar male voice.

"Mark?" I squint in the dark.

The lights go on. I put a hand to the back of my head. Beside me, I feel Ophelia's body stir. For some reason, every sense wants to stay turned this way around, not looking at her.

"Is it morning?" I ask, noticing that my words are thick.

"It's one a.m.," says Mark. He seems to cross the room in stages. One moment, he's at the door, then suddenly, he glitches to be right by me on the bed. Like a video cutting.

Then they're both sitting on either side of me. Ophelia and Mark. Ophelia is wearing lacy underwear in a nude tone that blends with her freckled body.

Why is Ophelia in underwear? Thoughts are jabbing at me, but I can't pull them into a huddle.

"I gave her sleeping pills," Ophelia is saying. "That seemed like the best way to be sure she was fresh for the wedding."

Mark's face looks as though he doesn't understand this at all.

He says something I don't catch.

"I thought she might choke on her vomit," Ophelia adds. "I wanted to be sure she was safe."

Mark says something else. About wanting to be alone with his fiancée. The way he says it sounds bad, but that realization is buffered somehow, like it's wrapped in cotton balls.

Ophelia leaves the room the same way Mark came in. Little snatches of color, like a movie on fast-forward.

"That was weird," Mark is saying. "Ophelia got into bed with you?"

The way he says it is like an accusation. Which I can't really handle right now. One fact rises up for my attention though. Didn't Mark say it was 1:00 a.m.?

"It's past midnight," I tell him, shaking my head experimentally. "It's bad luck to see the bride on the wedding day."

Mark's face collapses. "That's why I came," he says. "It's bad news. The storm hasn't blown itself out yet. None of the guests can land this morning." His brown eyes are liquid with sympathy. "I'm so sorry. I know you just wanted this thing done."

He starts talking about rescheduling. Moving things off and on the beach. Staffing. Logistics.

All I hear is white-hot noise. I can't stand it. I actually can't stand it. It feels as if my brain is boiling between my ears.

"No," I say. And my tone cuts through everything he's talking about. "*No*."

"Dri—"

"After *everything* I've been through," I say, aware I'm gritting my teeth, "after *all* of it, I'm not stopping now." I lift my eyes to his. "Mark," I say, "we don't need them. We don't need the guests."

His brow crinkles. "You need guests at a wedding. My mom would never forgive me. *Your* father—"

"I know, I know," I say. "But...can't we just do the celebrations tomorrow? Have the actual *wedding* photographed today?"

"Dri," he says quietly, "we don't have a celebrant. It isn't possible. We tried, but it isn't possible."

"It *is*! Sorry," I add. "I didn't mean to yell, but it is possible. We don't need a celebrant. That's just for show. Simone did all the legal documents. We signed everything official last week."

His face puckers. "But...wouldn't you *want* a celebrant?" he asks. "We spent hours deciding on the tone of the ceremony." Mark is being kind, because we both know I was the one obsessing over the format and how the words would seem to fans.

"I don't care about any of that anymore," I say. "All I want is you. And all we need is two witnesses." I take a breath. "We can do it, Mark. Just like you always said. You and me, right? We're the only ones that matter."

"You, me, and the sponsor?" There is just a shade of annoyance that I've never heard before in his voice.

"It's a two-million-dollar deal," I say. "Everything hinges on us getting pictures to them by noon. If we can do that, if we can *just do that*, everything will work out." My eyes are on his, searching, desperate. "Please."

He looks away. "There's more to marriage than sponsorship deals," he says quietly.

Part of me wants to slap him, because what does he know? My whole entire life is one big string of sponsorship deals. Marriage doesn't change that.

"My dad is here," I add, trying to think despite a sudden prickling sensation in my brain. "Hair and makeup. All the important people."

"All the *important* people? Hair and makeup? Dri, can you hear yourself?" For the first time in our relationship, Mark actually sounds angry. "Since we started planning this whole wedding, it's like you've become a different person," he says, shaking his head. "I put it down to stress but…"

I grab his hands. "That's what it is. Stress. I just need to feel safe. And I will. After we're married."

He sighs and looks deep into my eyes in that searching way he has.

"If it's so important to you, then yes," he says, "we'll set everything up for pictures. Just get some sleep."

It takes every ounce of self-control not to sigh with relief. This is going to work. I will be married, and this will work.

Mark's eyes slide to the door, and I wonder if he's thinking about Ophelia. An uneasy feeling swirls in my body. I dismiss it.

I am safe. I am happy. I am loved.

CHAPTER EIGHTY-ONE

HOLLY

I blink to consciousness on the cold floor of the panic room.

"Holly? Holly?" It's Fitzwilliam's voice. "Are you awake?"

"Am I awake?" I mumble, putting out a hand fuzzily in the semi-gloom and finding stone floor. "I think so." I look up into Fitzwilliam's pale-blue eyes. They look a lot less haughty than I remember.

Fitzwilliam breathes out hard. "Thank God," he says. "I thought… Never mind. Let's get you up."

I sit with effort, then squeeze my eyes tightly shut. "OK. Wow," I say. "That hurts."

"You fell down the steps," he explains. "Knocked you out cold." He hesitates. "We're trapped here, Holly. Someone shut us in. I've been pounding the door for hours."

"For *hours*?" I touch my head tentatively. "How long was I out?"

"I can't say for sure but…I'd guess it must be morning by now."

I turn my head to look up toward the dark steps out. "Adrianna's wedding day," I say thoughtfully. "Someone pushed me down the stairs," I add.

Fitzwilliam nods. "I figured. Do you know who?"

I shake my head, wince. The full extent of our situation is beginning to weigh heavily on me.

"The portrait door has resealed," says Fitzwilliam. "We're trapped down here."

"No one knows where we are," I say.

I get to my feet with Fitzwilliam's help and take a moment to absorb where I am.

"Wow." I pause to rub my eyes. "This is real, right?"

"It's real."

I take it in. "Jesus."

The room is furnished in the loudest, brightest kitsch imaginable. I have never seen so many colors, patterns, and textures all in one place. My eyes settle on slices of lime-green psychedelic wallpaper, hung in thick stripe formation, next to purple flocked paisley and a chintzy rose pattern.

Furnishings are velvet, in joyful pinks and blues. There's a bar set with gaudy bottles of liquor and retro glassware, and low seats have been scattered all around. Rococo cornicing has been repurposed into decorative wall shelves and stuffed with garish ornaments. A kind-faced plastic Jesus shares a shelf with a smoked-glass tiki tankard, three ceramic rabbits, and a battery-operated Hawaiian hula dancer, revolving languidly.

There's a kind of magnificence to it. Like someone put Fortune House's deep colors and colonial elegance through the looking glass.

But several aspects of the decor don't fit. Above the bar is a wooden family crest, which, by the pockmarked surface and peeling paint, looks to be antique. It depicts the famous Kensington swords and ravens, above the words DISCIPLINE, SELF-RESTRAINT, AND GODLINESS.

Then there's the wall art. Saints and apostles, painted in the same lurid colors as the interior, but somehow different. Less exultant. More macabre. One saint is being shot at on all sides by arrows, while another lies on a burning bed. A third, his round halo flaming, is being boiled in oil.

Finally, at the center is a Chesterfield daybed in soft chocolate-colored leather, sitting grandly. Nothing about it matches the decor at all.

"Do you recognize the bed?" asks Fitzwilliam. "It was the one Adrianna was manacled to for three days. I guess it's here as some kind of lurid memento of the kidnapping."

"Seems in bad taste." I catch a glimpse of myself in a flock-framed mirror with *Good Times* written on the glass. My blue hair is flat, and eyeliner is smudged around my round eyes.

"If you think that's in bad taste, look here." He beckons me a little farther in. Hanging from an elaborately corniced ceiling are three dresses. Bridal gowns.

"Shit." I move closer.

"Is that a scientific term?" asks Fitzwilliam.

I eye the dresses, and shiver despite myself.

"This was Ophelia's design, right?"

"Ophelia's and Silky's, I think."

We're interrupted by a soft beeping sound.

"Wine coolers," explains Fitzwilliam as the noise stops. "Looks as though they have some automatic temperature adjustment built into the racks."

He nods in the direction of the largest wine display I've ever seen. Hundreds of deep burgundy and olive-topped bottles glow expensively under the low light. They take up three entire walls.

"Did you take a look to see if Simone set anything up down here?" I ask.

"Not yet." He manages a small smile. "I was somewhat preoccupied." Fitzwilliam runs a hand sheepishly through his thick crop of black hair.

I smile back. My eyes land on the giant daybed where Adrianna was famously manacled for her three-day ordeal.

The wine display beeps again, soft and urgent. Frowning, I turn toward it. "Should it be making that noise?"

"Probably means the temperature is off for one of the racks," he says.

I look at the small LED displays topping each column of wine. Around a hundred in total, lined all around the room.

"Those numbers aren't temperature," I murmur. "That's a relative humidity reading."

"I'm impressed," says Fitzwilliam. "You know something about wine."

"I know something about cadaver storage," I correct him. "We use relative humidity in morgues."

I take a step back, letting my eyes range the digital displays. My finger tracks along the various displays. They all vary. My eyes light on one.

"This one is eighty-five to ninety."

"That would be high for wine," says Fitzwilliam. "You'd risk mold on the corks."

"It's the relative humidity used to preserve bodies." I turn to him excitedly. "Simone, this is just the kind of detail she liked to talk about on the show."

My eyes rove the rack. It must hold sixty or so bottles, floor to ceiling. Where to start?

"*Six feet under*," I murmur. Taking a breath, I stand on my tiptoes and count down six places from the top. When I reach the sixth bottle, I slide it free.

"Nothing out of the ordinary," I tell Fitzwilliam, disappointed. "It's just a regular bottle of wine."

I push a hand into the cavity. "Nothing here."

"I'm taller than you," says Fitzwilliam. "Let me look." He comes to stand beside me, peering into the space in the wine rack, then pushes a long arm deep inside.

"Anything?" I ask hopefully, knowing in my heart there isn't.

To my great surprise, Fitzwilliam's hand emerges, clutching a sheaf of documents.

"Crammed right into the back," he says, handing them to me. "You'd never find them unless you knew where to look."

My heart catches in my chest. "Fitzwilliam," I breathe, "this is it. The documents Simone wanted to reveal on *Wrongly Accused*."

CHAPTER EIGHTY-TWO

ADRIANNA

I close my eyes as Ophelia sprays a shimmering mist of dewy foundation on my face. She has already spent an hour fitting a heavy piece of chestnut hair into my own curling tresses, pulling and shaping it with a brush and tongs.

As she finishes, I sit staring into the mirror. Ophelia was always the best at doing my hair and makeup.

"I am Adrianna Fucking Kensington," I mutter, at my reflection. "I'm getting married today."

"Ready?" Ophelia's beaming smile is fixed in its usual place. She wears the magenta gown I carefully picked out so as not to complement her skin tone. I wonder briefly if I should have been kinder.

No, I remind myself, *it's not about me. It's about the Kensington brand.* The Kensington brand has to be perfect today.

"Did you see Petra?" I ask.

"Not yet." Ophelia shakes her head, still smiling. "She stayed up pretty late. I'm guessing she's nursing a sore head this morning. I'm sure she'll be here on time for the pictures."

"Petra stayed up late?" I don't remember that. But then again, I don't remember much at all from last night.

"How is your head?" Ophelia stands just a little too close.

"Fine," I say, slightly unnerved. "It's fine."

"Want me to check your breath?" she suggests. "Be sure you're not breathing tequila fumes on your groom?" She says it lightly, like a joke. Almost. But then, without waiting for my response, she leans in an inch from my face and inhales.

I sit rigidly in my chair.

"You smell *gorgeous*," says Ophelia, her head back but not far back enough to be a normal distance. "He's lucky to have you," she whispers.

Confusion is knocking my mind around. Things are fitting together.

"Ophelia," I say quietly, "why did you get into my bed last night?" There's a long tense moment where our eyes lock. Her narrow freckled forehead puckers.

"You asked me to," she says, mouth downturned, eyes flitting around the room. "Don't you remember? You didn't feel safe."

"But you told Mark you were afraid I would vomit."

"I…" She nods. Two tight inclines of her head. "Of course I told *Mark* that," she says. "I didn't want him to think you'd invited me into bed with you the night before your wedding."

I take in her amber eyes. Everything there suggests truthfulness. Dedication. Devotion.

And yet…it's all so confusing.

There's a knock at the door. I look up to see Dad. He has a small smile on his face.

"Well, you look beautiful," he says gruffly, "but that was never in any doubt."

Dad was always terrible at delivering compliments. "I got rid of the security like you wanted," he says.

I smile at him in surprise.

He shrugs. "Maybe you were right. Times have changed. You're taking the brand in a new direction. We don't need to be so heavy."

"Thanks, Dad."

"I...I got something to say..." He's rubbing the back of his neck awkwardly. "Won't take long."

I arch an eyebrow. Sounds like this will be good. He doesn't even seem to have registered Ophelia as a physical presence and talks on without regard to her hovering uncertainly in the room. It's easy to do that with Ophelia.

"Georgia says I never told you girls I was proud of you," he says.

"Dad, is this going to be a speech? Because—"

"When I married your mother, I thought that day was going to be the making of me. I changed my name from Leopold Kolowski to Leopold Kensington, and I was so sure the wedding would be us all coming together." His mouth twists. "'Stead, my father said I'd betrayed his name and refused to attend the ceremony, and your mother's family didn't even show up."

"I know this, Dad," I say. It's an old story.

"Then we had your christening," he continues, "and I thought this would be the one. The big family gathering. Your Polish grandpappy was dead by then. Grandma Kensington was actually going to attend. Along with a lot of newspaper reporters." He chuckles. "You know that lady didn't look in my direction once for the whole service? That's quite a feat. The papers ran with 'The Big Freeze: Lady Kensington Ices the Fish Vendor's Son.'" He shakes his head. "My guys found out later it was your grandma's people who gave them that headline."

"Granny can be mean."

"You don't know the half of it. Don't worry," he adds. "I'm nearly to my point. This isn't some story bad-mouthing your mom's family, though God knows"—he brushes a hand through his dark hair—"I have a lot of 'em." His eyes drift to the window. "All those years, trying to get with those people. Now fate conspires to keep the mighty Kensingtons from my daughter's wedding. And the best thing is, *you don't care.*" He beams suddenly. "And I couldn't be prouder. You taught me something today that I should have learned years ago. The Kensington name, you're bigger than that now." He grips my hand tight. "You've made your own name."

Tears leap into my eyes. "Thanks, Dad."

He stands in awkward silence for a moment as if deciding whether to speak.

"I do have one last thing to say," he adds.

I roll my eyes. "Dad, you can make a speech at the wedding."

"I messed up."

He can't meet my eyes. I feel the hairs on the back of my neck stand on end. Dad never, ever admits to being wrong.

"With Petra," he says. "I messed up."

This time, I can feel Ophelia tense beside me. Every part of her body is radiating high alert. I guess Petra's name has that effect on all of us.

"Me and Petra are done," he says. "And I should have listened to you when you were at school. I was too busy, but that didn't mean I didn't *care.* I would kill for you and your sister."

There's a long pause as we look at one another.

"I know, Dad," I tell him. "I know. Now quit making me cry. It took two hours to get this makeup right."

I don't risk a glance at Ophelia, but I notice her chest is high like she's holding her breath.

"So." Dad stands, his voice back to normal, shaking his head like he's getting himself in the game. "You ready to get married?"

CHAPTER EIGHTY-THREE

HOLLY

Fitzwilliam comes to stand at my side as I hold the documents we found in the wine rack.

Many pages, bound together in the same kind of format you find legal paperwork. But it isn't a case file. The front page is official, dated three years ago. Stamped with the logo of *Policía Nacional de Colombia*. I frown at the report, trying to fit my high school Spanish to the words.

"It looks like...a charge sheet," I decide. "*Cargos*...I think that's Spanish for *charges*, and the crime is *secuestro y tentativa de asesinato*. Is that *murder*?"

"Attempted murder." Fitzwilliam is reading over my shoulder. "Kidnapping and attempted murder."

"Petra Morka," I say pointing. "Her name is listed."

"*Sospechosos*," says Fitzwilliam. "I think that's...*suspect*. I wish Ortiz were here," he murmurs, pushing dark hair from his forehead. "OK. So it looks like...Petra Morka was charged. With kidnapping and attempted murder. Three years ago."

"For Adrianna's kidnapping? Or something else?"

I flip pages. Suddenly Fitzwilliam is tapping my arm frantically.

"What?" I look up.

The door to the safe room is now standing open, and a figure is halfway down the stairs.

It's Petra Morka. She is holding a gun.

"Holly Stone," she says, "and the cop pretending to be her assistant."

I eye the gun, my heart picking up a beat. "It was you," I say. "You pushed me down the stairs."

"Sorry about that." She shrugs, not sounding sorry. Petra points. "Drop the papers," she adds. "Now."

I let them fall. Petra gestures for Fitzwilliam to place them on the bottom step. Keeping her eyes on us, she waits until he backs away, then scoops them up.

Her implacable expression slips briefly when she sees the title of the document. Petra regards them for a moment, then flips to the back page. Her famous jaw sets as she reads. Nothing in her face gives away the slightest emotion.

Then Petra places the papers on the floor in front of her and kneels. Gun held high, she produces a lighter from her pocket.

"Don't!" My eyes are glued to the flickering fire. "Please," I say. "Whatever is in those papers, Simone wanted me to find it out."

"You?" Petra's mesmerizing blue eyes widen fractionally. "You think you meant something to Simone?"

She holds the lighter to the bottom of the documents.

"No!" Fitzwilliam lunges for the flames, but Petra fires a warning shot. He freezes halfway across the room as plaster rains down.

I watch helplessly as the tongues of flame lick at the pages. "It was you," I say, "wasn't it? You kidnapped Adrianna."

Petra backs away from the flaming documents, out and up the stairs.

"You won't be at the wedding, Holly," she tells me as she closes the door. "It took Adrianna three days to escape from here. Somehow, I don't think you'll be so lucky."

CHAPTER EIGHTY-FOUR

HOLLY

Fitzwilliam has made another attempt to open the door of the panic room, but it's hopeless. He troops back down the stairs, dejected. I've stamped out what's left of the flaming documents and rake through the remains with my fingers. There's nothing left of the police report but ash and a rising column of pale white smoke.

"Damn it!" says Fitzwilliam. "At least we know what was in that report," he adds thoughtfully. "It must have been Petra, right, who snatched Adrianna?"

I nod slowly. "Guess so," I say. "Now we just need to figure a way out so we can warn her."

"You think Petra is planning to do something bad to Adrianna on her wedding day?"

"It would fit with why she trapped us down here and burned the documents," I say. "Maybe something about the wedding affects Petra in a way we haven't realized." I'm thinking of Simone. The legal documents.

But why do I feel like an important piece of the puzzle is missing? My thoughts keep pinging back to the kidnapping. Somehow Petra doesn't altogether fit.

Something else is waving for my attention. About the way the smoke from the ashen remains of the documents is rising.

Slowly, I get to my feet. Fitzwilliam wears a hopeless expression on his usually stoic face.

"Sealed shut," he says. "With the wedding, I don't think anyone will think to check down here for at least a day."

"Airflow," I tell him, following where the last strands of smoke are curling white fingers toward the back of the panic room.

"Holly," he sighs, "you're doing the thinking-out-loud thing again."

"Look how the smoke from those burning documents is moving. It should be still."

"Maybe there's ventilation of some kind in here."

"Maybe," I agree. "But I've used vapor in forensics before to identify airflow, and that smoke is flowing smoothly. Not jerky, like with AC. That suggests a natural current of air." I scan around the room. "It never made sense to me," I say, "why you would put a panic room so far from the bedrooms."

"The wine cellar," says Fitzwilliam, "needs to be underground."

"Maybe," I say. "But we also have the mystery of how a masked kidnapper dragged Adrianna in here through a party full of people. Put those two anomalies together…" My eyes track the wisps of smoke. "The most obvious answer is there's another way in. Or out."

I follow the thin stream as it crosses the room and seems to pool around one particular spot. A large floor-to-ceiling mirror with a gilt frame. I watch it, assessing for a moment how the smoke curls and vanishes around the back.

"See that?" I point triumphantly, but Fitzwilliam doesn't seem to be keeping pace with my line of thought. "A secret behind a mirror," I murmur. "How very like the Kensington family." I stand back, considering, then reach out an experimental hand and push the mirror.

Just as I hoped, the glass recedes before springing back against my touch, peeling away from the wall.

The mirror is a door.

"Holly," says Fitzwilliam, moving toward me, "you found a way out!"

"Makes up for my general weirdness, right?"

There's a strangely loaded moment where we're both looking at one another. Fitzwilliam steps away first, looking awkward.

He looks to where a set of wooden steps is revealed behind the mirror.

"Let's get out of here."

CHAPTER EIGHTY-FIVE

HOLLY

We take the wooden stairs up several flights through a musty and cobwebbed stairwell until we eventually arrive at a small door. It's hotel room-style. White-painted wood with the kind of handle that fits a key card. But when I push down on it, the door is unlocked.

Fitzwilliam sighs in relief.

"Get behind me, Holly," he whispers. "We don't know what could be on the other side."

I let him push the door a crack and survey what's beyond before sliding his body through. After a moment, he beckons me to follow.

I emerge into a very familiar room. Wall-to-ceiling glass, with ocean views all the way over the island.

"It's the Tower Suite," I say. The room is decorated for the wedding. Orchids are scattered on the bed. Champagne sits chilling in an ice bucket. The infinity pool has a heart of flower petals floating daintily on the water by some clever trick of logistics.

"This bedroom connects to the panic room." I look back. "The wardrobe," I add. "There was a secret passage hidden behind the wardrobe door."

I turn back in amazement to see the entrance we just came through seems to have completely vanished.

"You would *never* find that," I say, "unless you knew it was there."

"The police didn't," Fitzwilliam points out. He takes it in. "Just like you said. Leopold connected his panic room to the suite the family sleeps in."

"I guess he wanted to keep his family safe."

"Fathers generally do."

I don't reply, because this hasn't been my experience. Not to mention this seems to go beyond what *safe* means to most people. "Adrianna saw a figure wearing a mask out on the balcony," I say. "Everyone assumed she'd imagined it, because there was no way anyone could have gotten inside. But if someone knew this secret entrance, all they'd need do is run downstairs to the panic room and come back up this way."

"All points to Petra," Fitzwilliam says. "If she was sleeping with Leopold, it's likely he would have let her in on the secret entrance, right? So she could sneak into his bedroom after dark without his daughters seeing?"

"If it was Petra," I point out, "she would have known that locking us in the panic room wouldn't trap us forever."

"Petra didn't figure on you being so smart," he says.

I nod, taking in the beautiful ocean view, wondering if Leopold ever appreciated it for anything more than a panoramic heads-up on a possible attack.

"Leopold Kensington is on a private island with views in all directions," I say. "Hires the best security money can buy. And still feels the need to build a concrete bulletproof bunker underneath where he and his daughters sleep. Doesn't that seem a little extreme?"

"Given his daughter was kidnapped, I'd say it was good foresight. Not accounting for how she was snatched, of course."

I sigh. "For all her money and comforts, I wouldn't want Adrianna Kensington's life," I tell Fitzwilliam. "Moving with an armed guard. Being constantly at risk of kidnapping or robbery."

Fitzwilliam is looking at the beach. "The wedding," he says, "it's starting."

Down in the white sand cove below, the entire beach has been decorated for the wedding. Deep hedgerows of tropical leaves and bright jungle orchids have been created on either side of a wide aisle.

Walking down it, a matching outsize bouquet in her hand, is the slim figure of Adrianna Kensington.

At the other end is Mark Li. And standing next to him, the unmistakably tall figure of Petra. Her camera is raised toward the approaching bride.

The blush-colored velvet chairs that surround the bride are empty. There is no celebrant. Two large black speakers take the place of an orchestra.

Mark stands under a two-foot-deep ceremonial archway of vivid flowers and dark green palm leaves, awaiting his bride. Next to him stand Ophelia and Georgia in their magenta bridesmaid gowns. Petra is taking a relentless flurry of pictures.

I hesitate, watching Adrianna's slow progress. A long train trails behind her. Leopold Kensington is at her side in a brash-looking suit.

"It's not a real wedding," I tell Fitzwilliam. "There's no one here." Something about the staged nature of this has jogged something very sudden and concrete into my mind.

Facts and theories begin to converge. "I think we've got everything the wrong way around."

"What do you mean?"

"*Wrongly Accused,*" I tell him. "Simone's show is *Wrongly Accused.* I don't know how I didn't put those things together before. I think Simone was trying to clear Petra's name. And the fingerprint access. If the kidnapper took Adrianna from this room to the panic room, she must have let them in that night."

"You're saying she knew her kidnapper? Does that mean Adrianna isn't in danger?"

"Not from Petra," I say. "But we need to get down to the wedding before it's too late."

CHAPTER EIGHTY-SIX

HOLLY

Fitzwilliam and I race out of the house, and the feeling of tropical morning sunshine on my face is the most welcome sensation I've felt since landing on the island.

The quad bikes have been driven out of view and decorated in pink and red flowers to match the wedding.

"There," I say, pointing.

I jump aboard, ripping the floral display from the handlebars and tossing it onto the manicured lawn.

"Orchestra music," I say as the first strains wind up from the beach. "We've still got time."

Fitzwilliam nods as I rev the bike and spin away from Fortune House, sending an arc of sand flaring behind us. We bounce through jungle and pass the open expanse of the viewing platform.

"Care to share your theory with me?" he asks as sand sprays up.

"The fingerprints on the birthday invitation," I say, "they were bothering me. Simone obviously meant for them to be some dramatic reveal. Why would she go to that trouble just to show that Adrianna was the only person to touch her birthday invitation? Then I realized." I bank the bike hard left. "It wasn't who the fingerprints belonged to, it was the way they were distributed on the invitation. That was what Simone wanted us to see."

We're nearing the wedding. Adrianna has almost reached Mark, standing expectantly ready for her. I put on a spurt of speed.

CHAPTER EIGHTY-SEVEN

ADRIANNA

As I stand at the foot of the aisle, everything has finally come together. The dress, a princess construction that took two people to lace me into, looks every part the Cinderella moment I dreamed of. It weighs so much I broke into a sweat walking here. If it wasn't for Dad, his arm keeping me upright, I honestly don't know if I could have made it.

But that journey seems symbolic. All the hardships. All the struggle and pain. They're behind me now. I'll walk up this aisle as Adrianna Kensington and back out again as a new person. Adrianna Li. A different family. A new start. No longer dependent on Kensington wealth.

We've already signed the documents. The only thing that needs to happen is for the bride and groom to say, "I do."

Mark's gently smiling face comes into focus, and my heart soars. Then my eyes settle on the bridesmaids: Ophelia and Georgia. Petra is standing to the side, taking pictures.

I'm struck by a sudden feeling that I've known for a long time, a thing I should have acted on. My three bridesmaids, lined up in their magenta dresses. I'm terrified to go any closer to them. Something really bad is about to happen.

I turn slightly to my dad.

"I can't," I whisper. "We need to stop the wedding."

Dad's face tightens into a pained false smile. "It's just wedding jitters," he says, speaking from the corner of his mouth. "Every bride has them. Your mom had them. You'll be fine."

"No." I'm wriggling against his arm, but Dad keeps his grip tight.

"You can't ditch Mark at the altar," he says. "He'll be humiliated in every press outlet the world over. Just get through this part. We can work it out later. Mark's a good guy."

It's all happening too fast. The heavy dress, the beating sun, the smiles of my bridesmaids, which now suddenly seem snakelike.

My feet plant themselves, one in front of the other. I have the strongest feeling that I'm walking right into a viper's nest.

I arrive at Mark's side. He smiles at me. A gentle, loving smile. Beneath the veil, he can't see my expression. Dad wipes a tear from his eye.

"You take good care of her," he tells Mark.

I'm looking at Mark, but in my peripheral vision, the bridesmaids are lined up in their neat row. One of the girls is raising something from beneath her bouquet.

As Dad reaches to lift my veil, he catches the movement too.

Ever on guard, he twists to be sure there's no threat.

And then, from behind the bridesmaids, I see a figure. Running toward me.

It's Holly Stone.

CHAPTER EIGHTY-EIGHT

HOLLY

I reach the aisle just as Leopold Kensington is about to lift his daughter's veil. His expression is one of blissful pride.

He switches around in alarm as I come to an ungainly halt between the bride and groom, panting with exertion.

"Holly?" says Mark, confused and angry.

Adrianna twists around in shock. "What are you doing?" she hisses, her eyes glancing across to where Petra has retrieved a different lens from the folds of her gown and is attaching it to her camera.

"You should know what you're marrying into," I tell Mark. "Silky was murdered."

As soon as the words leave my mouth, I see it. She knows. Adrianna must have figured it out, somewhere between putting on her gown and walking up the aisle. Her sapphire eyes fill with tears.

"Holly," she whispers helplessly. "Not *now*. Please."

Petra flashes another picture.

Adrianna glances miserably at the flickering camera. Opens her mouth to say something, then changes her mind, turning to me.

"I had it all wrong," I say. "I thought someone was obsessed with you, trying to stop your wedding." I take a breath. "But none of this was ever about that."

I turn to Petra.

"You threw me off track," I tell her. "Destroying the wedding cake. Sneaking into her suite wearing a cloak and mask. Writing threats in the sand. But all you ever wanted was to photograph Adrianna looking freaked out. Those images could get your flagging photography career back on track." I shake my head. "But you had nothing to do with Simone's death."

I turn to Fitzwilliam.

"You were right," I tell him. "And wrong. Criminal profiling is the key to this entire case. This whole thing, even Silky's murder, was one big publicity stunt."

My eyes lock on Leopold Kensington.

"The actions of a very gifted publicity person."

Leopold's eyes meet mine, and I know I've finally got it right.

It was him, right from the start.

"You had me fooled," I tell him. "I assumed whoever killed Silky didn't want the wedding to take place. What you wanted was to manage the publicity to a perfect storm."

Leopold's face switches, and just for a second, I see a flash of someone else. The fish vendor's boy who learned to be tough because he had no other option. Then the weight of the years settles back in. I notice his fists silently clench. I keep talking.

"You had it all planned out. Adrianna's kidnapper would be found dead on Elysium right before her wedding. It would be the story of the decade. Just the thing to get all eyes back on the Kensington brand and bring high-spenders to Elysium by the boatload."

I pause for effect.

"But then Simone died unexpectedly, and you had to rework the story quickly. Revive the kidnapper earlier than planned."

I glance at the cameras.

Leopold raises a single eyebrow. "I wasn't even in the Plaza when Simone died."

"No, you weren't." I agree. "Simone's death was an accident. An accident you made the most of. Silky called you the night Simone slipped through the scaffold to her death. I imagine she was hysterical. But she also knew she could trust you to cover for her. After all, you'd been supplying her with drugs for years."

It's a guess, but I can tell right away I got it right. Leopold blinks, considering.

"At some point during the conversation, you must have realized this could actually work in your favor," I continue. "You told Silky to put the body in Adrianna's dress case, knowing it would be wheeled into the Plaza ballroom the next morning. You arrived early at the Plaza, before the wedding demo, allowing you enough time to stage the body. You had the perfect alibi for when Simone was murdered, and no one suspected a thing."

"Interesting theory." Leopold raises a stocky eyebrow. "We can edit these photos, right?" he says to Petra, waving toward the camera. "Crazy fan tries to disrupt Adrianna's wedding."

Petra dutifully takes another snap.

I notice Mark's eyes widen slightly, like he's not sure what to believe. Leopold puts a reassuring hand on his shoulder and turns to me.

"The kidnapper has been identified," rumbles Leopold. "It was a tragedy. But Silky had mental health issues and a drug addiction. She was an old family friend. None of us had any reason to wish her harm."

"Except that Silky knew the big family secret," I interject. "Just like Simone did."

Something crosses Leopold's face now. Something a lot like fear.

"Can someone get this crazy girl out of here? Before she ruins my daughter's entire wedding." Leopold glances around for his ever-present security before realizing with cold shock that there's no one at hand.

He lunges forward and grabs hold of my arm. I jerk it free. "You've been buying Silky's silence for years. First with money, then with drugs. But she was becoming more demanding. Addicts always do. So you came up with a plan. Give her an uncut batch, strong enough to overdose, then frame her as the kidnapper. The perfect end to a clickbait story."

Georgia steps in. "How dare you," she says, her voice trembling. "How dare you come here on Dri's wedding day with these accusations. We were all traumatized by Dri's kidnapping, Dad more than all of us. He would never risk the real kidnapper going free."

"You're right. He wouldn't," I say.

"What are you talking about?" demands Georgia.

"The big secret Leopold has been trying to hide. The family secret Simone planned to expose on *Wrongly Accused*." I take a breath. "I couldn't understand how the kidnapper had bypassed such an elaborate security system and gotten into the Tower Suite that night. It's set for Adrianna's fingerprints, and any kind of breach would have shown up. The only way someone could have drugged Adrianna and dragged her through the secret route to the panic room would be if she had let them in. But there was a second possibility."

I whirl around, looking into Adrianna's frightened deep-blue eyes.

"Your dad isn't the only publicity genius in the family, is he, Adrianna? The entire kidnapping was a stunt devised by his twenty-year-old daughter." I turn back to Leopold, the groom, and the bridesmaids. "Adrianna kidnapped herself."

CHAPTER EIGHTY-NINE

HOLLY

The revelation of Adrianna's self-kidnapping ripples through the small wedding party like a detonating grenade. Mark's face explodes in wide-eyed disbelief. Georgia takes an audible gasp of air, stepping back, the bouquet lifting defensively to her chest. Ophelia looks devastated. Heartbroken even. Leopold flows through a full spectrum of anger and panic, settling on menacing calculation.

"There never was a kidnapping," I tell Mark. "It was a setup all along. Twenty-year-old Adrianna knew she needed a big splash to break into the media world. She'd been raised to do it after all. And Adrianna was smart enough to know how much attention stalker and kidnapping cases got. Her first move was to send herself a threatening birthday invitation signed by Trinity. But the spread of the fingerprints just didn't match the pattern of someone opening an invitation and reading it. There are extra prints, right where you'd expect the person who wrote the name on it to make them."

Petra snaps away, adjusting her lens to capture Adrianna's mortified face.

"It was easy to lock herself in the family panic room." I pause. "The simplicity of the plan was what made it so brilliant. But

Adrianna messed up. Used the manacles she'd seen around the island and didn't realize rust had damaged the mechanism, making them impossible to unlock once shut."

Adrianna swallows heavily. Something awful twists on her face, like she wants to hurt me.

"Was it the court case against the school you wanted to detract attention from?" I ask her. "Or did you just realize how much money your story could make for the family nightclubs after Leopold sank every cent into construction work on the Kensington graveyard?"

She shakes her head.

"Your masked captor's persona was an amalgamation of all the terrors you had suppressed from boarding school," I say. "The stories you so desperately wanted to tell."

I look into Adrianna's famous sapphire eyes.

"Because I think you *do* care," I tell her simply, "that the legacy of your ancestor's cruelty is still hurting girls sixty years later at Kensington Manor School. If you didn't care, how could you have dreamed up a kidnapper like Trinity?"

"I couldn't," whispers Adrianna, her voice choked. "Silky wanted me to testify against the school. I *couldn't*." Her eyes are pleading.

Petra snaps a picture.

"Put the camera down," Adrianna hisses. "Put the fucking camera down."

Petra hesitates. She looks as if she's considering the next angle to snap from.

In one quick movement, Adrianna dives toward Leopold and pulls a gun from his waistband.

"No!" Leopold acts on instinct, snatching for it. He's too late.

Adrianna points the gun toward Petra.

Petra actually laughs. "What are you going to do, Adrianna?" she says. "Shoot me? You always were a coward."

The gun wavers in Adrianna's hand. Her jaw tightens and untightens.

Ophelia steps forward smoothly. She wraps her hand around the gun, enfolding Adrianna's grip. She turns her face up, and their eyes meet.

"Don't let her win," says Ophelia, holding her gaze. Something childlike and tragic flares in Adrianna's cobalt eyes.

"You think you're her savior?" demands Petra, outraged. Her angular face twists in hurt.

"*I* was your protector," says Petra. "*I* protected all of you. What I did was for your own good—"

It all happens in seconds. The gun fires as Leopold steps in front of Petra. He jerks back like he's been hit. But it's Petra who the bullet catches, square in the chest.

There's a look of disbelief on her face, followed by shock. She brings a hand to the flowering patch of blood on her silk-clad chest, then collapses to the ground.

"Petra!" Leopold's face is stricken as he kneels by her side.

"That was for Silky," says Adrianna quietly. "And all of us girls who survived. I should have done it a long time ago."

Mark takes a step back, eyes wide. "Dri..." he whispers. "What did you *do*?"

"Fuck." Adrianna ignores him, ripping off her veil and throwing it to the ground. She addresses her father: "How are we going to fix this fucking mess?"

Leopold stands, his face unreadable, and takes the gun from Adrianna's unresisting hand.

He takes a long steadying breath, then turns it on me.

"It's OK," he says. "We have a forensic expert. Holly and I are going to have a meeting. Work out how she can fix this for us. She'll make it look exactly how we want when the police arrive." Leopold grabs my arm. His eyes land on Fitzwilliam.

"No one try to follow us," he adds, pulling me away from the wedding party at gunpoint. "Or Holly dies."

CHAPTER NINETY

HOLLY

Leopold walks me at gunpoint back toward Fortune House. I look back onto the flower-strewn beach where Adrianna is leaning against Ophelia, tears rolling down her face. Georgia is gesticulating, pointing at Petra's unmoving body. Mark stands alone, straight-backed with shock, staring at the three women. Fitzwilliam is looking desperately in my direction, clearly waiting for a chance to follow.

I see Georgia press a radio to her ear. She's calling security, I think numbly, all hope of Fitzwilliam rescuing me fading away.

"There's no way you can pull this off," I tell Leopold. "You can't cover up what Adrianna just did. Even if I helped you, and I won't."

Leopold wipes sweat from his brow and looks dolefully up at the morning sun. He's deathly pale, I notice, and the walk seems to be an effort.

As we reach the stone steps, he stops to lean a hand on the balustrade, breathing heavily, the other keeping the gun pointed at me.

"I'm sorry, Holly," he says, a wheeze to his voice. "I'm building a legacy here. Something to keep my family safe. My wife and daughters didn't grow up where I grew up."

"But *I* did, Mr. Kensington. And a whole lot of those people would choose to stay poor rather than make the choices you made."

"More fool them. I see what happens to poor people in New York. A good father doesn't put his kids out with the trash. In America, you need to take what you can with both hands."

"You murdered an innocent girl," I tell him.

He shakes his head. "Silky was a good kid. Used to be a good kid," he corrects himself. "The drugs changed her. She wasn't *her* anymore. Hadn't been for years." His eyes light on me. "Have you any idea how it feels, to grieve someone who's still walking around? Like a freakin' zombie got their body?" He talks on without waiting for an answer. "We tried everything to help Silky," he says. "For years. It was that school that messed her up pretty good. She would have died sometime soon anyway. I made my peace with her death years ago." Leopold takes a slow, juddering breath.

"I'm just a scientist, Mr. Kensington," I tell him. "You want a therapist, go pay one."

He laughs, winces, then stands a little straighter, eyeing the large house. "I'm sorry you had to get mixed up in all this. Let's get going."

I take in the grand Fortune House.

"The Kensingtons' prison never went away," I tell Leopold as he takes one step at a time, holding the left side of his body. "It's still here. Forcing women to fit the right image. The prison bars just turned into high heels and hair straighteners."

"This way." Leopold jerks the gun. "The Tower Suite."

We enter the Tower Suite to see the glass-walled room with its honeymoon decorations. Scattered flowers and iced champagne.

For a second, I can see the whole setup gives Leopold pause.

Then he regroups and collects himself.

"Stand there." He waves the gun, gesturing for me to walk out toward the edge of the infinity pool.

"Whatever you're planning—"

"Just step out onto the edge," he says. "There's something I want you to see."

I weigh my options, but it's incredibly hard to keep my thoughts straight with the gun pointed at my face. Swallowing, I inch out onto the lip of the infinity pool where the water flows over the edge, giving the illusion of pouring off into the sea below.

Warm chlorinated water washes over my feet. I look down onto the sheer edge of the cliff, and my stomach seems to rush up to meet my head. Closing my eyes momentarily, I force myself to look down. I'd been desperately hoping I could see some foliage to fall into or a jutting piece of rock. There's nothing. Just sheer, unforgiving cliff.

I always wondered how it would feel to stare death in the face. Now I know. It feels unreal. Like it's happening to somebody else.

Leopold walks out onto the edge, and the earlier breathlessness is overtaking his entire body. Each step seems to be costing him a huge effort. Is he unwell?

Pool water laps over his mirror-bright handmade leather shoes. The height doesn't seem to bother him, though he displays the smallest twitch of annoyance as water soaks dark patches into the leather of his footwear.

"You know," he says, "when I built this place, one of the guys supplying the coke told me this would be the spot for the perfect murder."

He looks down over the cliff. Fearless. My knees are shaking. "The guy thought from here, a body would be taken miles out to sea by the down current. Good chance no one would ever find it." He uses the gun to scratch his sweating forehead. "Simone was smart. I liked her." His face flickers in deep sadness. "When Silky rang me all hysterical, saying she'd pushed her...it was hard. Silky said they'd gotten into a fight," he adds, lifting his eyes to mine. "Simone tried to confiscate Silky's drugs. It was..." He hesitates, grits his teeth like he's in pain, then talks on. "Triggering," he continues. "Isn't that what you kids say? Something about having something precious taken away. Silky just reacted." A whisper of a smile plays out on his face. "That school had a lot to answer for."

"If you're going to kill me," I say, "get it over with. I won't help you fabricate evidence. And I don't see how my death will do you or your family any good."

He glances up at me with a small smile, his dark brown eyes surprisingly warm.

"I didn't bring you here to kill you, Holly Stone," he says. Leopold opens his jacket to reveal a growing patch of blood on his white shirt.

"My whole life, people think I'm a dumb Polack," he says. "Son of a dumb Polack. Fish boy." He laughs. "I'm not dumb, Holly. I know you can't make this go away. I didn't bring you here to kill you," he says again. "I just didn't want my daughters to see me die."

CHAPTER NINETY-ONE

HOLLY

I stare mutely at the bloody patch under Leopold's suit jacket.

He looks away from me, staring out over the island. The wound is in his lower abdomen. It's bad. I can't take my eyes off it.

"I thought... I didn't realize the bullet hit you," I say, staring at the blood-soaked shirt.

He nods. "You know, I barely felt a thing when it happened? Guess I was distracted." His face is sad. "Hurts like hell now." His mouth twitches. He pulls up his shirt and stares with mild disbelief at his own abdomen. It's distended with internal bruising, pumping a slow stream of blood from a small bullet wound. "I am going to die, right?" There's the tiniest shred of hope in his voice.

"Feels that way."

"Looks like it hit your intestine," I tell him, taking in the way the fluid and gases are pushing his abdomen outward. "You've got about an hour."

I don't tell him the rest. That he'll likely die in agony, poisoned by his own intestines.

He looks out to sea. "We can't get a medic out here for at least three hours."

"A medic probably couldn't help you anyway."

He smiles. "Thanks for not lying to me." Leopold is looking at the glass-walled sides of the Tower Suite.

"I built this place," he says. "From a patch of swamp and some broken old buildings. When people think of Caribbean islands, they think paradise. But I tell you, this was a hell on earth." He shakes his head. "Hard to imagine now, how I had the energy. Athena and I were a good team. In the old days."

The sun is rising in the sky, sending rays of gold and umber across the glittering sea. Leopold's eyes are distant, looking out over his island and the ocean beyond.

"What do you think, Holly?" he says. "If a person slipped and fell from here, would the body be swept out to sea?"

I look down at the rocks. The way the current swirls around them.

"If a person fell from here," I say, catching his meaning, "I think there's a good chance their body would never be recovered for forensic examination."

He nods. "When I was a kid," he says, "boys like me would disappear. Just disappear. Poof." He clicks his fingers. "No one gave a rat's ass about a sixteen-year-old goon from the Lower East Side. We were expendable." He fills his lungs, proud. "But if anything happened to *my* daughters, the *whole world* would notice." Leopold nods again, the slightest touch of pride on his pale face. "Fathers protect their daughters. That's what good fathers do."

We look at one another. Something passes between us. "Mr. Kensington..."

"You can call me Mr. Kolowski. I've been dodging that name my whole life. Might as well own it now." He sighs. "A good father also knows when to let go. Never was so good at that part."

Footsteps sound outside the room. Leopold takes a step toward the edge of the pool.

I instinctively move toward him. But it's too late.

Leopold drops from sight and is gone.

CHAPTER NINETY-TWO

ADRIANNA

When I saw the blood on the sand, I knew. I just knew. I even knew where Dad would go.

It was hard to run in the dress, and halfway up the hill, I ripped away the long train and threw it into the jungle undergrowth. Somewhere behind, I heard Mark's voice. Guess he must have finally pulled himself together. Because honestly, Mark was next to useless, standing open-mouthed on the beach while Georgia and Ophelia worked out a plan.

I made it into Fortune House, my dress dragging over the herringbone floors. I wasn't sure it would fit in the elevator, so I took the stairs. By the time I reached the door of the Tower Suite, sweat was pouring down the sides of my face.

I thought I could hear his voice on the other side of the door. But as I throw it open, Dad isn't here. It's just Holly, a strange look on her round face.

I follow the direction of her gaze. There's blood in the water, on the edge of the infinity pool. A flash of red that flows away and out of sight.

Dad has gone.

I knew it already, I realize. Before I opened the door or entered the house or even left the beach.

I close my eyes and sink to the floor of my honeymoon suite, the fifty-thousand-dollar bridal gown pooling around me. Dad always talked about the importance of family.

He was right. I'd give up all of it. Every last designer gown. Every multimillion-dollar sponsorship contract. Every pretty picture. I'd give it all up for one last minute with him.

I'm crying. Holly moves closer, looking uncertain.

"I knew he'd come here," I tell her, wiping my cheeks. "His whole goddamn domain, laid out before him. Why? Why didn't he say goodbye?"

Holly chews at her lip piercing uncertainly, then speaks.

"He didn't want you to see," she says. "But he loved you, Adrianna. Right until the end. That's more than a lot of us can say about their dads," she adds wryly.

I don't know how long I sit sobbing, but I'm suddenly aware of Holly kneeling at my side. She picks up the hem of my big dress and holds it out for me to wipe away the tears. Using a couture gown as a handkerchief is such a Holly thing to do, I actually laugh. Wipe at my eyes with the silken material. Guess it doesn't really matter anymore.

"For what it's worth," says Holly, "I think it was your dad's final gift to you."

I dab at my face, swallow hot tears. "How?" I demand.

"If your dad shot Petra," she says, "then the crime dies with him."

I open my mouth and shut it again. A weird laugh comes out. But actually, she has a point. Ophelia will agree to anything I ask her. Georgia's version of the truth has always been based on what looks good in the popular press. Mark...Mark didn't see, did he? It's a good plan, were it not for one obvious issue: Holly.

"You're not about to say *that* to the police, are you?" I say finally.

She considers. "Simone always thought perception and truth were two sides of the same coin." Holly moves to the edge of the pool. "Maybe he slipped," she says. "Slipped and fell."

I stand shakily, the dress resisting my movements. Walk thoughtfully to the edge of the pool. Water begins soaking into the hem of my skirts. The morning sun throws purple and pink shades onto the clouds. Elysium always did get the most beautiful mornings. I never quite appreciated that until now.

"Dad would have wanted a very dramatic death," I decide. "A cliff-top tussle with his long-term mistress. Maybe even pushed to his doom by one of my bridesmaids." My eyes track to Holly. "That would fit the family brand, wouldn't it?"

Holly doesn't reply.

I wipe a tear. "I'm glad he didn't go that way," I say. "I'm glad it was just a tragic accident. We can have a peaceful life now. Less drama."

CHAPTER NINETY-THREE

HOLLY

As Adrianna and I get down to the beach, Fitzwilliam runs toward us, closely followed by two security guards. He slows to a halt and stares. I guess we must look a sight. I'm helping Adrianna with the ragged remains of her huge gown, ripped from where she ran through the jungle and bloodstained from Petra's bleeding body. Her famous face is bloated with tears, the blue eyes swollen almost shut, airbrushed wedding makeup running in rivulets down her cheeks.

"Holly," says Fitzwilliam. "Thank God." His eyes switch to Adrianna. "What the hell happened?" he says finally. "Where's Leopold?"

"I'll fill you in later," I say as security clusters around Adrianna.

He nods. "Georgia put in a call to the mainland for a medic. Holly, Petra is OK."

"She is?"

"Yeah. Strangest thing," he adds. "The bullet seems to have been slowed down somehow. It hit Petra in the chest but only lodged a quarter inch deep. Enough to lodge in her rib cartilage and spill a lot of blood. She must have passed out from shock and pain."

A lot of emotions cross over Adrianna's face. "I need Mark," she says finally.

CHAPTER NINETY-FOUR

NEW YORK TIMES

ADRIANNA KENSINGTON WEDS

Heiress Adrianna Kensington and tech millionaire Mark Li married in a small private ceremony this week. After what an inside source referred to as "a series of distressing and personal incidents," Kensington and Li decided against a lavish wedding and refused official photography. The power couple elected to eschew a two-million-dollar sponsorship deal to marry privately on the Kensingtons' family island, which will be sold to an undisclosed buyer next month. The handful of family and friends in attendance praised the famous heiress for her dressed-down wedding and practical approach to the latest wave of Kensington family traumas. Sources close to the heiress claim she intends to step back from the nightclub business and concentrate on technology ventures.

PETRA MORKA NUDES SELL FOR MILLIONS

Images of Petra Morka's youthful indiscretions with an unnamed schoolgirl sold for $2.2 million last night. This makes them the most expensive set ever sold at a photography auction. The eight-figure sum was paid by the Saatchi Gallery, which described the pictures as "beautiful" and "haunting." They plan on showcasing them for a duration of eight months in an upcoming New York exhibition. Designer Ophelia Mills-Herd is slated to curate the exhibition, having won recent acclaim for her kitsch and unsettling interior design projects.

During the heated bidding war, Max Sutton, editor of *Titan Magazine*, walked out in fury. He claimed to have been tricked into bidding by Morka in order to inflate the bid. When asked about this tactic in an interview, Morka was typically candid and unapologetic.

"*Titan Magazine* has been exploiting women for years," she was quoted as saying. "Why shouldn't women get their own back?"

ELYSIUM ISLAND SOLD TO MEDICAL GROUP

Elysium Island, famously known for louche parties and all-night clubs, has been sold for an undisclosed sum to a private buyer. Elysium is due to be repurposed as a high-end luxury rehab, aimed to attract celebrities with addiction problems. The Kensingtons have refused to comment on whether the choice of buyer represents a kind of tribute to the late Silky Eversfield, who died of an overdose on the island. The new owner, Dr. Lutz of The Clinic Group, plans to roll out a range of luxury centers around the globe from its flagship facility in Seattle.

BODIES FOUND ON ELYSIUM

Mass graves have been found all over Elysium, the former party island of Leopold Kensington. Producers have released the last ever episode of *Wrongly Accused*, compiled from material gathered by host Simone Walters before her brutal murder. The feature-length show theorizes a dark history to Elysium in which hundreds of women were secretly buried on the island near a schoolhouse built with the explicit purpose of forcibly reeducating "fallen" women.

Elsewhere, prison cells and more graves were uncovered. In the 1950s, the island was part of a drive to turn out marriageable Catholic girls with a program of deprivation and penance. The model of "Discipline, Self-Restraint, and Godliness" was to be the founding principle of the famous Kensington Manor School in New York, which boasts several generations of prestigious alumni.

KENSINGTON MANOR SCHOOL TO CLOSE

After decades of educating schoolgirls in the famous Kensington ethos of "Discipline, Self-Restraint, and Godliness," the prestigious New York boarding school will close its doors next week. Founded by descendants of Lady Margaret Kensington, who opened the first Kensington Manor School on the Caribbean island of Elysium, the principles of indoctrinating girls with a firm religious education and hardy outlook have fallen out of favor in recent years. Founding pupils had their hair shorn and wore head coverings during their time at the school, but this practice was dropped in the New York iteration, with hygiene conditions improved.

The current headmistress, herself a former pupil, said "soft" parenting styles and use of cell phones to contact parents have made it increasingly difficult to maintain their traditional character-building techniques. The school denies that the decision to close is linked with accusations of negligence and abuse, which saw many wealthy families withdraw their girls. A spokesperson from the public school system claims Kensington Manor School was a relic of female oppression, where women were groomed as marital commodities.

GEORGIA KENSINGTON NEW CEO OF KENSINGTON BRAND

Georgia Kensington, best known for spectacular PR campaigns, got a promotion this month to become CEO of the Kensington brand.

She plans on working closely with supermodel Petra Morka to reimagine the famous nightclub empire. She assured fans that the door was open for Adrianna to return but thinks it unlikely.

"Adrianna likes a quiet life now," explained Georgia. "She probably always did."

CHAPTER NINETY-FIVE

HOLLY

The Realtor is handing me the keys to my new downtown office. There's a freshly carpeted floor, box-fresh desk, newly painted walls, and a great view of Central Park.

"Thanks," I say, smiling as I take the keys. "This looks perfect."

I notice she's looking me up and down a little too quickly in that way people have taken to doing of late.

"I've seen you before, haven't I?" she says, shifting to adjust the weight on her high heels. "You were one of Adrianna Kensington's bridesmaids."

She's taking in my pastel blue hair and toned-down eye makeup with renewed interest now. Like she can't quite marry my appearance with Adrianna's photo shoot perfection.

After the wedding was called off, Adrianna's sponsor pulled out, but she and Georgia worked around the clock on an alternative PR campaign for the aborted wedding. They left enough gaps to let the press fill in the blanks. The media speculated that Silky Eversfield died on the island and Leopold shot his mistress before vanishing.

The day it went to press, the Kensington nightclubs all over the world sold a year's advance tickets overnight.

"What did I tell you, Holly?" said Adrianna in response to my open disbelief. "Silky had four million followers. Her death got so many clicks, it almost broke the internet. And she was *exactly* on-brand. Glamorous, sexy, and drug fueled. The perfect snapshot of what people can expect when they visit a Kensington Club."

The joke was on me, since I'd agreed to pose for bridesmaid pictures thinking no one would want to run them. But I guess I didn't mind so much. And it benefited me in the end.

"I saw you in the *National Inquirer*," adds the Realtor, referencing the picture that became the most famous. Georgia's unerring intuition for publicity meant she released just the right images to grab worldwide attention.

Adrianna in the tatters of her gown, makeup running down her face, Petra with a bloom of blood on the chest of her magenta bridesmaid dress. Georgia and I helping them both back to Fortune House.

Ophelia is out of shot, since she took the picture. Since the wedding, she has decided to cut back her involvement with Adrianna's life. I wonder if the spell was finally broken when she processed the depths the Kensingtons would go to for publicity.

"I was also in *New York Magazine* for my forensic work," I tell the Realtor, smiling, "but no one seems to remember me for that anymore."

She smiles. "I thought you'd be like the rest of the uptight Kensington entourage," she confesses. "It's like they speak another language."

I nod. "Yeah," I say. "Took me a while to get my head around that too. I guess you could say I'm a little more bilingual nowadays."

I look around my new office. The paychecks I collected from post-Elysium cases paid the rental on this office for two whole years in advance, with enough left over to put down the security on my very own apartment. Nothing fancy, but it's good to have a place to store all my dungeon gaming cards and arrange my candles.

The Realtor is leaving as the door opens, and Fitzwilliam puffs in, looking out of breath and flustered. He has my computer screen tucked under his arm.

"Oh, hey!" He smiles in relief. "Thought I'd gotten the wrong office." He looks around, taking in the view. "Nice."

He crosses the room and kisses me on the cheek before depositing my screen on the desk.

"Not bad, huh?" I say. "For someone who was raised in a walk-up on the Lower East Side."

"Just be careful you don't turn into Leopold Kensington," says Fitzwilliam. He sounds like he is only half joking.

"On the subject of Leopold Kensington," I say. "Adrianna wants to hire me to look into his disappearance. The forensic part at least."

Fitzwilliam's eyebrows rise at comical speed. "His disappearance? The guy took a bullet right through his abdomen."

"True. His body was never found," I point out. "And he was a tricky guy. Possible he set the whole location up so he could disappear if he needed to. It's not impossible."

"Does this mean you'll be looking into the Kensington family?" Fitzwilliam looks unhappy at the thought. He reluctantly dropped the case of attempted murder against Adrianna and Ophelia when Petra refused to press charges.

"Lot of skeletons in the closet, right?" I nod. "I'll need an assistant," I add.

He sighs. "I guess I have some vacation coming up. You sure you want to take this assignment?"

I nod. "Absolutely," I tell him. "Like Adrianna says, I'm part of the family now."

Truth Is Stranger Than Fiction

Wondering how much of *The Bridesmaid* is based on fact? To find out more, go to www.catherinequinn.com/thebridesmaid

Reading Group Guide

1. Do you like attending weddings? Have you ever had to deal with a bridezilla? Would you consider Adrianna a bridezilla?

2. Why did Holly and Simone split from each other? If you were Holly, would you have joined Simone, or would you have gone your own way?

3. Due to their argument, Holly cuts off all communication from Simone. Is there a healthier way to express your disagreement with a friend's actions? How might Holly have handled the situation with Simone and her TV show better?

4. Holly loves forensics because they show the truth. Do you believe there's an objective truth? Why or why not?

5. What do you think of boarding schools? Do you approve of them in general? Should there be a minimum age of the children in a boarding school, or is any age fine? What might the benefits or disadvantages of boarding school be?

6. Are you a different person from who you were in college (or high school)? Have you ever met with someone you haven't seen in years and completely reevaluated your opinion of them?

7. How does Adrianna's fame cause her to distance herself from her friends and family? What would it mean to consider yourself a "brand" before considering yourself a person?

8. In what ways did the Kensington Manor School traumatize its students? Do you believe their methods were successful in creating proper young ladies?

9. Did you have a different opinion of Adrianna at the end of the novel compared to the beginning?

10. Did you solve the mystery before the reveal? What did you make of the reveal?

11. Do you believe justice was done in the end?

A Conversation with the Author

Where did the inspiration for this book come from?
I absolutely love weddings! But I have noticed all that stress can add a steely edge to even the gentlest of brides. I've been shocked to see personalities change completely in the build-up to weddings. I wanted to write about all those conflicts and eat wedding cake—what could be better?

Did you have a favorite character to write? Why?
I loved writing all those characters, but my favorite was probably Adrianna. I love discovering inner drives in powerful women who aren't striving to be liked. Adrianna has a huge weight of responsibility on her shoulders and a deep vulnerability that not everyone will see. I enjoyed seeing how clever she was managing that load.

Do you have any experience with bridezillas or being a bridesmaid?
I've been a bridesmaid several times and have had a fair few bridezillas to deal with. I found it all quite shocking until my own "sort of" wedding, which was a party in a field and the most casual setup you can imagine. I got the biggest dress I could find secondhand

for $50, encouraged all the guests to wear wedding dresses, and had friends each make a cake so we could stack them into one large tiered one. There was no stress, no drama, and no money spent—but I still ended up shouting at my kids to hurry up as we left the house! I remember thinking how stressed I would have been if it had been a traditional day—it gave me a new understanding.

What is your writing process like?

I usually get wildly excited at the beginning, very beleaguered in the middle, and happy again at the end. Nowadays, I keep the beginning very loose, as I know the end will likely be nothing like I imagined at the start of the process.

What kind of research did you do over the course of writing?

Research is my favorite—I do so much. As a former journalist, I like to go all out, making trips to experience things firsthand or visit locations—the more unusual the better. I also love interviewing people alongside extensive reading.

What would you like readers to take away from the story?

I always try for books where readers feel entertained but learn a little more depth about a world they might have seen on the surface. In this case, I think readers might be surprised to see just how much fakery goes on behind those media-perfect pictures. I also like to wrap things up with an emotional reflection, which might make a reader see human nature a little differently—and, hopefully, more optimistically.

Do you have any plans for Holly moving forward?

Holly may well appear in another book, but my lips are sealed!

Acknowledgments

Books are never the work of just one person, and good books take many, many people. I don't know if this is a good book, but I do know I couldn't have done it without the incredible support of so many amazing people. My supremely hardworking publisher, Sourcebooks; wonderful editor, Shana Drehs; and, of course, my amazing agent, Piers Blofeld. To the extended team at Sourcebooks, who work in publicity, editing, proofreading, cover design, and doing all the things to make sure a book emerges as its best self, thank you all so much.

Thank you as always to my incredible partner, Simon Avery, who is always my last reader, and my sister, Susannah Quinn, who also happens to be my favorite author. To my parents for all their love and support, and my beautiful children, Ben and Natalie. I am so lucky to have you all in my life.

For this book, I was able to draw on my past life as a travel journalist and had so much fun doing so. I always used to think it was a shame I got to see so many fabulous luxury places with no one to share them with, so this book has been a wonderful chance to bring everyone along with me for one last big trip. I also got to draw on a number of my past celebrity interviews to create some of the characters in this book, and while a journalist never reveals her sources, the eagle-eyed might be able to match some names and faces.

As always, the biggest thanks goes to my readers, and I hope you enjoyed reading as much as I enjoyed writing.

About the Author

© Emma Stoner Photography

Cate Quinn is a travel and lifestyle journalist for the *Times* (London), the *Guardian*, and the *Mirror*, alongside many magazines. Prior to this, Quinn's background in historical research won prestigious postgraduate funding from the British Art Council. Quinn pooled these resources, combining historical research with firsthand experiences in far-flung places to create critically acclaimed and bestselling historical fiction. Moving into contemporary fiction, Quinn now uses her research skills to delve into modern-day lives and cultures.